ALLANE MILLIANE

Heart Match

For the women who keep swimming despite the storm.

Chapter One

This could be the most humiliating moment of my adult life. I'm kneeling on my bathroom floor, trying to aim the acid that keeps flowing from my mouth into the toilet while struggling to maintain my composure—but failing miserably. The problem is, I'm not alone. There's a guy who I'd never seen before until a few moments ago next to me making soothing circles with a warm hand on my back, the other holding my hair back.

Oh God. I swear I'm never drinking with an empty stomach again.

Though my body demands my attention, my mind is reeling. I wish I could blame Lexi and Naomi—my best friends—because now our conversation keeps replaying in my head like a broken record.

The vomit that keeps coming up my throat pushes my thoughts away and I try to focus on the gentle hand comforting me to keep me grounded.

I try to tell him that I'll be fine alone, but just then I heave once again. I hope this was the last because not only is it embarrassing, it hurts. It's hard to believe there's anything left in my stomach considering I only had breakfast today. Oh and rosé, of course, otherwise I wouldn't even be in this situation. Did I mention it's Monday night?

God, how did I get here? And how am I going to fix it?

Two hours earlier

I'm with Naomi and Lexi at The Rose & Thorns, the pub we've frequented since we were college students. With its dark blue walls, pale green bar counter and oak tables—an attempt to make it modern, chic, but at the same time not losing the feel of a London pub, which in my opinion is impossible given the strong smell of stale beer and the sticky surfaces.

I summoned them for an emergency meet-up. I needed to rant about my boss—again—and my fiasco of a day.

'Oh honey, I'm sorry. I know how hard you've been working on this project, we've barely seen you in the past weeks,' says Naomi, touching my arm reassuringly.

The pub is actually busy for a Monday night, but not busy enough for people to occupy all the free tables, still, we choose to sit on the high bar stools, our favourite place—closer to the booze and the cute bartenders.

'I just … can't believe it happened again, you know?' I mutter, running my finger over the rim of my glass.

Caleb—my co-worker and friend—and I have been working day and night on this project with the team for the past six months. And for what? Why work in the creative market if you aren't allowed to be creative in the first place?

'But didn't she like the designs? I mean, they're amazing,' says Naomi as she orders us another round of drinks.

For some reason there is glitter in her short thick curly hair. That's so her. That's so part of her job as a social media consultant. It involves all kinds of photo shoots and props, ranging from glitter to paint to confetti.

'She did, but it doesn't matter. She wants us to go for another approach. She said, "Forget eco-friendly for now".'

'That sucks, Livvy. Why is it so hard for brands to embrace anything eco-friendly?' says Lexi, playing with her blonde ponytail with one hand, the other holding her strawberry frozen margarita.

'It's expensive, that's why,' I say, watching the cute bartender mixing up some blue coloured cocktail for one of the girls sitting next to us. He's cute.

According to Haley—my boss—our ideas are too innovative for the brand guidelines and image, not to mention costly. The company doesn't want to risk trying different designs and materials when the traditional ones already sell beyond expectations, which I suppose makes sense for them, but not for me. I want more. I want different. And I want to do the environment good along the way.

'You guys, I think I finally need to admit I'm starting to hate my job,' I say it aloud for the first time ever since I joined Secretive. I blame it on the rosé stirring in my empty stomach.

Both Naomi and Lexi stare blankly at me. I can't really read their expressions. They each sip on their drinks, studying me. Lexi has these thick long eyebrows that normally meet in the middle of her forehead if she doesn't pluck them, they usually give me a sign of what she's thinking, but not tonight. And Naomi has these inquisitive big green eyes that are almost never impassive like they are as she stares at me.

'What?' I ask.

'Nothing,' they both say in unison, and almost imperceptibly looking at each other.

Hah, I noticed that.

When they look at each other this way it's because they want to tell me something that I don't want to hear.

'It's just, you don't hate your job, c'mon. You're just working for the wrong brand,' says Naomi.

I knew it. Naomi and Lexi have been trying to convince me to quit my job for the past year. Saying what I just said only adds to their list of arguments.

I roll my eyes and tip back the rest of my rosé, because I know where this is going, a possible intervention.

'This was one of your most amazing works. I mean, eco-friendly luxury lingerie?' says Naomi.

Sorry, I forgot to mention I'm a lingerie designer.

There was once a time that working for Secretive was a dream. When I began working for them as an intern, it felt surreal. Today it feels like I don't belong there, like our visions don't match anymore. I guess I changed, while Secretive stayed the same. Certain relationships tend to make both parts grow apart, no matter how hard you try to make it work.

'There are so many great things behind this idea, it's hard to accept that she didn't even give you a chance. Your talent needs to be appreciated and I've been …' Naomi stops mid-way to amend her sentence, '*we've* been telling you for a while that maybe it's time for you to move on, honey.'

'Oh, so that explains your unreadable expressions. You've both been talking about my work situation again,' I say, getting the cute bartender's attention to my empty glass. His expression says *are you sure about this?* Who does he think he is to imply with his gorgeous face that I've already had enough to drink? I try to remember how many glasses I've had since I got here, but I lost count after the third, which makes me think I should have eaten before letting alcohol hit my system.

'Livvy, don't get me … *us* wrong. You're twenty-six, your whole life ahead, talented as fuck, great potential, but let's be honest, you're a workaholic and Secretive slaves the hell out of you. You breathe, and live work—you dedicate all your time to this company that, in my opinion, has such a different vision than yours. Isn't it time for change?' asks Naomi.

Change. I don't know what's changed for the past three years, apart from the fashion trends and my hair. Yes, I work. A lot. Yes, I'm unhappy with not being able to work on projects I'm passionate about. But no, I don't want changes. Changes are scary, and I've been avoiding them with all my strength, from the simple things regarding my daily routine to more complex ones related to my work life.

'Oh, and did I mention the fact that you haven't been in a serious relationship since … Ever since you …' I don't let Naomi finish.

'Stop right there. What has my work situation got to do with having a serious relationship or not?' I protest. 'It's not like I don't see people,' I remind them.

'Yeah, sure, you do see people. More like, you fuck them and dump them before they even get a chance to bring you flowers,' says Naomi in her scary bossy tone. I'd probably have felt terrified about it if I weren't so tipsy and angry. Naomi can be terrifying sometimes, like an authoritarian mother.

I let out an annoyed exhale and drink some more from my freshly refilled glass. The alcohol is helping me to be immune to the accusations, or at least to make them less hurtful.

'Livvy, I'm sorry, but Naomi is right. The last guy, who was it? Dan? He was so sweet, and gorgeous ...' begins Lexi.

'Yeah sure, he was way too sweet, like honey and sugar and sweetener all together in one glass of water. He just wouldn't stop texting, it was freaking annoying. Did I mention he wouldn't shut up about *Game of Thrones*? God, I loved the series, but that's all he could talk about, like he was living in GOT's world.' I might have gotten carried away right there. Poor Dan, his only real problem was that he wanted more than sex and I didn't.

'Oh, fine. But there were so many other cool guys. It's like you just use them and throw them in the trash, like tampons,' says Lexi, and this coming from her was new, and surprising. Did she really compare guys with tampons?

Naomi shoots me her raised eyebrows stare, agreeing with Lexi.

'So what? I'm happy with just having fun. I'm young, busy and you know being in a relationship right now for me is something out of the question.'

I keep taking big gulps of my rosé; it's starting to go down way smoother than the first sip. I begin staring at the bartender again to order one more.

Is he new? I've never seen him at the pub before.

I begin imagining going home with him, those biceps perfectly fitting under that black T-shirt. I bet he has one hell of a V under it. I'm tempted to slip my hand under the hem to feel him up. He's checking me out too. I smile at him and watch him flush. I don't even care that probably every day a drunk girl does the same to him.

'Oh my God, stop flirting with the bartender,' says Naomi in disbelief, snapping me back to the conversation.

'I'm not ... whatever. Is he new?' I say, still trying to save my ass from the not pleasant conversation.

'Livvy,' Naomi hisses. 'Anyways, we're just saying ...'

'What Naomi?' I snap.

I'm getting upset—I hate it when they decide to intervene. I don't need an intervention. I don't need to be saved from my work nor be pressured to open up to a relationship again. I called them today because I wanted them to listen to me bitching about my work, not to intervene as if I am an addict and need help.

'Maybe you need change. Also, you should question if not wanting a relationship is something related to your work life, or to, you know …' continues Naomi.

'Do I even have a chance on winning an argument against you tonight?' I say, defeated and lightheaded. Light like a balloon.

'No, you don't,' says Naomi with a devilish smirk.

'What happened to that dream of yours of founding your own brand?' says Lexi.

'That was a long time ago,' I say.

'Three years ago isn't a long time,' Naomi points out.

Three years ago a lot of things were different. I'm not that person anymore.

'It's a crazy idea,' I say, more to myself.

'Why? I'd be your first client,' says Lexi, beaming.

'Second, I'd be the first,' says Naomi, shaking her head from side to side, doing her happy dance, the glitter in her hair shining under the dim lights of the pub. I roll my eyes at them, hard.

'Oh, I've got another question,' says Lexi.

Judging by her bloodshot eyes, she's had more margaritas than her limit—she can only take so much. Her ponytail is already a mess from her running her hand through it unconsciously, her red lipstick in need of a touch up.

'Are we doing questions and answers now?' I ask.

'Last one. Promise you'll be honest?' pleads Lexi.

Oh God, this can't be good.

'Sure. Let me just order another glass.'

When my eyes meet the cute bartender's, he smirks in disbelief. He already knows what I want, and reluctantly pours the remaining contents of a rosé bottle into my glass. Did I drink that entire bottle?

Shit. This is not going to end well.

'Don't you think you avoid serious relationships because of what happened between you and Josh?'

Josh. Josh Lexington. The name shouldn't even be mentioned aloud. Because of him, I have an aversion to all the Joshes in the world.

I take a deep breath. I knew this was coming. Ever since they learned what happened between me and Josh, it became a sensitive topic. We have talked about it before, of course, right after what happened, but then it became some kind of restricted area, a forbidden topic. They helped me get my life back on track, and we buried the topic and the name Josh. Apparently until tonight.

'I don't avoid serious relationships. I just don't need it.'

'Honey, is that your honest answer?' asks Naomi.

'Yes.' It is how I truly feel; I'm not lying.

They eye me suspiciously, not really convinced.

'What?' I say, my nose inside the glass, my lips slightly touching the liquid.

'We just don't want you missing good opportunities to be with a nice person because you're afraid,' says Lexi.

'I'm not afraid. I'm not,' I snap.

Am I afraid? No, I'm not. Tsk.

'Okay, okay, don't get so defensive. It was just a question for you to think about,' says Lexi.

Was I defensive?

'Right, let's change the subject,' suggests Naomi.

I could hug her right now if I weren't so annoyed with her already. I hope the alcohol makes me forget this conversation.

'Thank you. And let's get another round because I'm thirsty,' I say, almost falling off the high stool. *Shit.* Cute bartender must have heard me and seen what almost happened, because when our gazes lock, he raises a very judgemental eyebrow at me. Whatever.

'While you're avoiding a relationship at all costs, I'm trying to be in one for what feels like ages,' says Naomi.

She's right. With Naomi it goes like this: she meets a guy, who according to her is perfect. Then the perfect guy has sex with her a few times, tells her he isn't looking to be in a relationship, they don't see each other anymore, then suddenly that same guy is dating someone else professing his love on every social media channel. I don't know if it's just bad luck, if guys are always such assholes, or if it's just because her perfect guy's still out there waiting for her to find him. I almost feel bad about the guys I've 'used' in the past years. Almost.

'What about Lewis?' asks Lexi.

'Yeah. I don't know. Lewis is different. It's almost as if—' she stops for a moment, as if trying to understand the situation herself.

Lexi and I wait.

'As if he's afraid of me,' she says, finally.

'What?' asks Lexi.

'I wouldn't be surprised,' I say. Only after the words were out I realise I actually spoke them.

'What do you mean?' asks Naomi with furrowed brows.

Uh Oh.

'I—I mean,' I stammer before continuing, she has her defensive look on. 'You are a bit intimidating sometimes, you're aware of that aren't you?'

She keeps watching me as if I just made the discovery of the year. Maybe she's having an epiphany and is finally figuring it out for herself.

'Maybe he's just afraid to take the first step. Being your co-worker means once he asks you out, it could either go really well or screw things up,' I say.

She seems to think for a moment. It looks like she hasn't considered this possibility before. She's had a thing for Lewis ever since he joined the company she works for. From what she told us, the feeling is mutual. But, she keeps on waiting for him to ask her out, and he never does. I've had my suspicions for a while that the real reason for that is quite simple: he's intimidated by my friend.

Lexi's eyes are full of excitement, my remark seeming to make a lot of sense to her now too.

'Don't be mad, but I think Livvy has a point,' says Lexi.

'Yeah, I think *you* should ask him out. Why wait for him?' I tell her.

Naomi's big green eyes tell me she's considering discussing this further, but before she can say anything else, Lexi says, 'I envy you guys.'

With furrowed brows, Naomi and I stare at our friend. I don't know about Naomi, but I'm shocked to hear this from her.

'What can you possibly be talking about?' I ask.

She hesitates for a moment and says, 'I don't know. You guys seem to have this busy sexual life, different guys, possibilities …'

My eyes lock with Naomi's and I know she's as surprised as I am with this confession.

Lexi has been with Thomas—the love of her life, her words not mine—ever since high school. They moved in together just when I moved out from the flat we used to share, three years ago. We all love him, and it's impossible to look at Lexi and imagine her without Tommy, so it really does come as a surprise hearing her confess this.

'Okay? What's going on?' asks Naomi.

Lexi seems to try to find her voice or words for a moment.

'It's been months since I had sex,' she says, flushing and unable to meet our gazes.

Oh.

'Elaborate,' I say.

She sighs, clearly frustrated.

'Okay, this was a bad idea. I don't want to talk about it anymore,' she says, looking away and sucking on the straw of her cocktail.

'No, no, no. We're not judging, honey, we just want to know what's going on so we can … help?' says Naomi.

'I don't wanna talk about it. Forget I said anything. Please?'

Naomi and I exchanged worried looks but decide to respect our friend's wish.

We end up all talking about work again, this time not about mine. I'm barely present in the conversation, my tipsy mind roams to a different place: an old dream that, to happen, something needs to change, and it has to come from me.

I don't recall the last time I was this hammered. Lately I have been getting wasted on green tea to keep me up and work like a slave. Right now I do my best to step out of the car without tripping on the pavement in front of my building. I don't even know how I ended up in an Uber. The driver offers help but I wave him off. The whole way he seemed worried staring at the rear-view mirror, probably afraid I would puke in his car.

I open the old, noisy wooden front door of my building after almost tripping on the front steps. My heels are killing me, and as tipsy as I am, it's like I'm walking on an ice rink, even though it's summer in London. I spot the lift on the ground floor, a guy has just stepped on it and the doors are beginning to close.

Oh God, I need to pee. Don't let the doors close on me.

I don't think I can climb the five floors of steps to my flat right now. I also can't wait for the slow old lift return to the ground floor before the need to release becomes unbearable. I hurry to catch the ride up.

I hope the bastard waits for me.

He does. He waits for me, and as soon as our eyes lock, I forget about my need to pee.

'Thank you,' I say, finally moving from where I was standing and stepping onto the lift as graciously as I manage on these heels.

He nods, with a half-smile. And what a smile. Not just the smile, the whole package.

He's wearing sports clothes. White running shorts and white T-shirt and black cap backwards, a big backpack slung over his shoulder.

How can he be so sweaty and still smell so good?

Our eyes meet, and the look on his face is a mix of shyness and confusion. I don't know why. Anyways, he takes off his cap, quickly runs his fingers through his inky and sweaty hair, only to place the cap back on. I can't avert my eyes from the muscles on his arm flexing with the movement. I almost feel sober again with the electricity running through me.

God, he's cute. Haven't seen him in the building before.

I'm now trying to balance myself on my heels, so I just lean by the metal bar under the mirror for support. If he weren't here I'd have taken off my heels by now. I keep watching him from my peripheral view. His profile is soft and rough all the same, it might be the combination of his sharp jawline and the stubbles. *Goddamn it, his stubbles are perfection.*

Am I staring? God I'm staring aren't I? Maybe that's why he's looking at me like that. Amused.

I close my eyes for a moment and take a deep breath. My heart is pulsing fast and funny under the effect of the alcohol. I really shouldn't have drunk this much. When I open my eyes again I'm staring at the button panel and realise that he pressed the button to the sixth floor to the penthouse. He's quiet, but I feel his eyes on me.

'Shit.'

Oops, did I say that aloud?

I forgot to press the button to fifth floor, and so I do it as fast as I can, but the doors have closed and it's too late for it to stop on my floor before reaching the penthouse. This lift is that stupid. So not environmentally friendly.

I hear a laugh-snort behind me, when I look back I see the gorgeous human being standing there at the corner, now relaxed, playing with a bunch of wristbands around his left wrist. His middle of the ocean deep piercing blue eyes catch mine.

'God you're cute.'

Was this my voice I just heard? Shit!

This time he lets out a delicious laugh, his gaze still connected to mine, his mouth twitching just a little on one side showing a dimple and his big white teeth.

'Is that so?' he asks, amused.

I'd say he's blushing but I'm not so sure of anything right now apart from the fact that I'm making a fool of myself. Even drunk, I'm perfectly aware when I'm making a fool of myself.

'God, I'm never drinking more glasses of rosé than my e-established limit a-again,' I stammer and do my best not to burp. Burps are disgusting. The words roll slow out of my mouth. I hide my face with my hands.

I hear him smiling through his nose.

'And what's your limit?' his voice is deep, but soft, and he has just dropped a cute accent, on the last word. He's not from around here.

'One bottle, it seems. After that I start doing and saying things I shouldn't,' I say, my voice muffled by the palms of my hands, still unable to look at him.

'I see,' he chuckles, possibly agreeing with my remark.

'Sorry,' I say, now peeking out of the hiding place I've improvised with my hands.

'There are worse things than being called cute,' he winks at me.

Oh God, why do I feel my insides stir up? Oh the things I could do to his body, how messy I could make his hair. Oh … it's so so hot in here right now. Stop it. Get it together Olivia.

Before I can say anything else the lift stops at the penthouse and the doors open.

'Guess I'll see you around.' Cute guy's making his way out just when I start to feel my acidic stomach complaining.

Oh no. Not now.

I tense and try to think of the fastest route to the closest bathroom. Until this lift has closed its doors and I get to my floor it will be too late. I step out of it, just behind him, and the only thing keeping the bile rising up my throat from coming out is watching his ass move inside the white fabric of his shorts.

He turns back suddenly and I bump into him, crashing against his hard worked chest.

'Sorry,' I say quickly, almost pushing him out of the way. He holds me, steadying me by my arms, the warm touch of his hands sends an electric current through my spine. Unfortunately, it's not enough to calm my raging stomach.

'Are you alright?' he fixes his gaze on mine, his expression of worry.

'I'm gonna be sick,' I say lifting my hand to cover my mouth, as if the gesture would avoid what's coming.

'I'm taking … t-the stairs. I live d-downstairs,' I say with effort.

He lets me go and offers me to use his bathroom. I shake my head and make my way towards the staircase, it's only one floor down.

I can do it.

I take each step as fast as I manage considering I'm wearing high heels, the black ones with red soles I insist on wearing when I have an important day. I'll be lucky if I make it to the bathroom before breaking my ankle. On the last few steps, when I see the door to my flat, I open my purse to take my keys out, but as always, it's a whole mess inside it and as usual I can't find it on the first try, nor the second, or third.

Of course I trip. Then I'm flying.

I can already feel the hard bang of my pretty drunk face hitting the floor, I wince with the anticipation of the pain that's coming my way, but something pulls me back, making my heart stop for a few long torturous seconds.

Am I gonna fall or what? Well, it seems not.

Chapter Two

I wake up to the familiar sound of my phone's alarm clock and to the vibration of my watch in my wrist, both set to go off at 5 am. The buggers don't know anything about hangovers.

Why do I feel like the first pancake of a batch, destroyed and useless? God, everything hurts.

I sit on my bed and try hard to remember how I got here. I smooth my thin, entangled hair as best as I can, but there isn't much hope of it looking any better.

I look around my room. My black heels are perfectly positioned next to each other by my bedroom's door. This gets my attention because there is no way I would put them this way. Even when I'm not drunk I kick them each to one side when I get home. I might be controlling with my routine, but that does not include my home's organisation.

Last night was …

How did I get home again?

I press my fingers to my temple and close my eyes, forcing my mind to go back in time, to last night. All I can think of is my conversation with the girls, the dreadful one about changes. Then, the cute bartender.

Shit. Did I bring someone home?

No, no, I didn't. I remember now taking an Uber. The girls ordered it for me—I was in no state to do it myself. In fact, I don't even know where my phone is.

Before I make myself step out of the bed, I look at myself under the duvet and realise I'm not wearing last night's clothes anymore. I'm still wearing the same lingerie from yesterday though. But I'm wearing a T-shirt too. A large men's T-shirt. I really don't remember taking my clothes off and putting this … *oh shit.*

I get up and cautiously go inspect my flat, feeling like the last zombie on Earth. Everything is as I left off, even the glass of water I had yesterday morning before heading to work. Then I spot something unusual again, my purse is hanging on the wardrobe. I never ever hang it there. It's always either on the kitchen island or on the couch.

Shit.

It all comes back to me in a frenzy rush.

Cute guy.

I remember him holding me on the stairs, avoiding my fall and saving my face from horrible damage. Then him helping me finding my keys in my purse, getting in my apartment with me, and …

Oh God. He helped me vomit in the toilet. He might also have turned away when I decided it was time to finally pee. And … he put me to bed after dressing me in his T-shirt.

I check my body for any strange signs, but I'm intact. I take a quick peek at my face in the hall's mirror and I almost scream in terror. My bangs look like I slept as a bat, upside down. Black smudges under my eyes. I'm a mess. Yesterday was a mess.

I drink a big glass of water and run to the shower. I'd normally be getting ready for my morning run, but today isn't routine and this already drives me nuts.

After a long shower, I open the left side of my closet. It's all there, perfectly arranged. I already feel calmer. My lingerie collection, my most loyal companions. Each set on their respective hanger. Thongs, hipsters, corsets, bras, bralettes, bodysuits—you name it. In every colour and material, all kept neat and clean, and scented with exotic black vanilla. There are no basic items apart from sports underwear, which are a necessary thing to have anyway.

Remember Carry Bradshaw and her shoes and clothes addiction—ok the woman was addicted to anything fashion-wise—in *Sex and the City*? In my life, I'm the Carry Bradshaw version of lingerie addiction.

I don't only create them, I wear and live through them. How can I design the perfect lingerie without wearing and feeling them? Are these all my designs? Most of them, but I've got no boundaries or restrictions to a work well done, so I do wear lingerie from the competition, but I only keep the ones I really love. Once I'm happy with my pick, a grey lace hipster and matching bralette, I put on my summertime home office clothes: ripped cut-off jean shorts and a white cropped T-shirt. I grab my purse and head out to Fresh Me Up, the café across the street, where I always get a smoothie after my morning run.

It's still quiet; there's just a guy with a suit on the line in front of me placing his order. The usual two elderly ladies on a table by the window sipping their coffees and the woman that always sits on the couch in the far corner is focused on her computer. No one different than normal, just the background music that changes according to the season.

I don't need to check the menu or today's specials on the chalkboards behind the counter. I always get the same.

By 6:30 am I'm standing in front of Andi, the nerdy guy behind the counter who already knows my order. Ok, he's not just a nerd guy—Andi knows my morning routine more than anyone else. Sometimes when I stop by after my run, he's already prepared my smoothie. But no, he's not *that* kind of guy, he's much younger than me and this is his student job. Besides, he's not my type, even though I have to admit he's cute with those glasses and timid hazel eyes.

'Make it double today, Andi,' I say, already holding my phone to pay.

'No running today?' Andi asks as he begins preparing my order.

'I'm hammered, if I go for a run right now I'm afraid I won't survive what's coming my way today,' I say.

Andi chuckles as he begins placing the ingredients into the mixer.

Then I hear a now familiar voice from behind me, and I briefly wish to be buried deep under the Earth.

'How are you feeling today?'

I turn around and it's him, *Cute guy*. He's taller than I remember, maybe because last night I had my heels on. He's wearing a cap again, this time facing forward, almost hiding his beautiful blue eyes. He's smiling down at me, and I feel my entire body blush. A memory from last night comes back as soon as our eyes meet. His warm hand soothing my back in circles as I spit fire. I also remember him carrying me in his arms and laying me on the bed, and as he does so his face is so close to mine I feel like swimming in his pool-coloured eyes. My heartbeat quickens a bit at the thought of it. This is the last memory I have before blacking out.

'Hey. Hmm. B-better than last night,' I stammer, completely embarrassed.

I can hear the mixer doing its work in the background.

'That's a start,' he says with a smirk on his stubbled, sexy face.

God, I almost forgot the damn stubbles, and how fucking hot he is.

'Here you go,' says Andi, giving me my big green smoothie.

'What are you getting?' I ask Cute guy.

'Which one is yours?' he asks.

'Green tea, spinach, coconut milk, parsley, frozen strawberries, hemp hearts, ginger and mint, no sugar,' intervenes Andi, a strange big grin on his face.

'It's called Sweet Relief,' I say, as if the name would matter.

Cute guy looks back from Andi at me and says, 'Sounds just like what I need. I'll get the same.'

God, why is his gaze so intense? Also, did he just stare at my lips?

'It's on me,' I say, and give Andi the sign I got my phone ready before Cute guy begins to protest.

'Thanks,' he says simply.

'I guess I owe you more than a green smoothie. I'm so sorry about last night, and thank you,' I say.

'Ahh, it was nothing. I'm glad you're okay,' he says and we exchange smiles.

It was nothing? The guy doesn't even know me, watched me vomit the first time he sees me, then puts me to bed in his T-shirt and doesn't even think it was a big deal?

Once my payment goes through and he gets his smoothie, we leave the café together. He hides his face a little bit more under his white cap and opens the door for me.

'I'm really, really sorry again for last night. I swear this isn't something that happens often to me. Yesterday was a bad day at work, *very* bad,' I explain myself even though he never asked for an explanation, but I do feel like I owe him one, considering he witnessed my most embarrassing moment ever.

'Sorry to hear that,' he says, then sips his smoothie with the paper straw without a care in the world, striding the pavement so casually, as if he owned the neighbourhood but it wasn't a big deal.

'And? Do you like it?' I ask, referring to the smoothie.

'It's pretty good.' He holds the transparent cup higher and looks at it, as if analysing its contents.

We are walking side by side on the pavement. Like last night, he's wearing sports clothes and is sweaty but still smells heavenly.

'Thank you for … you know, taking care of me,' I say again.

'It was no trouble.'

'I made a fool of myself.' I stare at the pavement because embarrassment's still pretty much the boss of me today.

'No, you didn't.'

'You're being nice. I totally did.'

'Pretty sure you're not the only one to have done it before,' he chuckles.

'Oh, so I did make a fool of myself.'

He laughs, then confesses, 'Ok, maybe a little.'

'Oh my God.'

Oh my God indeed, the way his mouth curls into a hard-not-to-stare grin almost makes me choke on my drink.

'What? You were the one who extracted the truth from me. I was trying to be nice,' he says in a teasing way.

'Fair enough.'

We cross the street, he holds the door of the building open, then step inside the lift. We both press our respective buttons and I suddenly feel the urge to ask if he'd like to have breakfast with me. What do I have to lose? The guy already put me to bed before without even knowing me anyways, an invitation for breakfast is nothing in comparison. Just, you know, to show him gratitude. Nothing more than that.

We ride in silence, contemplating our drinks—and each other it seems. I can't avert my eyes from his mouth sucking on the straw. When I lift my gaze, I catch him doing the same with me.

Oh.

The doors open at my floor. Before I say goodbye I find the courage to ask.

'Would you like to come in and have breakfast with me? My way to say thank you for last night, and give your T-shirt back?'

'Uhh …' he thinks for too long and I already regret asking and feel embarrassed once again.

'Sorry, was just an idea,' I say trying to make it sound like it's not a big deal.

'No, no, no … I'd love to. It's just that I have something going on today and …' he shifts his cap backwards and tugs a strand of his hair behind his ear.

'It's ok, you don't need to explain,' I say.

The doors begin to close for the second time, and this time he holds them open and, to my surprise, says quickly, 'How about dinner?'

I don't even give it one second thought, 'Sure.'

'Great. I'll knock at your door at eight,' he says with an almost imperceptible wicked smile.

'I'll be waiting,' I say.

'Oh, and you can keep the T-shirt,' he says, then the doors close, breaking the connection between our eyes.

Chapter Three

'Sometimes I wish I knew your secret,' says Naomi, on speaker.

I'm dreading my workday. After yesterday I have no motivation whatsoever to work on the designs. Not today at least. I decided to accept that today is one of those useless but necessary days to keep my mind sane. So right now instead of drawing new designs in my office, I'm checking what's in my fridge and brainstorming—mainly alone— what I'm cooking for tonight. I hope he's not allergic to anything. I should have asked him what he likes.

'Secret to what?'

'To attracting cute guys even when you're making a fool of yourself,' she says laughing.

'Thanks for the honesty,' I say.

'Always a pleasure. But seriously. I can't believe that in less than twenty-four hours you managed to get the guy to hold your hair while you vomit, take off your clothes, put you to bed wasted and still get a date with him,' she says.

'First off, when you put it that way it sounds really weird. Second, it's not a date. I just wanted to show how relieved I am that he didn't take advantage of me last night, more than for the fact that he held my hair while I vomited and put me to bed,' I say.

'Okay, now *you* are sounding weird. But you've got a point. Just don't tell him your real reason, it might give him ideas ...' she chuckles on the other side and I roll my eyes and let out a laugh on my side.

'How do you manage to have a dirtier mind than mine?' I ask.

'What do you mean? You learned it from me. I'm still your mentor, it's only natural my mind remains dirtier.'

She is indeed my mentor. After Josh and I broke up, she was the one to introduce me to the world of casual sex. At first, I wasn't sure about it. Would I be able to sleep with someone without getting attached and begin to expect more? I had my reservations. But once I realised it meant I didn't have to worry about fighting all the time and being kept from doing things I liked, or being myself for that matter, I got the hang of it. Not having strings attached worked pretty well for me.

'Ha. I know what I'm cooking,' I say staring at my fridge, excited.

Naomi's typing something on her computer, then asks, 'What's his name anyway?'

'That is a good question. One I intend to ask tonight.'

'Make it a priority. Does he know your name?'

'Now *that* is something I'm intending to tell him tonight, at some point.'

'I just can't believe you. Do you know how weird this all sounds?'

'It sounds worse than it feels, I can tell you that much.'

'Still weird. At least you know where to find him,' she smirks.

'HAHA.'

'Hey, are you getting some of the designs back? I might need new lingerie for the weekend.'

Sometimes I get to keep some of my designs, and the girls, of course, take full advantage of this. I don't mind; in fact I love it. We always have fun trying them on, and they have fun wearing them.

'Hmm, who's the lucky guy?' I ask.

'Mmmm ... Lewis,' she says.

'Whaaaat? Are you serious?'

'Yep. I literally just asked him. What you said last night, it made sense. So instead of waiting, I decided to try. I already had a no for an answer anyway, so why not?'

'How strange,' I say.

'What? Why?'

'You following my advice ...'

'Shut up,'

'Seriously, normally I'm the one following your advice, not the other way around.'

She laughs.

'Right. Speaking of … are you gonna consider my latest advice?'

'I gotta go. I need to head to the store and get some ingredients.'

'Olivia!' she hisses.

'I'll let you know when you can come over to pick your lingerie,' I ignore her.

'Right, thanks,' she says. 'And … Olivia?'

'Yeah, Naomi?'

'I don't remember you ever cooking for any other guy before.'

'Shut up!' I say, fighting back a laugh.

'Whatever, I gotta go too. I have a meeting. Use condoms. Tell me everything. Bye,' she says, leaving me alone with my chuckles.

He knocks on the door at 7:55 pm. I stop what I'm doing on the kitchen counter, the smell of black truffles in olive oil steaming through the air. I check my red lipstick on my very plump lips—thanks to my mum's genes—on the mirror. Then fix my bangs to one side and open the door without thinking too much.

I'm facing him right now, and what I see makes me swallow hard and lose control over where my eyes are staring. He's holding flowers for fuck's sake, their intense pink colour is stunning and they look insanely expensive. But that's not the main issue. He looks like a completely different person wearing beige Chino shorts, a navy-blue V-neck perfectly hugging his biceps, and white sneakers. It's the first time I see him without a cap on. His dark hair is wet, messy and glossy, long enough to have some strands hanging over his forehead. He smells like every man should smell, I can tell you that much.

'Hi,' he says first because I still haven't managed to speak.

'Hi,' my voice comes out sweeter and softer than I planned.

'I thought about bringing you a bottle of rosé but considering your hangover I decided to bring you flowers rather than come empty handed,' he says all this with one hand holding the bouquet, the other pressing against the door's frame, right above my head.

'Thank you, you didn't have to,' I say trying not to smile as widely as I know I'm smiling.

We stare at each other for a few seconds, then I realise I'm still holding the door half open and haven't invited him to come in.

'Who's there?' I roll my eyes, because I know this voice well. It's my next-door neighbour.

Cute guy throws me a quizzical look.

'It's Mrs. Thompson. She can't see well anymore, but boy can she hear. Problem is, every time someone's in the hall, she comes by the door to check who it is,' I explain all this almost whispering, so she doesn't hear it of course.

Cute guy chuckles and hands me the flowers. I might need to mention this to the girls: I didn't have to sleep with him before getting flowers.

Once inside, I pour water into a vase, and he's watching me with hands in his pockets, elbow propped on the kitchen island so that he's leaning sideways. For a moment I think it's best we skip dinner and go play on my bed. But I remember it's probably best I ask his name first.

Once the flowers are set on the black surface of the kitchen island, I offer him something to drink and he accepts water. I'm also drinking water tonight, there is no chance I will be drinking alcohol for the next month. Unless I really need it, which I hope I won't.

'It smells amazing,' he says, approaching me at the kitchen counter as I grab the package of pasta.

'I hope you like pasta,' I say.

'It's only my favourite food,' he says, our eyes meet and so do our smiles. There's something easy about the way we stare into each other's eyes at this moment, it's as if we're both searching for something only the other has. It feels familiar, and safe, and normal.

'Good. I hope you also like black truffles,' I say as I pour the pasta into the pan.

'Oh yes.'

He gets closer so he can smell the freshly made black truffle sauce. The proximity reminds me of him touching my back.

'I see you like cooking,' he says.

'I do. I find it to be very therapeutic, and fun,' I say, taking a little sample of the sauce with a spoon for him to try.

'This is amazing,' he says with his eyes closed, tasting the sauce.

I can't help but watch him attentively, noticing his thick long lashes.

'I know, right?'

If there's something I'm always proud of, it's my cooking. When I cook. Lately, I haven't been doing much cooking.

'Never tried this one at home before,' he says.

'Do you cook?'

'I do.'

Oh.

I'm facing the stove, he's right next to me with his firm gorgeous ass pressed against the countertop, arms and feet crossed in front of him. Again, we find ourselves staring at each other. No shame in it, even though my heart is already betraying me by beating faster than it should.

'So … I was talking to a friend of mine today and she thinks I should know your name before I feed you,' I say it matter-of-factly, but it comes out a bit weird.

He lets out the same delicious laugh from the lift.

'Do you want to know my name?'

Why does he look so amused? And what kind of question is that? Of course!

'I wouldn't mind if you told me …' I say, letting the corner of my mouth muster a smile.

'Funny, my brother also thinks I should ask yours, Miss Charlton …'

Now it's my turn to laugh. Of course he knows my last name, it's on my front door.

'Smart brother you have,' I say.

'It's Lucas,' he says it with a cute accent that now I'm sure is French. He has a funny grin on his face, like it's entertaining to say your own name to someone.

'What?' I ask, still trying to figure out what's so amusing about this.

'Nothing. You haven't told me yours yet,' he says.

'Olivia, but everyone calls me Livvy,' I say.

'Well, nice to meet you, Olivia Charlton. I like your name,' he says.

I swear to God, if he says my name like that again I'm definitely skipping dinner.

'Nice to meet you, Lucas.'

'You can call me Luc,' he says.

Luc it is then.

He helps me set the table, which is my kitchen island. We sit side by side on the high stools. He watches me intently as I serve him the steamy pasta and sprinkle some Grana Padano cheese over, then as I help myself.

'This is really good,' he says after the first mouthful.

'I'm glad you like it. Thank you again,' I say, referring to last night.

'How many times are you still going to thank me?'

'I don't know,' I say blushing, staring down at my food because I know his magnetic eyes are on me.

'I didn't do anything,' he says, turning sideways and propping his foot on my stool. I like that. The proximity—again. Should I put some music on or would it be too suggestive?

'We both know you did more than that. Let me remember, there was the part you might have held my hair, then the part you took my clothes off, and …'

'Olivia. It was nothing. I just put you on your bed and left,' he says, his eyes serious fixed on mine, because I have found the courage to look at him again.

'Exactly. That's the point …' I say, and watch him for his response, in the hopes he got what I mean.

He raises an eyebrow, in the way that says, *really?*

'So you're thankful that I didn't do anything … to you?'

'Hmm … I guess you can say that. I mean, you could have, I don't know …'

'… What?'

The shock on his face. Priceless.

'Taken advantage of the whole situation, you know …'

'Ha. Lucky for you I'm not that kind of guy.'

'Hmm. Lucky me.' Our eyes lock.

'If I want to do anything to you, I'm gonna need you to be fully conscious so you won't forget how I made you feel.' He drags his eyes from mine down to my mouth.

Fuck. Damn. Who is this guy?

He says this in such a calm voice you'd think he just said he's taking the trash out. I shift myself on the stool and try to quickly reorganise my thoughts so I can give him a good answer, because he just caught me by surprise. But, my eyes dart to his mouth too.

'And do you?' I ask, surprising even myself. Where is this going?

'What do you think?' his expression is serious and daring. He looks like a sexy devil with his thick inky black eyebrows. He's still staring at my mouth when I lift my gaze back to his eyes.

'I only just learned your name, not to read your thoughts …' I say it as a joke, but I know that he would, I'm not that naive. I'm back at staring at his mouth at this point, this time running the tip of my tongue on my lower lip.

A laugh brightens up his face and he says, 'Fair enough.' He goes back to eating his pasta, leaving me staring at his soft profile.

We talk. A lot. I don't remember the last time I talked so much with a guy without having physical contact in between. He tells me he's from Reims, France, where they make champagne. His grandfather owns a family champagne house. He also tells me he grew up between the grape fields of Reims and the busy Paris life.

He mentions that he rented the penthouse on Airbnb. I figured. Mr. Sorensen, the penthouse owner, uses it for short term rent, so I've seen my fair share of people staying there. None of them looked like Luc, by the way.

I tell him about my day at work yesterday and explain how I ended up wasted.

'What do you design, exactly?'

'Right, I forgot to mention that detail,' I say as we both are cleaning the kitchen island once we're done eating. 'Lingerie.'

'Oh,' he says as if he weren't expecting it.

When I look at him his shiny blue eyes are checking me out, as if he was actually seeing me in my underwear—well, I guess he already did, last night. 'That sounds fun.'

'I like it,' I say, trying to ignore how charged the air has become. 'I also like the fact that I work mostly from home.'

I lead him to my office, so he can get an idea of what I'm talking about.

'Wow,' he says once I open the door.

'Meet my creative space.' I'm glad I had time to tidy it up a bit, it's always messy otherwise.

I'm not sure what he thinks about the big wall completely covered with mood boards of hand designed sexy lingerie, with photos and fabrics pinned to it.

In the middle of the room there's a long table, which I use to draw and put fabrics next to each other, then a desk with my computer screen and laptop on the corner. I also have a cabinet where I keep my materials, books and magazines. And there's also the lingerie stand at the corner near the big window where I hang what I've been working on.

He checks out my designs pinned to the big wall first.

'These are amazing,' he says.

His words steal a smile from me because I know he's saying it from a man's point of view.

'Thanks,' I gnaw on my lower lip, pleased with myself.

'Which company do you work for again?'

'Secretive,' I say.

'What? Are you serious?' he turns to face me, surprised, recognising the brand. It's hard not to.

'Yes. Why? Familiar with my work, are you?' I tease.

'I might have seen some of it before, yes,' he lets out an innocent shy smile.

I didn't expect him to be honest about it.

Secretive is a luxury brand, famous worldwide. Some pieces are so exclusive that only a few units are made. Well, I normally make those. And, you know, Gisele Bündchen, Keira Knightly and Cara Delavigne might have worn them before. Just saying. I'm the head of their Private Collection, and Caleb is my right hand. All the pieces I work on are unique and exclusive, some are even custom made.

He moves to the lingerie stand where there are some pieces of the previous private collection, and some ideas for the new one. He doesn't touch them, he's analysing them with curiosity, hands in his pockets. The air in the room suddenly becomes hot and heavy. I don't usually show my work to the guys I hang out with, unless I'm wearing it.

He keeps on looking around and I keep on watching his ass when I can. When he's not looking, of course. It's hard not to. His hands in his pockets make the fabric stretch perfectly tight around his ass—it's impossible not to stare.

'Do you get to wear them too?' he asks to my surprise. I mean, not that I haven't been asked this question before. It's just that for some reason I can't explain why coming from him it's different. It makes me blush.

I watch him staring at me, playing with his wristbands, waiting for my response. A smile on the corner of his eyes.

'Almost all the time,' I say.

He fixes his surreal blue eyes on mine as he sucks in a breath.

'Lucky boyfriend,' he says to my despair.

Oh God.

'Do you think you'd be here if I had a boyfriend?'

He smirks with my question.

'I don't know. *Do* you have a boyfriend?'

'I don't do boyfriends and serious relationships.'

'Oh?' he raises an eyebrow inquisitively, as if I just challenged him on a bet.

'Do you have a girlfriend?'

'Do you think I'd be here if I had one?' He's serious, throwing my own question back at me.

'Would you?'

'I've been single for the past two years.'

'And I for the past three.'

'I thought you didn't do serious relationships,' he mocks.

How did this conversation become so intense?

'Not anymore,' I say, and for a long minute we hold each other's gazes, until I can't take it anymore of the heat building up in my inner thighs and climbing all the way up my neck.

Chapter Four

'Popcorn?'

I have no idea where that came from, but it worked to break the moment.

'Sure.'

Fuck. He needs to go.

I know when I shouldn't get involved. Luc makes me feel out of control, and I hate not being in control, especially over my emotions, and apparently my wobbly legs too.

As I prepare the popcorn, he steps onto the balcony. From the kitchen I have the perfect view to the living room and the balcony, where he's now quiet, leaning on the railing watching London's skyline just as the sun has sat. He looks tired. I join him as soon as the popcorn's ready.

My balcony is my favourite place in my flat in the summer months. I'm proud of how I decorated it. It's cosy and comfy and inviting. Big pillows, old wine racks and throw blankets make up the lounge seating area on one corner. Next to it there's a small table with the season's flowers and enough space for me to put glasses and the books I'm currently reading. Oversized plants and candle holders are on the floor in the opposite corner. Magical lights hang from the ceiling, and the view to London's skyline is my favourite part.

I turn on the little lights, as it's already dark outside. I offer him the bowl and he takes a handful of popcorn. We sit on the cosy couch, him on the corner, me right next to him, so that if he needs to get out I need to get out first. We prop our feet up on the balcony railing as we lay on our backs. Funny how it feels so comfortable and not one bit strange to do this with Luc, even though we just met.

The only thing between us is the popcorn bowl, sometimes not even that, as our hands lightly touch each other when we both reach for some more at the same time. We both lay there in silence—other than the cracking of popcorn in our mouths and the traffic below—looking up at the horizon that now has completely changed colour to black.

'So how come you don't do boyfriends? Bad broken heart?' he asks turning his face sideways to look me in the eyes as he runs his fingers through his hair, messing it enough to make my jaw hang for a brief moment.

'Yeah. I guess you can say that,' I say, hoping he won't press the subject.

'Can I ask what happened?'

'It's complicated.' I fidget with my fingers.

'It always is,' he says and waits for my answer anyways.

The white around the blue of his eyes are turning into light pink. He looks really tired, and the way he's watching me is somehow calming and soothing. I guess I'm very tired too, still from last night.

'It was a toxic and abusive relationship,' I say.

I can't even believe myself when I let out these words. Though I've always known it since I broke up with Josh, I never used these words loud and clear before, especially not with a stranger.

I turn my face to look at the dark sky and continue as he watches me attentively. My heart's pace has increased.

'He was violent and possessive,' I say it thinking of the time Josh shoved me in his car and held my face with one of his big hands and squeezed my cheeks so hard the inside of my mouth began to bleed. Later on I discovered my labial frenulum was ripped, never to recover again. Not that it makes a big difference in my life, but it bothers me that it's a reminder of him. I hate it that he left his mark on my body.

'I'm sorry to hear that,' Luc says.

I can see him watching me with his beautiful, tired eyes. He has now shifted to his side, and I notice his T-shirt has moved up slightly, enough to show the white waistband of his underwear.

'It's ok. Eventually I managed to end it,' I say looking back at him. It wasn't that simple though. There was nothing simple about the way Josh and I ended things. This part I don't feel like sharing with him.

'It must have been hard … to put an end to it.'

It's as though Luc can read in my eyes how hard it was. I sigh, slowly, trying to slow my heart rate. Thinking of Josh messes me up.

'It was. It took me way too long to see that nothing about our relationship was normal, and that I deserved better.' My voice comes out soft and low, as if I'm saying it more to myself than to him.

Why I am saying all these things to him is beyond me. It's like he has the secret power to persuade people to tell him their deepest secrets. It's probably his deep soothing voice, or how relaxed he looks right now. Or maybe it has to do with the fact that he's not a part of my life. I don't know.

I don't think I've ever spoken about this with a guy. Until today, Naomi and Lexi are the few people who know what happened, and only after it was over. I never found the courage to tell them about what was going on in our relationship while it was happening. I was ashamed and afraid of what they were going to say. I wish I had told them sooner—I could have spared myself at least one more year of Josh in my life.

'I'm sorry you had to go through that,' Luc says softly.

'Thanks. It's been over for a while now. I'm a different person.'

There is a long moment of silence between us, and all the while our eyes are like magnets attracting each other. Our hands lying on each side of us, I shouldn't be surprised by how I wish they were touching. I bet his hands are warm right now, like they were when he was rubbing my back. I can almost feel his fingers threading through my hair, playfully. I begin imagining his heat enveloping me, his smell adhering to my clothes.

'You know, not every guy is gonna hurt you like he did. And as you said, you're now a different person,' he says, filling in the silence and preventing my thoughts from going any further.

'Sounds simple when you say it. But it's not. Not for me.'

'Do you think you closed yourself to love?'

His question makes me think of the girls last night, and consequently of all the nice guys I turned down in these past three years. I made sure to only get involved with men who weren't expecting anything from me other than sex. Every time I felt like I was getting too attached, I moved on to the next. It has been easier and safer this way.

'It's possible,' I confess, to my surprise even.

How did this conversation get so deep again?

'I get it,' Luc says, and he means it. I can see it in his eyes as I look into them.

There's no popcorn left in the bowl, not even the kernels. We finished them too. It so happens that he also likes them.

I should stop looking at him, it doesn't feel healthy to stare at each other for so long without touching. This is the main reason I decide I don't want to see him again after tonight. I don't and I can't do this kind of deep staring—it makes me feel naked, an open intimate journal, limpid water, but mostly without control.

I look up at the sky again, but he keeps watching me. I hope he doesn't notice how my breathing has changed, how hot my skin feels.

'How long are you staying in London?' I ask, just so I know for how long I'm going to have to avoid him.

'Two weeks tops, maybe less,' he says taking a deep breath, as if this is something complicated for him. There, one even better reason to avoid him. He's leaving soon, and right now I'm pretending I don't feel the little weird pain in my heart.

'Are you here because of work?'

'Yes,' his voice is lower, almost a whisper.

I turn to face him again only to find his eyes closed. He fell asleep. It makes me smile. I take the chance to watch him, and I do it for a long time. I watch his chest rising up and down under his now wrinkled V-neck. I notice the dark stubbles along his jawline, the fine shape of his nose, his messy hair—now dry and softer—being lightly moved by the wind. Is it too creepy of me to take advantage of his vulnerability and check him out?

The hand over his chest moves rhythmically up and down with his breathing. The other's by his side, palm facing up, and I notice it's covered in calluses and fresh, reddened blisters. I realise I still don't know much about him, but right now I think it's better this way.

I wake up to the sound of a ringing phone that is not mine. My head's on someone's shoulder, someone's nose is breathing on the top of my head. The phone keeps ringing and I realise where I am and with whom.

Luc wakes up startled by the noise too. We break apart as fast as we manage. He gets his phone from his back pocket and as soon as he checks the caller his face full of worry.

'*Merde.* I gotta go. It's 2:00 am,' he says, startled after ignoring the call.

I move out of the way so he can get up, he moves at the same time and somehow he's now hovering over me.

'Sorry, sorry,' he says quickly and jumps over me and onto the floor.

I follow him to the front door still half sleeping, not really understanding what's happening and how we fell asleep and drifted until 2:00 am, how I ended up with my head on his shoulder, who was calling him and how we should say goodbye after all that.

'Sorry and thank you,' he says smoothing up his hair, but it's still very much messy, and even sexier with his sleepy face.

God. Just go and never come back. I can't see you ever again.

'It's ok, I ...' before I say anything else he gives me a quick kiss on my cheek, turns around and takes the stairs, three steps at a time, back to his apartment above mine.

Chapter Five

I have the feeling my life has gotten quite messy in the past two days. Things seem to be chaotic. First, my work issue, then I get way too drunk with the girls and because of that I get myself a Luc in my life and waking up today feeling like I should stay in bed the whole day. This never happens.

As I snooze my alarm for the second time, I stare at the ceiling and wish last night never happened and that Lexi and Naomi would be already up so we can do one of our emergency video calls. But when my alarm goes off once again, I decide I should do at least one thing that I still can control: run.

I've found running to be the best therapy for anxious days, which have been present more often than not in the past three years of my life. Today's no exception. It's 5:30 am when I'm in front of the building wearing running shoes, shorts, a cropped top and a ponytail warming up before I head toward the Thames.

I love it how quiet London is at this time of day, when the whole city is still getting ready to leave for work cramped in the tube, running around like lost ants and zigzagging like bees to make it on time for work. Since I only work in the office two days a week and the rest from home, I don't have to worry about being one of the ants or bees today. Instead, I enjoy the summer breeze by the Thames, here around Richmond, which is even more quiet than most other areas of the river.

The fresh breeze brings all sorts of smells, mainly morning coffee and freshly baked bread. And well, I refuse to complain about the bad smell that comes from the water once in a while, especially today that is sunny and such a beautiful early morning.

I've been focused on organising my thoughts while running for almost half an hour. I never wear earphones and listen to music when I'm running, I like to listen to the city noises or quietness, so I immediately hear when someone begins running alongside me and starts talking to me.

'Thought it was you,' says Luc from beside me.

All my focus is gone and my stable pulse has now been compromised.

'Oh, hi.'

I'm not sure if I should stop or keep going. But he keeps on running, so I just do too.

'Do you run often?' he asks matter-of-factly.

'Everyday. Well, apart from the days I have hangovers,' I say.

He lets out a smirk.

'You?'

'Same,' he looks at me and winks.

We run in silence for a few minutes. His pace is, of course, faster than mine, but he doesn't seem to mind slowing down a bit so my short legs can keep up with his long ones.

'I wanted to apologise for the way I left ... and well, for falling asleep at your house in the first place,' he says between his controlled breathing.

I smile to myself, then look at him and say, 'Don't worry about it.'

We run together for more than half an hour, and on the way back we stop at Fresh Me Up after he confesses he enjoyed the smoothie from yesterday.

'Two Sweet ... what was it again?' he turns back to look at me, waiting for me to help him remember the right word.

'Relief,' I say.

'Relief,' he repeats to Andi, who chuckles after pushing his glasses up on his nose.

'Sure thing,' says Andi looking between me and Luc, amused for some reason. Maybe he's wondering why for two consecutive days I'm here with a guy, the same one. I'm never here with a guy, let alone the same one twice.

Once we're out of the café, Luc turns his cap backwards, checks his watch and suddenly starts walking faster.

In the elevator we are on opposite sides, sipping our smoothies. The rational part of me honestly wishes we hadn't bumped into each other today. The irrational part of me is jumping with joy that this gorgeous man who slept beside me just a few hours ago is standing in front of me, sweaty from our run together. If we keep meeting like this for the next few days, I don't know how much willpower I'll have to ignore his existence until he leaves.

I watch him. The strong muscles above his knees, how his white shorts make his cock pop, the T-shirt stuck against the sweat of his abs, his hands holding his smoothie cup, and his eyebrows curved as he stares at me, also checking me out with no shame. For a moment it seems like we're both holding ourselves back with all our strength, fighting the urge to get our hands on the other. I feel sweat dripping from my neck down my back, drops wetting my skin as I try to recover power over my legs, which are now numb, not only from the run.

'Headed to work?' I ask him, trying to break the silence and the magnetism between our eyes.

'Yes. You?'

Our eyes are still locked.

'Working from home today, but yes, I've got loads to catch up on. Yesterday wasn't my most productive day at work,' I say.

The lift reaches my floor and I'm glad. I don't think I can stand one more minute trapped with him and his good, sweaty smell and his looks without things getting physical.

'See you around, Olivia,' he says, getting off the elevator with me.

'See you,' I say, watching him take the stairs to his flat.

I close the door behind me and try to even my breathing again.

I cool off with a long shower, make myself breakfast, and while eating I enjoy Naomi and Lexi's company on a video call. They're both getting ready for work. Naomi works for a PR company not far from Secretive, while Lexi is a fashion photographer.

I met Lexi first. It was during my first year at London College of Fashion. I was working on a project that required some good professional photos of my designs. She was also on her first year and was happy to help me as long as she could use the photos for a project of her own as well. It was perfect. And we became so close we shared a flat near LCF. A couple of years later, Lexi met Naomi during one of her own projects and introduced me to her. Since then, the three of us have been friends.

'Tell us everything,' says Lexi as she puts her makeup on. I know exactly where her phone is, propped up on her bathroom mirror's handle so we can still see her as she applies her mascara.

'We had dinner, we talked … a lot, mostly me, and fell asleep on the balcony couch after having popcorn,' I say while I'm still chewing on the bread like it's no big deal. If I had spoken to them today early before my run, I'd have made a big deal of it, but right now, if I do that, things will only aggravate and turn into something that's not.

'What? You didn't have sex?' Naomi asks as she sprays something on her hair.

I know, it's a surprise for me too. I don't remember the last time I had a guy over and didn't have sex with him.

'It was a thank you dinner. No secondary intentions, I told you.'

It's true, I wasn't planning on having sex with him, even if he took the initiative. Ok, I might have thought about it more times than I should, but truly it wasn't the initial intention.

'Course it was,' says Naomi.

'When was the last time you slept with a guy and didn't have sex?' asks Lexi.

We all laugh in unison; they know me too well.

'It was with Nate, last Christmas,' I laugh.

'Shut up, he doesn't count,' says Naomi.

She's right, he's my brother.

'Nothing happened, and to be honest nothing will,' I say it, already knowing there will be protests.

'Why not? Has he left already?' asks Lexi, interested.

'No. Though he will soon. It's just, you know, he's too much. I can't have casual sex with him. He's brought me flowers for Christ's sake,' I say.

'He what?' Lexi stops mid-way from applying her red lipstick.

I ignore her question.

'Here you go again with the "he's too much" thing, which only proves our theory of you ditching the good ones. Why do you sabotage yourself so much?' says Naomi.

'Naomi, it's not self-sabotage, I just … I just know when I shouldn't get involved.'

Or better, I know when I'm in risk of getting hurt. Why give it a chance if I already know where this is going?

'And how do you know that?' asks Lexi.

'When the guy makes me feel out of control.'

'Oh for fuck's sake, you can't control everything,' says Naomi.

'How does he make you feel out of control by bringing you flowers?' asks Lexi.

'It's not about the flowers. It's more than that. I don't know, Lexi. I can't explain it. I just … whatever. I don't want to talk about it.'

I start to think it was a bad idea to tell them everything that happened last night in detail.

'Then why did you call?' asks Naomi, annoyed.

'I don't know,' I'm asking myself the same question.

'You like him,' says Lexi.

'What do you mean by like him? Like I have actual feelings for him or like as if I'd like him to fuck me?' I ask.

'When did you become such a heartless bitch?' says Lexi again.

Right now Naomi is just listening as she drinks a glass of orange juice and keeps rolling her eyes up at our conversation.

'I'm not a heartless bitch. On the contrary, because I still need my heart I don't want to break it again.'

Silence. *That was probably too deep, wasn't it?*

'You like him,' now it's Naomi's turn.

I roll my eyes and sigh.

'If you didn't you wouldn't be making such a big deal about it,' says Lexi.

'I don't. I'm not, *you* are making a big deal out of it. And it's not like that. I simply wanted to share the info with you,' I say, and I know I sound defensive by the way it all comes out.

'Keep lying to yourself …' sings Lexi, she's even dancing to it.

'1,2,3 … I'm out,' I say, ending the video chat session on my side, though I'm pretty sure Naomi and Lexi kept on talking without me.

I spend the rest of the day focused on work. I find the courage to look at the designs I made and begin to rethink them, one by one. I end up deciding to put them in a drawer and start from scratch. They are too good to be changed, I'd rather work on entirely different pieces. Caleb is going to have a heart attack when I tell him we'll start from zero. He'll recover, I'm sure. Though I'm not sure he has recovered from Monday's fiasco. The disappointment and desperation written all over his face when I silently tried to tell him to shut up and not continue the presentation was heart breaking. He's so hardworking. The only problem is he gets too attached to projects and ideas, which makes him suffer when he needs to let go.

I make some green tea, put some music on, open the big window, spread paper and pencils on the large table and begin sketching. Though many designers don't do paper sketches anymore, I can't stop doing them. It gives much more control than a computer program.

I decide to give Haley what she wants, even if it's for the last time. She wants boring? I'll give her boring, my best version of it. Worst thing is, she's going love it, and I won't be proud or happy with the final result. It drives me crazy.

I first started working for Secretive as an intern in the last year of my Fashion Contour course at LCF. I always had this crush on lingerie, it always made me feel good about myself. I began wearing them even before I had sex for the first time. To me, lingerie isn't only about sex, it's about feeling powerful and sexy. I pick my lingerie based on my mood or occasion. Some days I feel like wearing rose silk lingerie, other days I want the full black lacy embroidered set with suspenders and all their glory. What matters is, I'm never wearing plain and boring.

Sometimes, someone else gets to see me wearing them, but most of the time only my mirror does. I wear them anyways, for myself. The simple fact that I know how sexy they make me look is already enough for me.

I stop working at about 6:00 pm because I begin to feel hungry. I realise I skipped lunch. The whole day went by so fast I didn't even think of Luc, which is great. Every time my mind revisits our talk from last night and how cute he looked sleeping beside me, I shove it back in an imaginary box. It's the best thing I can do for myself.

Chapter Six

It's Thursday. I don't see him when I go for a run. I don't see him at Fresh Me Up when I get my daily green smoothie. I also don't see him in the lift. I'm glad, but I'm not.

Today is office day, so I leave after breakfast and there's still no sign of him. Why do I want to see him again? I thought I was happy, managing not to think about him most of the day yesterday.

It's the first day back at the office after Monday's fiasco. I'm hoping Haley won't ask for a private meeting to remind me how I should do my work. I'm not in the mood.

I have meetings with other designers to discuss trends and materials and budget. I also meet with my team to discuss the changes we need to make so the collection gets approved. ASAP.

'Are you planning on killing me, Olivia?' says Caleb, with a hand on his heart.

I knew he would freak out. His bugged out cartoonish eyes behind his rose gold framed glasses only confirms his desperation.

'Sorry, Caleb. It is what it is. I can't even look at those designs anymore, they are too good to be fixed. We'll recreate them. We can do it,' I reassure him.

'In less than two weeks? No, we can't,' he's throwing me a painful smile, crunching his face, showing all his very white teeth, matching the pearls on his ears.

Caleb Kingston is a workaholic, and we've been working together since I was promoted after my internship, almost three years ago. He's the kind of professional that makes things happen and is not at all familiar with procrastination. He gets my designs, we share the same vision and we complement each other's ideas. But what I love the most about him is that he always, always gives his all. He puts his heart into everything he does, and this means he's capable of making almost everything possible.

'Caleb, I'm going to pretend you just didn't say *we can't*, because I pretty much know you're the queen of making the impossible possible'—hence my nickname for him, Queen—'so cut the drama and let's make it happen. Besides, we've done worse than that in a much smaller time frame,' I remind him.

'Cruel,' he says, and darts his narrowed eyes at me. I know he didn't take it personally, we are used to being *this* honest and straight up with each other.

'Steph, send me some ideas by Monday. Taylor, set up a meeting with the suppliers and start quoting. As for delivery, beg if needed. Everyone else, you already know what to do. Let's meet again on Monday and check the progress,' I say.

Once everyone leaves, it's only me and Caleb in the meeting room.

'You like it complicated don't you?' he says, standing up to follow me as I walk toward the glass door.

'And you like the challenge,' I wink at him.

He tips his head back and laughs without a care in the world.

'That's why we're the perfect team,' he says.

Later in the day I attend a photoshoot of the collection that soon will be released, explaining to the models how to wear some of the pieces. I also fix any tiny detail that needs attention so everything looks impeccable on the photos. I get the rejected pieces of the collection back and immediately text the girls to inform them.

Today at 4:30 pm
Me: Saturday, my place.
Then I send a photo of the pieces lying on my desk.
Naomi: I love you.

Lexi: Can't wait! I'm hoping these will help me spice things up in bed!

I finish my day at the office replying to as many emails as I manage before my stomach starts complaining that it's dinner time. I actually could have done this part at home, but I was kind of avoiding going home early.

Back in my building I'm checking my phone as I'm waiting for the lift holding the bag with the lingerie. Then I hear his voice. I pretend not to, but my heart is a traitor. I look up and see him coming through the front door talking to three other guys, one a lot older than he is—could be his father. One just a bit older, and the third, a younger version of him, only with shorter hair and tattooed arms and neck impossible to miss.

Luc's carrying a huge black and white HEAD's bag on his back—possibly the same one from the night we met—and so is the younger guy. The older man has a rolling suitcase. The other has a bag slung over his shoulder. All four of them are wearing sports clothes.

As soon as he sees me, Luc smiles. I smile back, there is no way you'd see that smile and not smile back. You can fight as much as you want. You will fail.

'Hey, good to see you,' he says, and by the look on his face he really means it.

'Hey,' I say.

He gives me a kiss on the cheek. While we have our moment—if you can call it that—the others are talking among themselves in French. I don't understand much. The lift arrives and we all step in. He stands beside me, while the others stand opposite to us. They are still discussing something that seems serious and interesting. I'm basically a ghost to them. Not for Luc, he can't keep his eyes off mine, only briefly to check out my legs, all the parts my mini dress doesn't cover.

'Were you playing tennis?' I ask this because of his bag, I know the brand. As soon as I ask this I get the full attention of the others too. For a moment I think I might have said something wrong.

Luc half-smiles and looks to the guys then back at me and says, 'Yes, I was. Do you like tennis?'

'Not really. To be honest I don't even know how you score on a tennis match.'

All men laugh and the only feasible explanation for that is the fact that I am clueless about the sport they clearly enjoy.

They didn't laugh in a way that made me feel stupid, but in a way that made me feel like I told them the best joke of the day. I don't mind. I smile back, innocently.

Once the lift reaches my floor, they say goodbye. Luc places his hand on the small of my back, an unexpected touch that sends an electrifying thrill throughout my body, and touches his cheek to mine as he says in my ear, 'See you around.'

This time he doesn't get off with me and take the stairs. He stays with the others until his final stop.

Today is one of those incredibly hot days of London's summer. No open window could make up for this crazy heat. I decide to take another shower, risking missing Amazon's delivery guy who might arrive at any minute; I'm waiting for some supplies to arrive. As soon as I step out of the shower I hear the doorbell ringing. Just in time.

I wrap myself in a towel and head for the door. No time to wrap one around my wet hair. It's not the first time a delivery guy will see me in a towel. I hate it when it happens, but it's better than missing my package or having it delivered to Mrs. Thompson.

I open the door and to my surprise is not the delivery guy, it's Luc.

'Sorry, didn't mean to disturb you. I can come back another time,' he says, trying to avert his eyes from my collarbone, but failing miserably. He's flushing.

'No, no, it's okay …' I say even though there's nothing okay about this. Though he has already seen me in my underwear, it doesn't make it any less weird that he's now seeing me in my towel. Ok, last time I wasn't sober. Now I am, and I'm fully self-conscious of my appearance.

'Come in, I'll be ready in a minute.'

I let him in anyways, because even though I want to stay away, I can't.

'Are you sure?'

'Who's there?' I hear Mrs. Thompson.

'It's me, Mrs. Thompson, Olivia,' I shout, to Luc's amusement. 'Yeah, I'm sure. If the bell rings you can answer the door, it's Amazon. But do it fast because, otherwise, Mrs. Thompson will get it first. Then I'll have to get the package from her and she'll want to talk for an hour and invite me in for tea,' I say with a serious face.

He doesn't look serious to me, he's suppressing a smile, his eyes betray him.

First thing I do when I close my bedroom door behind me is head to my closet and pick my lingerie. Don't get me wrong, it's not because I'm planning on showing it to him, but rather to give me some shield against this crazy attraction I feel for him. It sounds crazy, I know, but lingerie makes me feel safer somehow.

I pick a lacy black botanical embroidered set with a bra and a hipster brief that is mostly transparent. It's too hot for anything other than thin and transparent fabric. I feel powerful already. I slip on a black crop top and white ripped high-rise shorts, put some simple makeup on, my favourite Chanel perfume and let my hair dry naturally—with this heat it will happen fast. I hurry up, I don't want him to wait too long. I'm curious to know what he wants. I swear that's the only reason.

'Hey,' I say as I catch him sitting on one of the kitchen island's stools. His hair's fresh from a shower too. He's wearing chino shorts again, this time navy and a white V-neck. There's something about him and V-necks that makes his collar and neck irresistible.

Oh for goodness' sake. Stop it.

'Hey,' he gives me a once over as he gets up from the stool to greet me with a kiss on the cheek, only this time his hand goes to the hair on the back of my neck with full purpose. The touch of his long fingers threaded through my wet hair is better than I expected it to be, it makes every pore of my body awaken.

'What's up?' I ask as if it weren't a big deal to have him here right now, and his hand on my neck, like this. The thud thud from my heart tells me this is a big deal whether I like it or not.

'I won't take much of your time, just wanted to ask if you'd like to have dinner with me on Saturday,' he says.

What?

Ok, now the intervals between the thuds thuds are shorter. I wish I could pause this moment and weigh the pros and cons of the possible answers I could give him. But I can't. Even asking for time to think about it would already be a complicated answer.

'I …' I begin, but before I continue I take a deep breath. I'm sure that after I say what I'm about to, I'll push him away. And though it will be a shame not to see those eyes staring at mine again, it will be better than the heartache I'm destined to have if I keep this going on for longer.

'Listen, Luc, I don't think it's a good idea.'

His face now is the most confused I've seen. His eyes, though connected to mine, now seem lost.

'Why not?'

Were his eyebrows that perfect all along? Why am I thinking about this right now anyways?

'You know why.'

'Do I?'

The slow way he drags his eyes from mine to my mouth, makes me chew on my lips.

'Yes, you do.'

He closes his eyes and takes a deep inhale. When he opens them again he says, 'I promise not to take advantage of you. Unless you want to,' he grins.

Oh God, why?

I feel my face get hot. As we stand there in front of each other I lose my willpower provided by my lingerie to keep away from him almost instantly.

Would it be too bad if I slept with him? Just once?

'That's the problem,' I say.

The shock on his face as he hears this is priceless, it makes my pulse go wild, it sets my insides on fire. He closes and opens his eyes in slow motion, as if he has just had the kind of pleasure that makes you feel doped, like when smokers take their first drag, or when an addict takes the first sip of alcohol in a long time.

He takes one step closer. I don't know how long I will resist being this close to him looking at me like that, like things only make sense if we are as close as we possibly can be. He takes another step, and now I feel the heat of his body embracing mine. For a brief torturing moment I know if he touches me I will let him, and I won't have any more control over the situation and what can happen next. Then I'm saved by the Amazon guy.

I head to the door as fast as I can and get the package and set it on the kitchen island. He's watching me all the while. Right now the kitchen island is separating us, the vase with the flowers he gave me between us.

You know what I want right now? Him. I want to know how his lips will feel when they meet mine, find out what he tastes like when his tongue pushes inside my mouth, how my skin will react to his hands exploring every inch of my body, his smell all over me penetrating my nostrils, him inside of me until I lose myself. Yeah, that's what I want, that's the only thing that could put out this fire I feel between my legs right now. But then I don't let my mind go there, I keep reminding myself that he also has the power to hurt me badly, of making me lose control of everything I have power over, including my heart.

'Right. I should go,' he says heading towards the door.

I watch him striding across the room and wonder if I'll ever get this chance again. Contradiction and temptation get the best of me. He's leaving, right? So I won't have to worry about dumping him, like the others. This time will be easier. An experiment maybe? And like a magnet and metal, I can't let him go without giving it a try. Because, as Caleb said, I like it difficult.

'Are your brothers and father going to be there?' I ask.

He turns around with a wide grin on his face, a gleam of excitement in his eyes.

I'm so going to regret this.

'Maurice isn't my father, he works with me, as does Daniel. Jules is my brother, I guess there's no doubt in there considering he's a younger version of me,' he smirks, before continuing, 'And no, they're not going to be there. I won't be cooking, I'm taking you to a place I like. Only you and me, if that's ok.'

Oh God. The way he says *only you and me* already implies so much it shoots a thrill of anticipation through me. I'm definitely regretting this, eventually.

I fidget with my fingernails, because I don't know how to feel comfortable in this situation. Why is it so hard to control myself when I'm standing in front of him?

'When should I be ready?' I ask.

I can't even believe I'm doing this. So much for making him go away, so much for self-control.

'Seven?'

'Sounds good.'

I don't accompany him to the door, I stay as far from him as I can just to be on the safe side.

Chapter Seven

I'm running and trying to push away any thoughts and expectations about tomorrow's dinner with Luc, but my mind keeps going back to what I should wear, where he's taking me, whether I should tell the girls or not. I'm so focused on trying not to think about him that I almost don't notice that he's running in the opposite direction, with his brother, Daniel and Maurice.

Both him and his brother are shirtless, wearing some kind of black elastic belt around their chests, like those that are used to measure your heart rate. When Luc sees me he smiles and nods at me, then keeps his focus on his run. It's a vision of hell, or heaven, depending on your point of view. His torso is toned to perfection, his shorts are hanging low on his waist, and because he isn't wearing a T-shirt, somehow his glutes are more displayed than usual.

Again I have trouble pushing my thoughts of him away. Almost an hour later I finish my run a few blocks before Fresh Me Up. When I'm about to open the door I see him there with his brother getting smoothies. Andi isn't there today, Lesley is. She's only there in the mornings when Andi has the day off. She's ok, if I don't consider the fact that she never remembers my usual order. I mean, really? I always order the same thing. But the problem is, what I see right now really bothers me. She's all smiles and blushing while Luc's writing something on a piece of paper, which he's giving her back.

Oh for fuck's sake.

The guy has a date with me tomorrow and needs to give his phone number to the girl at the café the first time he sees her?

Did I just say date? And since when am I the jealous type?

I don't know what's gotten into me. I decide to skip my smoothie routine today. I don't remember the last time this happened. Oh, wait, of all the three years I've lived here it's never happened unless I was travelling.

I go home as fast as I can and pretend I didn't see anything.

As crazy as it may sound, this weird feeling I have inside of me—something comparable to rage and jealousy, which doesn't even make any sense—makes me madly inspired. And so I drown myself in work. I basically create enough designs for two different collections, even though I know only two or three tops might be used. I skip all the meals that follow breakfast. This happens when I'm too focused on a project, or when I'm too anxious about something. I decide to have a glass of milk before falling hard on the bed before it's even dark outside.

The next day I'm woken by the doorbell. I check my watch: 10:00 am. Why didn't my alarm go off? Oh—because it's Saturday. It must be Naomi and Lexi to take a look at the lingerie.

I look like a mess—I'm still in yesterday's clothes, even my makeup's still on. I press the button to open the front door downstairs and wait for them to reach my floor, still trying to fully wake up.

'Were you still sleeping?' asks Lexi, as if she's just caught me doing something illicit.

'I guess I was,' I say, letting out a yawn.

'Who are you? Where's my friend?' jokes Naomi as she gives me a hug. She smells so good, like honey and jasmine. I love her taste in fragrances.

I welcome them in and tell them to make themselves at home and get something to eat from the kitchen while I change into something fresh and brush my teeth.

When I get back to the kitchen feeling a bit more like myself, Naomi is making scrambled eggs while Lexi watches her, sharing today's gossip.

'I can't handle the Hemsworth family,' says Lexi. Yes, her gossip updates are usually about movie stars, or singers, or athletes; any famous person really.

'Yeah, they're hot. I like Chris best,' says Naomi

'Me too. I mean look at those abs and arms. I wonder what's like to be Elsa Pataky and have children with him,' says Lexi.

'Oh my God, why are you talking about children?' I ask.

'It's not about children, it's about the Hemsworth family. Come sit, Naomi has your breakfast taken care of,' says Lexi.

'What about them?' I ask as I sit on a stool next to her.

'The males of that family are blessed,' she says and Naomi lets out a laugh.

'She's horny,' teases Naomi.

'Shut up, Naomi,' hisses Lexi.

Lexi's browsing her Instagram and shows me some pictures of Chris Hemsworth shirtless on some beach in Australia. Then she shows me some of Liam's and Luke's too, to make a fair comparison, according to her.

'I prefer Liam,' I say.

'I respect that,' she says, serious.

She keeps browsing on her Instagram, jumping from one profile to another, figuring out who's dating who and travelling where.

'You're so addicted to that thing,' I say.

'Yeah, if you had a profile you would be too, all the world's gossip and news is right here,' she says.

'Not interested,' I say.

I'm not a social media kind of person. Ever since Josh and I broke up I deleted all my profiles from the web and haven't created one since, not even on LinkedIn for work. But even before we broke up I already hadn't used it much, he used to get angry anytime a male friend liked or commented on a status or picture of mine. There were many fights over the same subject over and over, and so I kind of developed an aversion to that. And well, there was also the stalking after the breakup.

'Are you hungry?' asks Naomi from the counter.

'A bit,' I say.

Having Naomi fixing me breakfast reminds me of when she took care of me after the breakup, precisely the day after, when my face was swollen and my ribcage hurt every time I breathed. I was so grateful that day to have her taking care of me without questions or accusations. I was glad I didn't have to go to my parents', considering the state I was in.

'Thank you Naomi, you didn't have to.'

'Have you been eating?' she asks as she transfers the eggs from the pan into a plate. She sounds like Dad, always worried about me eating enough.

'Of course I've been eating,' I say, defensively.

She eyes me suspiciously, as if by doing so she could extract truth from me. She doesn't, but she knows I lied.

'What?' I ask looking between my two friends who are watching me in the way they do when they want some kind of confession.

'You haven't been like yourself lately,' says Lexi. 'And you're hiding something.'

'I'm not hiding anything, and I'm still myself. What makes you think that?'

I take the plate Naomi gives me with eggs and toast and use it as an excuse not to meet their eyes.

'You never wake up late, you are always defensive when we talk to you lately, and you seem anxious,' says Naomi. 'I know you don't eat when you're anxious.'

Why do they know me so well?

'What's wrong with sleeping until late? I worked a lot in the past two days. I just want to finish the new designs as soon as possible, it's making me anxious, of course,' I say as I chew. Swallowing is hard.

They keep watching me.

'Is it the cute neighbour?' asks Lexi, teasingly bumping her knee to mine.

'Is there something about him you aren't telling us?' says Naomi widening her eyes in excitement, urging me to tell something juicy.

'No and no. You guys, would you just leave it? There is nothing going on,' I lie, of course, there is no way I'm telling them I'm having a date with him tonight. Not when I myself don't even understand what's going on between us. Not when I don't know how I feel about this, about Luc. Soon he will leave and I won't have to talk about him to them anymore. Besides, I don't want them to make a big deal about tonight, I'm already doing the job myself. I'm even considering cancelling. Why did I agree to this dinner anyways?

'Fine,' says Lexi, now defeated, seeming to have finally accepted I might truly have nothing to hide.

'Is he on Instagram?' But she continues, to my annoyance.

'How am I supposed to know that?' I say, my mouth full of toast.

'Yeah, right, sometimes I forget you live in a non-social media world. What's his last name? I'm gonna try to find him,' she says.

I don't know his last name, is that weird? I mean, I didn't think knowing his last name would be important, I've only met him five days ago, not that I'm counting or anything.

'Lexi, stop it,' I say, making it sound like I'm only annoyed by the fact that she wants to find his Instagram profile and not because I don't want to admit that I don't know his full name.

'Oh my God, you don't know his last name, do you?'

'Is it that important?' I ask, lying to myself. 'It's not like I'm going to see him again.' I'm such a liar.

'Of course it is. I mean, he's been in your home, he's cute—or so you say, because you know, we haven't seen the guy yet—and how are you supposed to stalk him on social media once he leaves?'

'I'm no social media stalker,' I say, and she immediately regrets saying it. She knows very well this is actually the main reason I'm not on social media anymore, not even with fake profiles.

'Where is the lingerie?' asks Naomi, changing the subject.

Once I'm done eating we head to my office. Yesterday I hung the bodysuits, robes and babydolls on the stand, the other pieces are spread out neatly on the big table, each bra and bralette with matching knickers, thongs and panties. There are also suspender belts.

'I've been crazy about this one since I saw you designing it,' says Naomi, holding high-waisted silk knickers in pale pink with golden botanical details.

'They are gorgeous, just feel this,' says Lexi holding the matching bra feeling the silk fabric between her fingers.

They amuse me. I love it how they make me feel better and how they love my work. I imagine if I ever have my own brand they will be my first clients, no doubt.

'No, seriously Livvy. What would your brand be called if you were to have one?' asks Naomi, as if reading my mind.

I roll my eyes at her, pretending I haven't been thinking a lot about it lately.

'Yeah. Let's discuss names,' says Lexi.

'Guys, let's not.'

'C'mon, are you saying you haven't been considering it?' Teases Lexi.

'I might, but—'

'But what? You're talented, you have experience, you've got the money and support. What else do you need?' says Naomi.

I just watch her. I don't know what to say, because she does have a point. The problem is just, I'm afraid. There are so many things involved.

'Just … think about it, Livvy,' says Lexi, moving on to the next lingerie set.

I'm glad when we move on to the next topic, Lewis. I haven't seen Naomi excited about a date in a long while. I know it's because Lewis is a big deal to her. Then there's Lexi and Thomas's lack of sex issue, which she's still hesitant to talk about.

'When are you going to talk to him about it?' I ask Lexi.

'I don't know how to do it or what to say. Tommy is a bit closed up about the subject,' she says.

'Are you saying you guys never talk about sex?' asks Naomi, unable to hide the surprise in her face.

'Why? Should we talk about it?' asks Lexi innocently.

Naomi and I exchange looks.

'Hmm, yeah? You guys have been together for how long? Almost ten years?' says Naomi.

'Yeah. He was my first and only.'

'Exactly, Lexi. Talk to him, sometimes a simple conversation can do wonders,' says Naomi.

They stay until late afternoon. I almost kick them out when I check the time and realise I should probably start getting ready for dinner.

The dinner they don't know about. The dinner I refuse to consider a date. Is it bad that I'm hiding this from them? I know eventually I will probably tell them, in a couple of years when they have already forgotten there was ever a cute guy in my building. They will probably be mad, but they'll forgive me, it will be better than having them putting pressure onto all this right now.

Chapter Eight

I have three lingerie options laid on the bed in front of me, one next to the other. It wasn't easy to narrow it down only to three—it's not gonna be easy to pick just one. Each will make me feel different about myself, will serve a different purpose, will mould differently on my body, and yes, of course, will look different too.

The first option on my left is a killer look. The combination of a high-waist black bra and brief with suspender. Tule and lace are the main materials, and what I love the most are the lace panels at the hips, they are like wings. This one won't let me feel intimidated, it goes with the fact that I'm still annoyed that he was flirting with Lesley.

The second option is completely the opposite. It's a very light rose bralette and a hipster brief both made of incredibly delicate lace so thin you almost don't feel it between your fingers. The bralette extends just under my ribcage, and it has satin straps in a bow on the back. This is one of my designs, one that only I know exists. Today, it would make me feel like myself: vulnerable, sensitive, but daring.

The third option is a bodysuit. Completely transparent if not for the nude-coloured flowers spread out through it. It's back is almost completely open, thin straps hold it around my neck. It would make me feel impassive, neutral and powerful because my nipples will show to anyone who dares take off my dress.

Why is it so important to me to choose the right one? Today of all days? Because right now I don't feel control over anything related to him, it's only fair I feel control over my underwear, at least. Even if I'm not planning on showing it to him.

I leave the three options there waiting for me while I take a shower. It will help make up my mind. Eventually I make a decision. Today, number two will be my companion, under my tight dark red dress matching my black Louboutin heels. Let's see what the night will bring us.

I leave my flat at 6:55 pm to find Luc by the stairs in front of my door checking his phone. He's wearing skinny navy-blue chino pants, a white polo shirt, a blazer matching his pants and white sneakers to complement the outfit. For a brief moment I wonder if there's still time to cancel our plans. I'm like a teenager on her first date. I feel like someone getting cold feet before a big moment. But the way he looks at me when he sees me makes me feel like the only beautiful woman he has ever seen, and like the best thing that happened to his day.

'Hi,' he says, his voice husky.

'Hi,' I reply, closing the door behind me.

He greets me with a kiss on the cheek, his warm lips lingering longer than normally. His big hand lightly holds me by the waist; the simple touch makes my stomach flutter. We take the lift and outside there's a driver waiting for us. Where he came from might have something to do with Luc.

We both sit on the back seat of the black BMW, each by a window, on opposite sides.

'Didn't see you at the café yesterday, nor today. Did you get your smoothie?' he asks, bringing back thoughts of him flirting with Lesley, but at the same time, I'm glad that he noticed.

'I skipped it,' I say, avoiding eye contact, staring out the window where London's life goes on, busy on a Saturday night.

'Hmm.'

'Was Andi there?' I don't know why I feel like I should test him. As soon as I ask it I feel like a jealous stupid teenager. So what if Luc was flirting with her? I'm the one he's taking on a date tonight, besides, wasn't I trying to avoid him anyways?

'Nope. There was a girl there, not sure what her name was,' his answer is sincere, his eyes don't even blink as he says it.

'Lesley. She takes over sometimes,' I say.

We are staring at each other, as he lets out a curious smile at me.

'What?' I ask.

'You look beautiful. I mean, you *are* beautiful,' he says making me blush.

'Thank you,' I say. Always take a compliment.

The honesty in the way he says it makes me feel like it's the first time a guy's told me that. I rest my head back on the seat and look out the window once again, avoiding his gaze, but failing at containing a smile.

'Is it your first time in London?' I ask after a while.

'Not really. I've been here a few times,' Luc says running his hand through his hair.

'Do you like it?'

'I do, yeah. It's a big city, a bit different than Monaco,' he says, getting my full attention.

'Why are you comparing London to Monaco?' I ask.

He's smiling, it's that amused smile again. I get the feeling I'm a great source of amusement to him.

'I live in Monaco.'

Wait, what?

I stare at him surprised, probably more than that. He's making a funny face, as if I already should have known that he lives in Monaco. I mean, who lives in Monaco? Seriously, how many people have you actually met that live in Monaco? He told me he's from France, but never mentioned where he lived. Okay, I never asked either. I'm beginning to get worried about all this. I uncross my legs and cross them in the other direction, shifting a bit uncomfortably on the seat, and pulling down my dress, which has slid up my thighs.

I wonder what the girls would say if I told them Luc lives in Monaco—all the outrageous assumptions they would make.

Isn't he weird? He undresses me, puts me to bed without even knowing me and leaves my shoes neatly placed, is nice, cooks, has an athlete's body, runs with me, likes to eat the un-popped kernels, takes me on a date in a BMW with a driver, and now he tells me he lives in Monaco like it's the most common place to live. If he's royalty I don't want to know. I really don't want to know, because knowing it might ruin this once and for all.

I decide not to ask him if he belongs to the Monaco Royal Family, first because this sounds outrageous, and second, why would a prince from Monaco choose to stay at a penthouse in Richmond? I thought they had a room in one of the British Royal Family palaces, don't they? Whatever. He's not royalty, and I'm not in some kind of common girl meets prince romcom movie.

After crossing half of London all the way to Mayfair, we finally arrive at the restaurant. Once we step out of the black BMW, after Luc opens the door for me, he threads his fingers through mine. The gesture takes me by surprise. I know this is a big deal not only for me, but for him too by the way he looks at me searching for my approval. My tiny fingers welcome his long rough ones and I follow his lead. We walk towards the restaurant's entrance holding hands.

The restaurant's inside a white building with high windows. After being gritted by a man at the door and once we're inside, I realise where we are. It's Sketch. I have never been here and it's nothing less than one of the most exclusives restaurants in London, Michelin starred and all.

The place is loud, bright and colourful. Art and music and *haute cuisine* blend in one place. As I take a look around, Luc lets go of my hand to speak to the hostess. I barely hear them talking—I'm enchanted by the ballerina dancing around the room for the guests. I've never seen anything quite like it. There is a mix of expensive perfume and exotic food in the air. Some people are clinking champagne flutes, while some girls are taking selfies in front of a flowered wall. This place is popular amongst influencers and stars, I know that because just the other day Lexi wouldn't shut up about it when she saw some photos of Taylor Swift here.

I'm brought back to where I am when I feel his hand take mine again, as if he's claiming me. I don't know why, but it feels goddamn good. And right.

A guy wearing a suit leads us to our place. I secretly wish our table is in this room where everything is pink, floor, chairs to ceiling. But our table is nothing compared to any restaurant table I've ever had. It's a table for two, in a private room. How about that for a dinner night out?

The room is in gold, red and beige colours. A big fireplace stands behind the table, on the left side is a big window framed with red velvet curtains and crystal chandeliers hang from the ceiling. Thick velvet curtains separate us from the rest of the restaurant, just like the ones framing the window.

'Welcome to the Lecture Room and Library,' says our host. He introduces us to our private waiter and explains how the menu works once we take our places at the table for two. We both agree that the wine pairing menu is out of the question, I'm the first one to say no to alcohol tonight, and I suppose this makes him decide not to have it either, which I think is thoughtful.

'So. It seems to me I know nothing about you,' I say.

I generally am not one to ask many questions to the guys I hook up with. The less information, the better. Why search for something I'm not willing to give a chance to?

Luc's playing with his wristbands, something I notice him doing a lot, and looking at me with thoughtful eyes.

'What do you want to know about me, Olivia?'

I think by now it's fair to say he's the only person to give me goosebumps when calling me Olivia. Otherwise, in general, hearing my name means something serious.

He has his face of amusement on, he seems relaxed and curious to know what's coming his way. I feel pressured about the questions I'm thinking. There are many things I want to ask, I don't know where to begin. I haven't been on a real date in years.

'Should I be worried that you live in Monaco?'

He lets out a sexy delicious laugh, his voice almost hoarse.

'If you mean worried by having a date with someone from the Monaco royalty, you can stop worrying about it now. Not only royalty live in Monaco, you know that?'

I almost feel stupid about my question, but at least now I know he's only rich and not royalty. I'm not sure how I'd feel if he belonged to the Monaco Royal Family. I never imagined myself as a princess, or living in a castle, or having paparazzi stalkers following my steps like Lady Di.

'Now I'm relieved,' I say, teasing Luc. And he cracks another one of his smiles. He's looking so delicious sitting across from me with his powerful daredevil eyes fixed on mine. It makes me unconsciously cross my legs, as if by doing so I'd calm the desire building between my thighs.

'Why's that?' he puts on a curious face, frowning a little, making his eyes smaller.

'I don't like paparazzi,' I say, a smile tugging the corner of my lips.

He crosses his arms and watches me with his curious eyes. The way he stares kind of makes my chest warmer. I tighten my leg around the other even more.

'Tell me about your ex,' I regret it as soon as I say it.

'I thought you wanted to know about me,' he grins, making me blush. But before I say, 'never mind', he says, 'We weren't a match. There was nothing easy about our relationship, work demands, busy schedules, long-distance relationship and all.'

I feel jealous already, even though I know they've been broken up for two years. It makes me jealous too because their relationship sounds nothing like mine and Josh's.

'What?' he asks, he's watchful, eyes trying to read me.

'Sounds complicated,' I say.

What I don't say is that it all sounds like normal problems in a relationship. I wish my problems with Josh were busy schedules, or even a long-distance relationship. Actually, in our case, a long-distance relationship could have been a very positive problem.

It doesn't take much for me to drift from reality and have my mind revisit unpleasant memories. Now I'm thinking of one of our fights, the one which we were arguing about me having a weekend getaway with the girls. He didn't want me to go, and I said I would go anyways. We were in his flat. Lately I had been spending more time in his flat than mine. He pushed me into the bed, grabbed a pillow and pressed it against my face for longer than he should have, leaving me gasping for air. Every time I think about it I feel breathless, and hot, and like my soul's leaving my body for a while. And ...

'Olivia?' I hear Luc's soft voice, pulling me back to where I'm supposed to be. 'Did I say something wrong?'

'No, no, it's fine,' I pretend and put on a smile on my face.

Because we decided not to have alcohol, the waiter suggested making a special homemade drink for us. They surprised us with a ginger, mint and peach lemonade, which had a light touch of pepper. Not long after, another waiter brings our first course and puts our plates before us, as he does so, Luc's eyes keep trying to find mine. As soon as both waiters leave us alone in our private dining room, Luc says, 'Do you want to talk about it?'

'About what?'

'Your ex.'

How can he possibly know I was thinking about Josh?

'Not now,' I say, and I mean it. Even though for some crazy reason I feel comfortable talking about Josh with him, I don't want to do it now, tonight. I don't want to ruin the vibe.

'Ok,' he accepts my choice with an understanding gaze. 'My turn,' he says.

I smile and nod.

'You told me you don't do serious relationships. What could change your mind?'

His question takes me by surprise.

'Why? Are you asking me to be your girlfriend already?' I tease.

Luc snorts at my question, but he's waiting for a reply.

Truth is, I don't know the answer to his question.

'I haven't thought about it,' I say

'Have you banned all men from your life?' he asks, making me chuckle.

'No, I still have a brother and a father.'

He laughs.

'And I'm here with you, aren't I?'

I don't mention I've done one-night stands more times than I can count in the past years. I don't think he needs to know.

He takes a sip of his drink and watches me with heat in his eyes. He doesn't say a word, he watches me running my hand through my hair, studying me or searching for some answers I can't give him right now, because even I don't know them. His silence makes me want to talk.

'What?' I say self-conscious of the way he's staring.

He shakes his head. 'Nothing, just thinking of how you make me feel,' he says it as he plays with his wristbands.

'And how do I make you feel?' I'm so curious right now to know where this conversation is going.

'Confused, but certain all the same.'

Oh.

'Elaborate.'

'I can't. I don't even understand it myself,' he says.

I don't either.

He's so focused staring he doesn't blink. We keep our eyes locked.

'You make me lose my focus on everything else but you.'

Oh God.

I cross my legs even tighter, but it's pointless, I can't control my attraction for Luc. No table, legs, food, glasses, waiters or anything can keep me from wanting him. That's why my words betray me.

'Do I drive you crazy then?'

'Something like that,' his voice comes out hoarse, and I feel sparks running from my stomach down to my core. It's like the adrenaline of a free fall.

God.

I wish I had a glass of rosé to drink all at once right at this moment. No, tequila shots would be best—a quicker effect.

We stare until I give up. I smile the kind of smile that gives away how the other person makes you feel. Staring at him makes me want to crawl out of my skin. I think he drives me crazy too.

'Favourite colour,' I say.

'White. Yours?'

'Pink.'

'Favourite drink? Oh, let me guess, rosé,' Luc says.

'Yes,' I chuckle. 'Yours?'

'Champagne.'

'Ooohhh fancy,' I tease.

'Do I have another choice coming from a family who owns a

champagne house?' he says.

'I wouldn't complain if I were you,' I say.

'Who's complaining?' He smirks.

'Favourite place?' I ask

'The beach. Anywhere. Yours?'

'Same.'

'You should visit Monaco sometime.'

'Is that an invitation?'

'Would you accept it if it were?'

Luc throws me completely off balance. I flush, and by the way he's looking at me I can see a dare. The blues of his eyes have turned into flames, and it might have started burning me in the process.

'Maybe,' I say.

No, would I? No, I wouldn't.

'There's hope then,' he says, his face now turning serious, but the blue flames are still pretty much alive.

'For what?'

'Us,' he says, making me let out an unexpected laugh.

I regret not ordering the tequila shots.

'What could change your mind? About me?' I ask.

'Nothing,' he says.

Oh God.

'You don't give up easily then?'

'You'd be surprised,' Luc runs a hand through his hair. 'What could change *your* mind?'

'I don't know, I already told you.'

'Your answer is unacceptable.'

'God, you're impossible,' I'm burying my face in my hands, hiding from his intense stare. When I look up after a few moments, he's still glaring at me.

'Ask me again another time,' I say, knowing this time may never come and I'll be able to get away with it.

'I will,' he says, and it sounds like a promise.

Chapter Nine

When we get outside, it's pouring. Luc takes his blazer and covers me, protecting me from the rain. We are holding hands and he's taking me to the car that's already waiting for us. Though we were probably under the rain less than five minutes, it's enough to get his hair wet.

This time, on the back seat of the car, we sit right next to each other, me by the window. He takes my hand in his and rests both on his leg, which is pressed against mine. We exchange smiles and stay silent for the entire ride, our glances, however, speak more than our voices could muster. The minimal skin contact between us is lighting me on fire. He caresses the palm of my hand with his thumb while his serious face keeps staring at me with those blue eyes shining in the dark, city lights catching them every now and then, his hair messy and damp from the rain.

London lights keep flickering into the car as we drive across the city. Raindrops are running down the windows. There's something about this moment that tells me I'm going to remember it for quite a while. Something has shifted in me and it's almost palpable, I just can't tell what.

The way Luc observes me is as if though he has already taken off my clothes more times than I can count, and has kissed every inch of my body. There is so much desire and longing that I'm glad we're not alone in the car. My heart is finding its way up my throat once we reach the front of the building, anticipation is running through my veins.

He holds the car's door open for me, and once we're out, he clasps our hands again. I never hold hands with the guys I go out with. Actually, we are either at my place or the guys' place, not having romantic fancy dinners or walking the streets together holding hands.

The way Luc is firmly holding my hand right now makes me feel safe, and special. It's as if he knows what he's doing, when I don't. It's a good feeling, surprisingly.

The lift opens its doors for us, and once we're inside, I don't know what's going to happen. I don't know if he will press his button and I will press mine and we're both saying goodnight inside this lift. I don't know if he'll invite me to his place, or if I should ask him to go to mine. I've been fighting over what I want and what I should do the entire ride home.

We don't press any buttons, at first. Instead, Luc gently and slowly presses me against the metal walls of the lift, so that I take a few steps back until I feel his hot breath on my face, his hands both on each side of my neck, holding me in place. Goosebumps spread like an electrical current through me. The air is charged and I'm suddenly aware of every hair on my body. His powerful and intense daredevil gaze is holding mine like a magnet. I'm on fire, my face is burning.

'What?' I find my voice to ask, and it comes out breathy.

The doors close, but the lift doesn't move as we haven't pressed any buttons.

'You know what I really want to do?' he asks softly.

'Hmm?' I murmur more than say.

My eyes are burning, only staring at him. My mind is swimming in dirty thoughts, thinking about the things I'd like to do to him.

'Taste you right here,' Luc says, running the rough pad of his thumb over the skin of my neck.

I feel my heart pulsing in my ears, throbbing in my temple.

'And then?' I dare to ask, joining his game.

He grins a wicked grin, one I'm starting to enjoy more each time.

'Lick you right here,' he whispers in my ear, lightly brushing the shell with his soft lips.

Now I'm losing power over my legs; my knees are going weak.

'And then?' I whisper back.

He looks at me. Now we're face to face, our noses almost touching.

'Kiss you right here.' He touches and parts my lips with his thumb as his eyes focus on the spot he's touching, drinking me in.

'Why don't you?' I say, breathless, watching his heavy-lidded eyes.

He closes the remaining distance between us and presses his body against mine, one hand lost in my hair, the other pressed against the metal, just above my head. When the skin of his lips meets the skin of my neck, I decide I can't fight against this. I'm too weak to resist Luc, I'm already too involved to say no.

His tongue strokes my neck, gently. Its warmth against my skin makes my panties wet and my heart beat louder against my chest. I sink my fingers into his hair and it feels just as goddamn good as I thought it would. I tug hard on it, pulling him towards me, possessing him, just as I tilt my head enough to give more skin for him to taste.

The doors open, and startled, we pull apart as fast as we can, as if we were caught doing something unlawful.

It's Mr. and Mrs. Warner from the third floor. He clears his throat, she lets out a shy smile. Luc exchanges places with me, placing me in front of him holding me by the waist, and I know exactly why he's done it when his hard erection presses against the small of my back. I do what I can to ease my breathing and put on a poker face for the Warners. They are old enough to be my parents, in fact, they know my parents from when they used to live here too, in my current flat. They've known me since I was born.

'How are your parents doing, Olivia?' asks Mrs. Warner.

I clear my throat before replying, just to check my voice's still there. 'They're good, thanks.'

I let out a forced smile, and both of them smile back. Luc gives a gentle squeeze on my hip. I'm sure the heat on my face reveals what we're up to.

'Send them regards. We hope to have dinner with them again sometime soon,' says Mrs. Warner, politely as she has always been.

'I will,' I say with the most innocent face I can muster, but very much aware of what's going on behind my back, literally.

The ride to the third floor is excruciating. All the while Luc holds me against him by my waist. As soon as we are left alone in the lift again he presses the button to my floor, not his. He then places his lips on my ear, giving me goosebumps from head to toe taking me by surprise. He's now tracing his warm and soft tongue along my ear, picking up where we left off. I close my eyes and lean my head back against his chest closing any possible distance we still might have between us.

He spins me around and presses me against the mirror facing me. He looks drunk, I feel giddy. His magnetic blue eyes fix on mine and it looks like they're begging for something. He pulls me by my hair towards him, his long fingers threaded through my hair, then his warm wet lips are on mine. His demanding mouth parts my lips and his tongue fills me, satiating my need of him. I welcome his gesture in full force, my hands are buried in his dark hair, and his are now tracing my spine down to my ass.

The doors open and we manage to step out of the lift without breaking apart, our kisses growing more frantic by the second. We are all hands on each other, until he holds my hands up above my head and against my flat's door. He's the only one touching now. He chooses my nipples to play with his free hand as his tongue's still inside my mouth. I moan, losing my mind. Right now he has all the power over me and I can't do anything but accept it and let him do what he wants.

I normally am the one who dictates how this goes, but against Luc I have no chance, unless I still had some remaining willpower within me, but it seems that I don't. I try anyway, 'Wait,' I say, gasping for air as I break our kiss.

'What?' he's as breathless as I am, and his blue eyes are dilated staring into mine, his mouth red from my lipstick, his hair a complete mess. He smells like sex even though we haven't had any. Yet.

He's still staring at me waiting for me to say something, but I can't speak. All I can do is try to make my mind think rationally about all this.

Think about tomorrow. You're going to regret this.

I try as hard as I can to make my mind behave, but it's pointless, no rational thoughts come. All I see is him, all I feel is him, all I want is him.

'Who's there?' shouts Mrs. Thompson, this time she seems really annoyed. She probably got way too many packages from Amazon today.

We both chuckle on each other's mouths.

'You were saying?' he whispers.

'Nothing,' I say.

Oh God, why can't I say no to him?

He smashes his mouth against mine, demanding all of me. *Fuck tomorrow.* I want him, like I never wanted anyone in my life before.

In between his free hand finding its way under my dress, his tongue crashing against mine and my hands still held by his above my head, I realise it would probably be best if we didn't continue this outside.

'Keys,' I manage to say against his mouth.

'Keys. Yes, right,' Luc says with heavy breathing and a lot of effort.

Eventually, I manage to open the door. As soon as we're inside he lifts me up and I wrap my legs around his waist, dropping my clutch and his blazer on the floor. He walks with me straddling him across the room and sets me on the kitchen island. He kisses me desperately as I tug hard on his polo and pull it up over his head.

Oh the sight of his abs.

'What?' he asks with a sexy as hell grin plastered on his face.

I smile back at the beautiful mess he is right now, running my eyes all over him. Shamelessly. Considering I'm fucked anyways, I might as well take advantage of the view.

'You're looking at me like when you saw me for the first time in the elevator,' he rasps.

'And how was that?'

'Like you wanted to fuck me,' he says this with a serious face and a hoarse voice in his French accent.

Oh God.

I answer him with a laugh. With my legs still wrapped around Luc's waist, I dig my heels onto his ass and pull him closer. He tilts his head and analyses me for a moment, contemplating what he's seeing. His warm hands travel under my dress from my knees to my behind, until he grabs hold of the soft stretchy fabric and slowly pulls it up my head.

When my head is free from the dress and I open my eyes, I find him staring at me as if I were his muse. He half opens his mouth and runs the tip of his tongue along his lower lip before his mouth is on mine again.

'Is this one of your designs?' he whispers against my mouth.

'Yes,' I whisper back, almost trembling with so much need for him.

'Good,' he whispers in my ear, then his lips, tongue and teeth begin their journey down my collarbone to my hard nipple, inducing an uncontrollable gasp. He's driving me insane with the sucking, licking and nibbling. The sensations send me to a parallel universe I've never visited before. I hold tight to his hair. When he reaches his destination I bury my nose in his messy hair and feel inebriated by the combination of both its smell and the thrill of him sucking my nipple through the thin fabric of my bra. Gentle, wet and slow. I moan. My sex pulses between my thighs, begging for more, for him.

He cups my breasts with his hands, one nipple he's sucking on, the other he's pinching with his fingers. My head falls back with another moan. Luc does it slow, and that's what kills me. Hearing my moan he goes back to kissing me. He sucks hard on my tongue, devouring me, eating me up. It's a kiss with need and urgency, as if he were barely containing himself under his pants, which I'm reaching for to open the fly. He doesn't stop kissing me while I do it, but as my hand lands on his erection straining his underwear, he takes little breaks between kisses and sucks air through his teeth.

I hear my phone vibrating on the floor, inside my clutch. Naomi and Lexi have been texting me, but I haven't replied. I ignore it and focus on where my hands are. But Luc stops for a second, eyes closed, panting. When he opens his eyes and they meet mine, I know he's hesitating. He's holding himself back.

'What's wrong?' I ask through my heavy breathing. My hands are tugging on his waistband, so I let go of it immediately.

His hand finds its way around my neck, his fingers touching my nape, his thumb stroking my cheek. He watches me for a moment and presses his forehead against mine. It's so unexpected my heart stops for a few long seconds.

'As much as I don't want to stop, I think we should,' he says, softly and breathlessly.

What?

'I don't want to be a one-night stand for you,' he says.

Oh God.

I'm so surprised by the fact that I'm not disappointed with what he just said—if any of the guys I've been with in the past had said anything close to this I'd definitely be annoyed—I can't even respond to that. My mind's all over the place now, in a battle between the high it seems to be on and his words. I don't get the chance to say anything, because right then, something begins to vibrate in his back pocket, breaking the moment completely. Luc growls in frustration and puts some distance between us to check his phone. Worry takes over his face when he sees who's calling. He runs a hand through his hair and says, 'I'm sorry. I have to take this.' His eyes meet mine briefly, he looks genuinely guilty.

'*Oui*,' he says, pressing the phone to his ear. The person on the other side starts talking as he listens attentively with furrowed brows.

He helps me down from the island, picks his Polo from the floor and helps me into it. He presses his soft, swollen and smudged-with-lipstick lips against mine and gives me a reassuring smile. Shirtless, his pants hanging low on his waist, still with a hard-on, he strides across the living room and to the balcony, leaving me speechless, wanting and confused.

Chapter Ten

From his sharp tone and the way his hand is raking through his hair, I can tell the conversation he's having is serious. I don't know how much longer he's going to be on this call. I want to give him some privacy, and debate whether I should go to my room or sit on the couch. I decide for the latter, it's not like I can understand much of what he's saying.

I make myself comfortable between the cushions, propping my feet on the coffee table. I can't help but watch him. It's almost midnight and who can possibly be calling him at this hour on a Saturday night?

'Margot, *je sais. Mais … non, non. Est que tu peux au moins essayez?*' It sounds like he's begging.

I wonder who this Margot is. My guess is, it's work. It sounds a lot like work to me. But on a Saturday night?

Once in a while he glances my way and his eyes smile at me, but his mouth keeps on talking. At some point, I lay down, my eyelids are getting heavy and the delicious scent emanating from his Polo all over me is soothing.

'Hey,' I hear his voice, low and sweet. His hand slowly skimming my arm up and down, gently forcing me to open my eyes. I guess I drifted for a few minutes.

Luc's kneeling on the floor.

'Hi,' I say. His face is so close to mine, I can't help but lift my hand to touch it. He welcomes the touch, leaning his head onto my hand.

His mouth curves into a boyish smile. He looks vulnerable, and his skin is hot and flushed.

'I'm sorry it took so long,' he says, guilty.

I don't say anything, because I'm still trying to figure my emotions out. While he was on the phone and before I fell asleep, I kept on thinking about what he said, about him not wanting to be a one-night stand.

'I should go,' he says, after a long moment of silence.

The disappointment I'm feeling can be added to the emotions I'm trying to interpret. I wish he would stay. I never ask or let any guy stay the night, especially when we didn't even have sex, but I was hoping he would stay. Is that insane? Somehow I can't get enough of his presence, or the way he makes me feel, which I can't yet put into words. And so I do what I never do, surprising even myself.

'Stay,' I say.

It might be because I'm sleepy, but right now I don't want anything more than for him to stay.

'Are you sure?' his voice is raspy. A smile tugs on his lips as he brushes my bangs off my face.

'Yes,' I whisper.

He helps me up from the couch, I take his hand and lead him to my bed, turning off the lights on the way. He tucks me into his chest where I can hear his heart beating against my ear. He interlaces his fingers through mine and I can feel the calluses on his skin. When I look up I see him watching me in the dark, though I can tell he's already half asleep, as comfortable in my bed as if it were his own. Right now he looks satisfied and relaxed, exactly how I feel. I realise that that's exactly what I needed, and it worries me.

I wake up sometime in the middle of the night. It's still raining outside, I can tell by the water drops running down fast on the window glass reflected by the lights coming from outside. I watch him sleep, deeply and peacefully. His breathing makes a little soothing noise. Though it's dark, my eyes are adjusted enough so I can see the shape of his perfect nose, his lips parted.

I raise my hand and touch the tiny little hair growing along his jaw and chin. Asleep, he puts his arm around me and tries to spoon me, but I'm facing him. His sleepy eyes open and look right into mine. I turn my back to him so that now he can effectively spoon me, our warm bodies complementing each other.

To me, there is nothing normal about this. The way he makes me feel so comfortable around him when we've only just met, me accepting an invitation to dinner, cooking for him, and letting him stay the night and sleep on my bed and lying about him to my best friends. This is all different from everything I've known since I left Josh, heck, of everything else I've experienced. I haven't done any of this with the guys I had sex with in the past three years. I have never let any of them get this intimate, and I also never allowed myself to get this close to someone. Why I'm letting it happen now is a mystery I can't decipher.

Of course, I had no deadline planned for when I'd finally let anyone get this close to me again, I just didn't expect it to happen anytime soon. In fact, sometimes I wondered if it ever would. I worked hard to close the walls around me in the first year after Josh. Yes, because there was me before, during and after Josh. There was the naive and unexperienced girl of before, the abused and deceived of during, and the woman who knows she deserves better after. Almost everything that can go wrong in a relationship, I had it with Josh, and considering he was the only serious relationship I ever had, I don't know what can go right in one.

Letting Luc occupy all this empty space I have in my life in a matter of days, naturally, makes me feel out of control. And not having control scares the shit out of me, because controlling is the only way I know to protect myself from hurting inside and out.

All these thoughts are playing tricks on my mind, sabotaging the way I truly feel right now, a kind of bliss that I experience when I'm around people that care about me and I care for in return. I shut my eyes and try to tell myself it's going to be okay.

Now it's too late to undo this.

Unexpected sunlight is cutting through the window. It doesn't even seem like it was pouring outside just a few hours ago. Luc's still asleep beside me. I study him sleeping, the light touching his bare chest, his body half covered by the sheets we shared last night. I look at the clock on my bedside table and it says it's already 9:00 am. My stomach growls, begging for food, something that can provide my body more energy to start the day.

I don't wake him when I leave the bed. I head to the bathroom and brush my teeth, on the way, I spot his pants on the floor. I smile to myself thinking of how we fell asleep last night.

When I return to the room, he turns to his side, moving his handsome face away from the sun. I watch him from where I'm standing, sighing as my mind travels back to touching his body last night, feeling the warmth of it, enjoying what that mouth and hands can do to me.

Still wearing his Polo, I head to my closet to pick lingerie, when I slide the door he mumbles something in his sleep. I choose a champagne silky set of bra and briefs embroidered with peach flower ornaments and put it on. I love how it hugs my body. I look at myself in the big mirror on the front of my closet and I'm happy with my choice. I smile for no reason in particular, and it feels weird and unforeseen. In the mirror I notice his eyelids fluttering and the moment he opens his eyes.

'Good morning,' he says, wiping his eyes with his knuckles.

'Morning,' I say, turning to face him with a smile.

There are lines on his sleepy face and he holds back a yawn.

'Whoa, that's a lot of lingerie,' he says as he glares at my open closet, then at me.

I laugh. I'm aware of his eyes on my body. We hold each other's gaze for a moment. There's some kind of intimacy that wasn't there before.

'What time is it?' he asks, seeming a bit lost sitting up on the bed and smoothing down his messy sexy hair that's sticking up in random places.

'Around 9:30?'

'What?!' he doesn't take it well. '*Merde*. I gotta go.'

I'm pretty sure he just swore in French. He might be really worried about something by the way he says it and how fast he gets up from the bed.

'Got somewhere to be?' I ask watching him walking towards me in a hurry, spotting his morning erection.

'Yeah, sorry. I should have woken earlier.'

Seems as though, as me, he also likes his routine. Despite the hurry, he grabs me by my hair and his mouth takes mine in a hell of a good morning kiss.

Wearing nothing but white Calvin Klein boxer briefs—for my absolute despair—he heads to the bathroom fetching his pants on the way. He finds his phone in the pocket and takes it.

'*Putain*,' he admonishes it.

He puts his pants on quickly, then splashes water on his sleepy face. I enjoy it all from my point of view by the bathroom's door frame. He comes to me, presses me against the frame, sucks on my neck and whispers, 'Up for a run?'

What?

'Right now?' I smirk in surprise.

'Meet you back here in half an hour?'

'Deal.' There's no way I'm saying no.

His reply comes with a smile, then a kiss on my lips.

He then quickly heads towards the door shirtless and holding his shoes. One hell of a sexy scene to watch on a Sunday morning. The thought that I almost fucked him last night right here on the kitchen island sends electrifying waves through my body.

I go change into sports underwear and put on running shorts and a tank top instead. As I tie my hair back into a ponytail in front of my bathroom's mirror my phone vibrates with a call from Naomi. I don't answer it. I wait until she gives up. But before she does it, she tries two more times. I feel like the worst friend in the world ignoring the girls' texts last night.

I'm pretty sure Naomi wants to share about her date with Lewis—and trust me, I'm dying to know too. But right now I can't possibly talk to Naomi, not if I don't want to tell her anything about Luc, which would lead her to know that I lied yesterday, and not when he's all over me in every way and everywhere. She will immediately recognise in my voice that I'm hiding something. I turn on the silent mode and go put my running shoes on.

I'm about to open the door when I hear Luc knocking.

'Hey,' I open the door to a sporty version of him, the one that always has a cap on; right now it's backwards. I don't ask him why he left in such a hurry if his only plan was to go for a run.

'Hi, Olivia,' he says pulling me into him and crashing his mouth against mine. The kiss lasts longer than it probably should, and it's a fierce version of a simple hello kiss, but I'm not complaining. He walks backwards taking me with him. Eventually we break apart and he presses the lift button. We kiss one more time before the car arrives, then again once we're inside.

'What have you done with my focus?' he stares down at me with questioning sexy eyes and frowning eyebrows. He seems serious about his question.

I beam at him, because I can't possibly know the answer to his question. I confess it makes me feel good knowing I make him lose his focus, even though I'm not sure on what.

Before we share another kiss, the doors open on the ground floor. As soon as we're out, he turns his cap forward.

We do some stretching in front of the building and start running alongside each other checking our watches turning on the running mode. I always run alone, if you don't count the time he caught up with with me a few days ago, so I'm not used to having someone beside me to keep a similar pace or to talk to.

We run a total of seven miles, taking the route to the Thames and around the Royal Botanic Gardens. I try my best to keep up with his pace as he effortlessly waits for me.

At some point during the run it finally occurs to me to ask, 'You know, I've been meaning to ask but it never comes up … what's your last name? Since you already know mine I figured I should also know yours.'

He smirks, drying the sweat from his forehead with a tennis wristband he has around his wrist.

'Are you going to look me up on social media?' he grins glancing at me sideways.

'I'm not on social media.'

'Is that so?'

I nod. He seems surprised.

'It's Lamaire. Lucas Lamaire,' he looks at me as if waiting for some kind of reaction, when I don't react to whatever he's expecting, he puts on his trademark amused grin. I seem to get that a lot from him.

'What?' I ask.

'Nothing.'

We keep running, mostly in silence but very much aware of the other's presence. Once we reach our street again we don't even ask each other whether we should get a smoothie, when our eyes meet after hitting stop on our watches, we know we're going in the café.

I hadn't had anything to eat before the run and my stomach has been complaining since I woke up this morning. I'm glad that instead of just ordering our smoothies to go, he asks me if I'd like to have a full breakfast.

We pick a table by the window in the far corner of the café, on the cosy green velvet couches. It's still quiet, which is no surprise considering it's before 11:00 am on a Sunday. We study the menu and place our orders with Lesley, whose eyes are fixed on Luc. I watch to see if he reacts to this in any way, he doesn't. She's staring nonetheless, with a not innocent smile on her face, it's annoying.

I clear my throat so she can pay attention to my order, and not to the handsome sexy as hell man sitting across from me.

'Oh, hi there, didn't notice it was you,' she says, seeming genuinely surprised to see me.

Hi *there*? Doesn't she know my name by now? She has envious eyes for me, her smile fading instantly at the sight of me.

'I'll have the omelette with champignons and rocket, a glass of water and the same smoothie as always,' I say.

'Which one is it again?' she asks.

Luc snorts, his beautiful blue eyes almost hidden under his cap staring at me in contentment. Even he can't believe she still doesn't know my order.

'Same as his.'

'Oh, ok.'

God, why is it so difficult to remember it?

She makes the order on the device she's holding in her hands and stands there watching us, more precisely watching him. I can almost see the drool on the corner of her mouth.

'That will be all, thanks,' says Luc, making it clear she can leave us alone now.

When she turns her back, he smiles at me, his eyes tightened in amusement meeting mine. I can read so much in those eyes, there is some kind of inexplicable chemistry with the way we can communicate to each other by just staring. It's absurd. When did that start?

Once our order arrives, I'm glad Lesley doesn't stick around to join us, though I'm sure that's what she'd want. She didn't even look at me when putting my plate in front of me. I'm impressed by how Luc handles this harassment, kindly dismissing her with a friendly smile and immediately turning his attention back at me.

'Why were you in a hurry today?' I ask him.

'Huh?' he lifts his gaze from his food.

'You seemed in a hurry earlier today …'

'Oh, yeah. I was supposed to meet my brother but he had already left.'

'Sorry about that.'

'What for?'

'Making you late?' I say guiltily.

'Not your fault,' he gives me a reassuring smile.

'Does that have anything to do with me making you lose your focus?'

'A little.'

I love how his eyes smile when he says it.

'Oh, really?'

He replies with a wink and goes back to his food.

I'm entertained by watching him eating. Sunlight's touching his eyes, turning them into an exotic shade of blue, popping even more on his perfect face. I can't get enough of them. He still has lines from sleeping. With me. On my bed. Why do I feel like I just slept next to a man for the first time? Everything feels intensified this morning.

He pulls out his phone and aims it at me.

'What are you doing?' I ask embarrassed, unconsciously tugging on my ponytail.

He grins and says, 'Taking a photo of you.'

'What for?'

He holds his phone up closer to me so I can see for myself and waits for my reaction.

I look at the photo on his screen and there's nothing I haven't seen before. It's just plain me, after a run. I glance up at him curious to know what he thinks it's so special about it.

'What is it?' I say.

'That's your I-want-to-fuck-you face.'

Oh God.

I flush, letting out an unexpected laugh. That's not what I was expecting.

'May I keep it?' he asks with a boyish grin on his beautiful stubbled face.

'If you promise not to sell it to a porn website, go ahead.'

Now it's his turn to laugh.

'Ahh Olivia …' he sighs.

His expression is of someone who's imagining or daydreaming about something they are longing for. He bites his lower lip and I'm certain of what he's thinking about, because it's just what I'm thinking about too.

Our moment is broken by something he sees on his phone. His face, suddenly serious, turns to look out at the street through the window.

It's Jules, Daniel, and Maurice walking towards the café. This makes Luc uncomfortable and unsettled. I wonder why they're always together, I'm guessing it's just the fact that they're staying at the same place. Also, why would his teenage brother be on a business trip? Maybe he's just in it for the fun to be in London.

'I might have to go now,' he says gesturing to Lesley who's behind the counter, that he'd like the check.

In the meantime the guys enter the café and are coming our way.

'Maurice, Jules, Daniel, this is Olivia Charlton,' says Luc once they're hovering over us. The way he introduces us is as though he didn't want to share me with them.

'Hi Olivia, happy to officially meet you, I'm Jules,' says his brother with a wide smile.

'Nice to meet you, Jules,' I say shyly. I wonder how much he knows about me and Luc. Not that there's much to know.

'Hi, Miss Charlton,' says Maurice politely. I immediately get that he isn't excited about the encounter. What I don't get is why he uses my last name. The way he's staring at Luc tells me he's cross with him. Maybe he's Luc's boss?

'Hey, Olivia, I'm Daniel,' says the slim blond guy, who seems to be about Luc's age.

'Are you ready to go?' asks Maurice, intensifying his displeased stare at Luc, now completely ignoring me.

'Yeah. Let me just …' Luc begins, but it's interrupted by Lesley who's attentively and excitedly waiting for his command like a little puppy.

Luc stands up and gives her his credit card. I begin to protest, but he mouths 'I got this.'

While Lesley and her device process the payment, Jules winks at me and says, 'Bye, Olivia,' and turns to follow Maurice who's already at the door waiting impatiently for the Lamaire brothers. Daniel's already outside on the phone.

Luc comes to me with a hypnotising gaze and whispers in my ear, 'Sorry, I gotta go. Will I see you later?' and faces me waiting for a reply.

I nod and he smiles. He holds my face with one hand to plant a warm kiss on my cheek and disappears to the street following the others. I watch them as they cross the street back to the building, Maurice is talking and gesticulating at Luc, while he seems to be trying to explain himself about something. My attention drifts to my phone and an incoming call from my Mum.

Chapter Eleven

'Hi Mum,' I say standing up from the chair and heading out of Fresh Me Up.

'Olivia! Thank God. Where are you?'

Oh, oh.

'What happened, Mum?' I say alarmed that maybe something bad happened to Dad or Nate. She sounds desperate.

'Naomi called and said you haven't been answering her calls or Lexi's. I also tried to call you a few times and you didn't pick up. I just got here in your flat and you aren't home. What's going on?'

Mother of God!

Mum in my flat is a bad combination. She inspects everything, under the bed and even the bin. She doesn't understand the concept of casual sex, so to avoid raising unwanted questions, I'm always careful not to leave compromising items around the place when I know she's coming over. This time though, I didn't have time to prepare.

'I went out for a run and was having breakfast at the café across the street, Mum!'

I'm so indignant I almost shout as I stride across the street to head back home before she finds evidence of Luc. I mentally try to remember if Luc took all his belongings today when he left, but then I remember his T-shirt and Polo are somewhere in my bedroom and hurry up. Maybe she's still inspecting the kitchen.

When I open the door she's all over me like an infestation of wasps.

'Livvy, oh my God,' she's so relieved to see me, I can't even be mad at her. I almost feel bad to think the worst and compare her to a wasp.

I give her a hug and she kisses me on the cheek, possibly leaving red lipstick on my skin. Her perfume is so good and strong it has already impregnated the air, eliminating any scent of Luc that remained.

'Mum, everything's fine,' I head towards my bedroom, checking on the way for evidence that Luc was here last night. She follows behind me, clinking her heels on the floor. You'll almost never see my Mum's feet in anything but high heels.

'You know how I get when you disappear like that.'

As soon as I spot my bed made and my and Luc's clothes neatly folded on top of each other on one corner of the mattress, I close my eyes and take a deep breath.

Shit.

'Mum, you're overreacting,' I try to pretend it's not a big deal that she has found men's clothes on my bed and head for the bathroom. Not giving her a sign that I know that she knows a guy has been here.

'Naomi says she's trying to reach you since last night, Lexi too.'

Yeah, I've been ignoring them on purpose, but I hadn't thought it would lead my mum to pay me a surprise visit.

'Does it have anything to do with your new boyfriend?'

See? That's the reason her surprise visits drive me crazy. I roll my eyes at her as I begin stripping down my clothes and tossing them in the laundry basket.

'I don't have a boyfriend, Mum,' I say, turning to face her. Her expression is nothing close to amusement, she's genuinely worried and I know exactly why.

'It's not like you to ignore the girls' calls, so of course I was worried and decided to come over. You know …'

Guilt takes over me for a moment. I can see what she's thinking in her eyes.

'I know Mum, I know.' I take a deep breath and try not to think about the day Josh tricked me into a conversation in his car, trying to convince me to go back to him. It did not end well. For me.

'It's been almost three years, Mum. I haven't heard from him in a long time.'

Thank God.

I don't mention the nightmares, how Josh's still pretty much alive in my head, haunting me. Sometimes I wake up in the middle of the night thinking he's in my bed. Some nightmares take me back to fights, to being his girlfriend again. I never have good dreams of him, as much as I try to remember just one positive memory of him, I can't. Even the moments I considered good and happy at the time make me sick now.

'I know, but you never know.'

'You're right Mum, sorry,' I give her a comforting smile before stepping into the shower.

She goes to the sink and starts retouching her makeup, our gazes meeting in the mirror.

'So, do you or do you not have a boyfriend? You can tell me, you know?'

'I don't have a boyfriend Mum. When I do, you will know,' I say, hoping she'll accept the answer and not mention it again.

'Right, right. Casual sex, isn't it?'

I almost wince hearing her say it aloud. It's so weird to talk to her about this stuff.

When I roll my eyes, she doesn't press anymore. Instead, she begins to give me all the family's updates. How Nate's new girlfriend's high-pitched voice annoys the hell out of her and that she hopes it won't take long before they break up.

'You'll meet her today. She talks so much it makes you wonder how she manages to breathe,' she says, making me chuckle under the water.

Then she mentions that Dad got a new car without telling her first.

'I don't know how many cars your father still needs. He barely drives the ones he already has,' she's putting more mascara as she complains. I don't even think she needs to retouch her makeup, she does it when she's anxious.

My Mum never understood my dad's passion for cars. What he enjoys the most about having vintage cars is spending time and money fixing them, more than driving itself. Truth is, his cars have always been one more way for him to bond with me. I always loved to listen to his explanations about engines, and designs, and special editions.

'It's different when you're a collector,' I say as I wash my hair, thoughts of Luc from last night playing in my mind.

'The Walters said you should do dinner sometime soon. I met them in the lift last night,' I say, trying to spare me from the unnecessary family drama, turning the conversation in another direction.

I close my eyes to enjoy the warm water running through my hand and down my face. I direct my thoughts to how warm Luc's body felt against mine, how our bodies fit and moulded each other as we slept.

'I'll give Beatrice a call soon,' she says, now checking the wrinkles on her face. Once she's done, she checks my cabinet and goes on and on about the anti-ageing products I'm currently using—she's a dermatologist.

I finish my shower and go pick lingerie and something casual to wear. Almost every Sunday Nate and I meet at our parents' house for brunch, late lunch or tea in the afternoon. Sometimes, dinner. Today it's late lunch and tea afterwards. I skipped last week because I was too stressed about presenting my new collection on Monday. So much stress for nothing, really.

I drive with Mum, considering I don't have a car despite Dad's constant insistence that I get one. But I mean, a car in London when I mostly work from home doesn't really make any sense. So whenever I need to go to their place I ride with Nate or take an Uber.

My parents live outside the city, in a mansion they bought when Dad's business picked up when I was about five. Before that we lived in my current flat. They still keep it as an investment, among several other flats across London. Dad works in construction, so he knows the real estate market well and buys properties that seem attractive.

After Josh, Mum convinced Dad I needed to have my own place and that our old flat would be ideal. Dad didn't really get why I needed to move, we never told him what really happened between me and Josh, if he knew, he'd probably have killed him or died of a heart attack himself. So once the previous tenants left, I moved in. Besides, Josh had never been to this flat. He wouldn't find me easily.

I don't have many memories of the time I lived in my current flat with them as a child. But I know they were always close to the Warners. And I also remember Mrs. Thompson, when she was younger and her husband was still alive. She used to give me and Nate lollipops, and sometimes she would even babysit us.

The big house is where I spent the rest of my childhood and my teenage years. It was nice growing up out of London. We had enough space to play, to throw big parties, to have our dogs, to have all our friends over. Nowadays it seems empty and quiet, except for when the Golden Retriever family we have are barking at and running after the birds in the garden, or Dad turns on one of his cars' engines to find out some sort of problem.

I'm greeted by Zeus and Athena—our Golden Retrievers—in the garden, which takes quite a while, at least until I've given them enough attention for them to find the next interesting thing. Then I finally manage to get inside the house.

'Hey, Dad,' I say as I come into the living room to find him sitting on his favourite chair, a leather brown one by the window, reading newspaper with black framed glasses on and watching TV at the same time.

'Hello, love,' he smiles and holds his arms wide open to me. 'You're skinnier than the last time.' There goes his worry that I don't eat enough.

'Dad. No, I'm not,' I roll my eyes at him. I sit on his lap and give him a kiss on the cheek. I haven't stopped greeting him this way even though I'm twenty-six, it has always been like that. We have always been close.

'What are you watching?' I ask.

'Wimbledon,' he says.

'Hmm. Tennis?'

'Yes. I'm hoping Moretti will kick Papadakis' ass,' he says. I have no idea what he's talking about.

'Boring,' I say, standing up. 'I'll go check what's for lunch.'

Before Nate arrives and lunch is served, I text Naomi and Lexi on our group chat.

Today at 1:04 pm

Me: You guys, I'm alive, ok?

Me: There was no need to call my mum, she showed up in my place and was freaking out.

Lexi: Oh my God, Livvy. Where were you?

Me: Slept at home, woke up and went for a run then had breakfast at Fresh Me Up …

Naomi: Why didn't you reply to our texts or answer our calls?

Before I get angry because everyone sometimes treats me like I'm a helpless lost child and to avoid further discussions, I swallow my pride and text again.

Me: Sorry guys. Won't happen again. Thanks for worrying about me, but everything's fine.

Lexi: Where are you now?

Me: Family lunch

Lexi: Call us later then.

Me: I will, I'm dying to know what happened with Lewis last night…

Naomi: A lot my friend. A LOT happened.

Me: emoji with heart eyes

I can't hide from them forever, so I start to play excuses in my head before the call, preparing myself to lie and not be discovered. Now that things have escalated from a simple thank you dinner into Luc staying the night and having breakfast with him in public, there's no chance in hell I'll tell them the truth. How will I even explain that *I* asked him to stay? And that we didn't even have sex?

'Hey, sis.' It's Nate, overly excited to see me, followed by a, wait, a brunette? I can't believe she's Thea, his new girlfriend. I've never ever seen him date a brunette before.

He notices my surprised face, but in his eyes I read a perfectly clear 'shut up'. When he hugs me he quickly whispers, 'Don't mention it.' Sure thing. I'll keep it to myself until the next opportunity I have alone with him.

'You must be Thea,' I say giving her a hug.

'And you must be Livvy,' she says with a strong southern American accent. I give Nate another stare, raising my eyebrows and widening my eyes at him. This must be the reason why Mum's been complaining about her voice. She speaks as if she's singing, and it doesn't help that her voice is high-pitched.

'It's really nice to meet you, Thea,' I say.

Behind Thea's back, I see Mum rolling her eyes.

'Thank you, it's finally nice to meet you too, Nate talks a lot about you.'

'I bet he does.'

I raise an eyebrow at him, making him grin like a naughty child.

When lunch is finally served on the big mahogany table in the dining room, Dad asks why Mum went to pick me up in London when I could have driven with Nate and Thea. While she makes up an excuse—something about she needing to stop by a friend's nearby—Nate's studying me. I avoid his gaze. He can tell we're hiding something. I'm glad Thea is sitting beside me making conversation non-stop. Boy the girl can talk. If she ever marries my brother Mum is going to wear invisible cancelling noise earplugs every time she visits.

'Nate told me you design lingerie,' she says in a low voice, so she doesn't interrupt my parents' discussion, which now is about whether I should or shouldn't get a car. Again.

'I do,' I take a sip of the refreshing watermelon lemonade.

'Do you think I can get an exclusive one?' she whispers, half covering her mouth with her hand, such a girlish thing to do. I can't help but laugh, she looks so innocent and she doesn't even seem to care.

'Yes, of course.'

It's not the first time I've gotten this kind of request, especially not the first time from one of Nate's girlfriends. Even though I find it awkward that my brother will be having sex with someone wearing one of my designs, for some very strange reason I don't mind if it's with Thea. I like her. Or maybe I just like how my brother looks happy around her.

After lunch we linger around on the couch, watching TV, discussing politics and cars with Dad, the most recent anti-ageing treatments with Mum and eating a bombastic caloric cake, which, as my Mum always says, *on Sundays it's ok.*

I drive back home with Nate and Thea. She talks during the entire ride, telling me how she ended up in London after getting a job offer as an architect. She works with one of Nate's friends, who introduced them. All the while, Nate watches me in the rear-view mirror as I sit in the back. I've never seen him want approval of a girlfriend so much, but apparently he concludes I've approved of her by his satisfied smile at me on the mirror. I, in fact, like her. Mum, I'm not so sure.

Nate parks the car and gets out to talk to me before I head back home.

'Hey, did something happen?' he asks.

'What do you mean?'

'You and Mum seemed to be hiding something from Dad today. And why did she pick you up, really?'

Nate is like a danger detector, ever since Josh happened in our lives.

'Oh, that? It's because I kind of didn't answer the girls' call last night and today in the morning. Naomi got worried and called Mum, so she appeared at my place freaking out.' I roll my eyes. 'You know how it is.'

'Hmm. And where were you?' he insists.

'Don't give me that stare, Nathaniel.'

It's the doubtful one.

'So you aren't telling me?' he asks, folding his arms over his chest squinting at the sun, the light turning his eyes even greener.

'Tell you what? There's nothing to tell.'

'Sure.'

'What about you? A brunette, huh?' I tease him, before he makes me confess about Luc.

He laughs, shyly. 'Do you like her?' he asks.

I'm glad my question gives this conversation a whole new direction.

'She talks a lot, but yes, I like her. But I think you shouldn't care if anyone else likes her, the important thing is how you feel about her,' I say.

'Did Mum say something to you?'

'She might have mentioned a thing or two, but you know Mum. She always has a lot of opinions,' I say, hitting his chest with my fist.

'Yeah, yeah. Well then, I guess I'll see you next weekend,' he says, giving me a hug. I hug him back.

As soon as I get home I video call the girls, but I make sure I'm doing something other than talking to them so it's easier to lie.

I decide I should organise my closet, even though I don't need it. I'm spraying my favourite vanilla fragrance on the lingerie and they both question me about the hours of my disappearance. They do believe me when I say I was focused working on my new designs and went to bed at the wee hours—it's a common excuse of mine anyways—woke up late and went for a run. I tell them I didn't answer my phone because I was too busy cursing at my boss and the next day I was simply too tired to talk about my rage. I guess organising my closet worked, because they totally bought my excuse. I tried not to talk looking at the screen, I'm not *that* good at lying.

'Next time you can write us something like "don't bother calling, I won't answer you",' says Naomi.

'Yes, ma'am,' I promise. 'Now, tell me about last night. Did you get to show off your new lingerie?'

Naomi grins, a gleam of naughtiness in her eyes.

'Oh, you have no idea,' says Lexi, who by now already knows more details than I do.

'Was it as good as expected?' I ask, curious, making myself comfortable on the couch in the balcony.

'Better. But I have a confession to make ...' says Naomi.

Lexi and I wait anxiously.

'I hesitated before going all the way,' she says.

'What do you mean you hesitated? I thought you were crazy about him,' I say.

'That's exactly why. I don't remember the last time I was on a date and didn't mind not having sex right away. I mean, it was just for a brief moment. We ended up going all the way, but still, this time felt different somehow. It's as if I was afraid he just wanted a one-night stand and be like all the others, you know?'

'Wow, I'm shocked. You really like him,' I say.

'I think I do.'

I'm so happy for her. Hearing her confessing something like that almost makes me confess about Luc. Almost. It also makes me compare her hesitation to his.

I'm glad I hold my thoughts until the call ends.

With my feet propped up on the railing, I grab a book and begin to read. I'm in a good mood. I enjoy the breeze and the fact that there's still daylight. I'm thinking of him, actually I've been thinking about him the whole day, plagued by last night's and this morning's shared moments. Right now I'm wondering if he's going to show up tonight when I hear someone at the door.

Chapter Twelve

It's him. Dark jeans and white V-neck on, naughty hungry gaze and furrowed brows.

'Olivia,' Luc says, towering over me, hand propped on the door frame above my head.

'Hi,' I almost don't find my voice.

A long moment of staring stretches between us.

'I can't get you out of my mind,' he rasps.

A shot of adrenaline runs through my veins, speeding my heartbeat absurdly.

'You're not a one-night stand.' The words are out before I can rationally measure them. I don't even know why I said them. Is it true? Or I said it because I want to fuck him this bad?

The smile tugging on his lips reaches his eyes that now are diverted to my mouth.

'Good,' he says.

He takes one step forward and presses his body against mine, making me take steps back until he closes the door behind him. His hand slips around the nape of my neck and through my hair as he lowers his face closer to mine. My breathing is so uneven and loud in my ears, I know Luc notices what he's doing to me. Still, his eyes ask for permission when they lock with mine. And I give it to him—I give him all the permission he needs to kiss me. When my lips part, he tightens his grip around my waist and neck and his mouth crashes onto mine. I rake and tug on his hair as his tongue slips into me, relentlessly kissing me, claiming me.

His mouth makes love to mine in a demanding way, showing that he too has been craving it the whole day. Right then, I have no doubt he wants me just as much as I want him, in every single way.

He cups my ass and lifts me up. I wrap my legs around his waist and dig my fingers deeper into his hair, desperately wanting him. He moans against my mouth and the sound rushes all my blood to my core.

He takes me to my bed, sitting me on the edge of the mattress. He tugs under the hem of my tank top and pulls it up. His eyes are on fire when he catches sight of my very much transparent nude bralette. I open his jeans, unzip them and pull them down his legs, leaving him only with his sexy white Calvin Klein boxer briefs. He's so hard under his underwear it makes me pool my panties. He's looking down at me, his eyes begging, imploring.

Propping one knee on the bed, his hungry wet mouth takes mine as he lays me on my back so that now he's on top and I'm between his knees. Luc's hips begin to move back and forth, grinding against me, and I immediately welcome the movement. His erection is pressed against my sex, the fabric of our underwear keeping them apart. He's so hot, so gorgeous, so fuckable.

He stops kissing me and I almost protest, craving the touch and the taste of him on my tongue, the closeness. He stares at me for a moment to study my face long enough to make my heart pulse harder on my extremities. His eyes are dangerously dark, filled with lust, his breathing just as fast and heavy as mine.

'What's wrong?' I ask, breathless.

'You have that face on—it drives me crazy.'

'Should I stop then?'

I'm serious, staring hard into his eyes, and so is he.

'Don't,' he rasps.

He frees his cock from his boxer briefs and strokes himself as he watches me. My sex tightens at the sight of it, I don't know where to focus my gaze. His heated heavy eyes, the ridges of his abs contracting as he touches himself, or the very part of him being stroked by his hand.

Fire bursts from between my legs to my chest. The scene is beyond arousing, the muscles of his biceps flexing as he plays with himself, the crest of his penis red and swollen. I could come by only watching this.

He stands up, discards his underwear on the floor and reaches a condom in his jeans. All the while I keep staring, watching every movement he makes with hungry, eagle eyes. The anticipation is driving me out of my mind.

He throws the condom next to me and joins me again on the bed. His mouth lands on my sex, he pushes his tongue against the fabric of my panties and the feeling makes me quiver, my toes curl. He sucks on my clit, and gently bites it, then flickers his tongue, tasting me through the silk. I tug his hair, pulling hard; a groan escapes his throat and the sound of him motivates me to move my waist to meet his mouth, with more pressure.

He then traces a path from my clit to my belly button, where he sinks in his warm and wet tongue. My core contracts in response. Luc moves up to my breast, and there he pinches my nipple under my bralette with his lips. They're soft, and warm, and wet. He reaches my neck and sucks on it, making me moan. I have the feeling I won't hold on much longer if he doesn't stop with the teasing soon. I'm so ready for him.

'Do you want to fuck, or do you want to make love?' he whispers in my ear.

What? Oh God.

The question and the way he asks it is beyond provocative and sexy, it almost makes me come in my underwear.

'Can we do both?' I rasp, barely recognising my voice.

'I'll do my best,' his voice comes out hoarse and warm, his hooded eyes staring down straight into mine.

I leave one hand on his hair, the other I slip down onto his warm and hard shaft, making him groan and bury his face between my breasts. The smell of his hair teases my nose, taking me to places I haven't been before.

He slowly begins sucking and licking and nibbling my skin, driving me insane. All I can smell is Luc, all I can think about is him inside of me and those eyes connected to mine.

He takes control of his length and plays with it against the fabric of my panties. My sex is so sensitive to the friction and warmth of it I'm almost coming. He slips a finger between my panties and my sex, feeling me. He closes his eyes and swallows hard.

'You are so ready,' he says opening his eyes to lock with mine.

'I am.'

He reaches over to the condom next to my shoulder.

'Let me,' I say.

He smirks, but doesn't protest.

I open the packet and begin to put on the rubber on his length. I do it slowly, teasingly. He's enjoying watching it, his hands on his hips, the muscles on his navel tensing, his eyes fixed on what my hands are doing. His chest rising and falling with his ragged breathing.

Once I'm done, he tips my chin up and kisses me, slowly. His tongue taking its time to play with mine. Then he softly bites my lower lip, sucks on it. I can feel the stubble on his face gazing my chin. While he makes love to my mouth, he tugs my panties to one side and fills me with his cock.

His thrusts are deep and hard, I welcome each and every one of them with need and voracity, saying his name against his mouth. He groans, and trembles. His movements become erratic and I welcome his release. I lose all my senses as my body convulses, my feet curl and my sex climaxes in shock waves pulsating strong and fast around his erection.

'Fuck, Olivia.'

My head's on his shoulder, we're both watching our hands as they interlace each other. I'm still intoxicated by the fucking and love making of a few moments ago.

'You like to play tennis, don't you?' I ask running my fingers over the calluses on his palm.

He chuckles. 'Yes, I do.'

I know he's looking down at me so I glance up to meet his eyes.

'I'd like to see you play some time.'

'I'd like that too.'

His expression is serious.

'But you might have to explain the rules for me. I confess I have no clue. Everything I know about tennis is that you need a racket and several yellow balls to hit.'

Luc laughs, then gently plants a kiss on my head. 'I've got you covered.'

'Once I was on vacation with my family in Mallorca, we stayed in a resort that had a tennis court. My brother and I borrowed some balls and a racket from the hotel to play. It didn't take more than fifteen minutes for us to give up playing. I couldn't even hold the racket, it was too heavy, let alone hit the ball with enough strength for it to reach the other side of the net. Nate was really annoyed that I couldn't play. He ended up finding other friends to play with him. I went and enjoyed the pool.'

Smirking, he kisses me softly on the mouth, holding my chin to face him.

'You need a proper racket based on your weight and height.'

'Good to know,' I say beaming at him.

I go back to focusing on his hand, the one with the wristbands. He has a silver one, a thick black one and a transparent plastic one with tiny blue bubbles inside.

'What's this one about?' I ask running my finger over the plastic one.

'It's from a brand that makes them out of plastic found in the ocean. All the money they get is used to save marine animals,' he explains.

'That's nice. I like the idea.'

'So do I, that's why I have a partnership with them,' he says.

I realise that's the first time he's talked specifics about his work, so much has happened in the past days I didn't bother asking what he does for a living, apart from maybe being part of the Monaco Royal Family. But in a way, I did imagine he worked in the business branch.

'So that's part of your work then, representing brands?'

'Yeah, part of it.'

'You know, my friends keep telling me to found my own brand. Quit my job.'

'Oh yeah? I must say, I don't know your friends, but I think I agree with them,' Luc says, sounding excited about it, his eyes widening.

'You do?'

'As a customer I can guarantee the quality of the product. I'm very satisfied,' he says seriously, arching an eyebrow.

I chuckle, placing myself on top of him, propped on my knees, one on each side of his muscled torso. 'What are you talking about?' I trace the path down his happy trail, the trail to sin. He's still naked and warm beneath me.

'I don't wear them, but I get to see and touch them, so I can speak from my customer experience,' he says, his voice hoarse.

He's watching my finger moving down his body.

'Also, I like the designer.'

'Oh … do you now?'

Our eyes meet.

'Oh yeah. I think she's really talented,' he says pulling me into him.

I prop my hands on his chest, he reaches closer so that he can kiss me.

'When do you leave?' I ask as if it weren't a big deal. I want to know because I need to prepare myself. This is not lasting long, as good as it may feel. And this time the reason isn't me.

'Are you trying to get rid of me?' he teases, running his beautiful and perfectly shaped nose along mine. The intimacy makes my chest burn.

'Maybe,' I tease.

'Is that so, Miss Charlton? In that case let me—'

He pretends he's leaving, but I start laughing and dig my nails into his chest, pinning him back on the mattress, forcing him to stay where he is. He laughs, his mouth curving into a wide self-satisfied smile, showing his sexy dimple, where I place a soft kiss.

'If everything goes right, then I leave next Monday,' Luc says, gently stroking my cheek with his rough fingers.

'And if it doesn't?'

'Then I might leave on Tuesday.'

'This Tuesday? The day after tomorrow?'

He nods.

'You look disappointed, Olivia.'

'Maybe,' I tease him once more, and ignore the annoying pain my heart just experienced.

He shifts me so that he stays on top of me, and starts to tickle me everywhere. I shriek underneath him.

'Oh yeah?' he tickles on my belly, under my ribcage, then he begins to spread soft bites around my breasts. I laugh hard, screaming 'Stop,' but he's unforgiving.

'It's not true, it's not true,' I beg, and my own words shock me.

He stops and stares down at me.

'Do you have something to say to me, Olivia?'

His expression is serious.

'I am …'

'What?'

'Disappointed.'

Even though I say it so he stops tickling me, I feel truth behind the word.

A wicked grin stretches his mouth, the satisfaction that comes with it is as if he has just discovered new land to colonise. I give him my I-want-to-fuck-you stare.

'Don't do it,' he says, serious.

'What?'

I pretend I don't know what he's talking about.

'Don't look at me like that.'

'Why not?'

'You're making me hard.'

'So? Are you tired of me Mr. Lamaire?'

'Never.'

Oh. Good to know.

'Then fuck me.'

Luc closes his eyes, exhaling sharply, taking in the dirty words that just came out of my mouth. Then in one move he pulls my panties down, leaving me fully naked and exposed beneath him.

His face turns serious and he studies me for a moment before pressing his hot burning erection to my core, gliding it against my skin. He teases me, applying pressure on my most erogenous zone as he massages my swollen sex in back-and-forth movements, then in tiny circles.

One hand is holding his length, the other holding me tight by the waist. I keep staring at him, waiting for his next move in anticipation, until he pushes into me.

At first, his thrusts are slow, but deep. His hips rolling in a tantalising rhythm, inviting mine to play along. I follow his lead. His thrusts get deeper, stronger, faster, making me moan every time he fills me again, and again.

I raise one arm to keep me from crashing against the headrest. The sounds of his groans and growls echo in my ears and go straight to my pulsing sex. We're drenched in sweat, our bodies gliding on one another. He fucks me senselessly and mercilessly until we both call out our names into each other's necks.

He rests his head on my chest, his stubble tickling my skin. I bury my nose into his freshly fucked messy hair. We're both panting, trembling from the climax. He's still inside of me and I like that. I like the feel of Luc whole inside of me.

Once he recovers he props himself on his elbows, catches my mouth with a kiss and says, 'I can't stay tonight.'

I'm disappointed.

'I've got a very important day at work tomorrow,' he says, and presses his mouth onto my forehead.

'Does that mean if you have a good day tomorrow you're staying longer?'

'Yes,' he smiles and steps out of bed.

I follow him as he grabs his clothes from the floor. He watches me walking naked towards him and throws me his T-shirt. 'Put this on or I won't be able to leave,' he commands.

'Yes, sir.'

This makes him chuckle.

He puts on his boxer briefs and jeans. By the front door he puts on his shoes and kisses me goodnight.

'I'll see you tomorrow,' he says.

Then he's running up the stairs to his flat, shirtless. I watch him as I wear his T-shirt impregnated with his smell. I go back to bed and fall asleep thinking of him.

Chapter Thirteen

I wake up at 5:00 am. My weekdays normally follow a set routine. I love having my days planned out. Structure not only organises my day but also helps me avoid unwanted surprises. In other words, it makes me feel in control. It looks like this:

5:00 am - wake up

5:05 am - get up and brush my teeth

5:15 am - pick sports clothes and get dressed

5:30 am - stretch before running for at least one hour. In good or bad weather, but not if hungover, which is almost never.

6:35 am - green smoothie for energy (hopefully it's Andi's day at Fresh Me Up)

7:00 am - shower, pick lingerie and clothes, dress

7:45 am - leave for work (Mondays and Thursdays are office days) or home office

- I will fit in lunch whenever if I find time, if not, then I'll have a banana and cashew nuts at my desk.

- Work until my stomach starts complaining, which normally is about 6:30 pm

- Eat something I cooked

- Read a book in the balcony/couch or depending on the workload, work some more

- Sleep

- Start over

But today's different. After my watch tells me it's time to wake up, I don't get up right away. I linger in bed, sniffing Luc's T-shirt, which brings me memories of last night, which leads me to very imaginative and graphic thoughts.

I only manage to start stretching at 6:00 am and spend my time running looking to see if he'll be running too. I don't see him, and I'm disappointed. When did that start to happen?

I get my smoothie from Andi. Luc's not at the café either. I resist the temptation to ask Andi if he's seen him today. I don't even need to, he shares the information anyways.

'His brother came for his smoothie,' he winks.

How the heck does he know who Luc's brother is, and how in the world can he tell I was looking for Luc is beyond me. I'm glad for the unrequested information anyways. I nod at him and leave as fast as I can.

I get on the lift hoping to see him, nothing, which makes me realise we still haven't exchanged phone numbers yet. When I'm finally ready to leave for work it's already 8:00 am. I curse myself all the way to Secretive.

The point I'm trying to make by mentioning every detail of my routine is, now it's been messed up for almost a week, ever since Luc appeared in my life. That's what happens when you let people in, when you get too attached. Without noticing you start changing what you do and what you are, and by the time you realise, things are different, and you feel like you can't control what you used to be able to, because your days now include another person.

The thing is that for the majority of people, this change is good. Not for me. It makes me anxious and fearful and insecure. It drives me insane. I hate changes.

I'm out on the street, and in front of the building there's some kind of commotion, a black car is driving off while photographers and a bunch of girls are overly excited. Sometimes, stars appear in the neighbourhood, and together with them come the paparazzi and fans. I ignore it, as I always do, and make my way to work, taking the tube to central London.

By the time I'm at Piccadilly Circus it's almost 9:00 am. Secretive's head office is just a ten-minute walk from the Underground station. As

I'm walking, I get the impression I'm being watched, something seems off. It's strange, but it's a familiar feeling, *déjà vu* most probably.

I try to remember when I last I felt this way, but I can't. I keep walking, I cross a street discreetly looking around, my eyes searching for what, I don't know, but there are dozens of people, maybe hundreds, minding their own lives. I turn a corner, I look back. Nothing. I only relax when I'm at my desk and Caleb and I go over our check list for today's meeting with our team, then with Haley.

'Hey, I was thinking. What if we try to convince Haley to use at least the steel boning? It can be easily sourced here in the UK,' says Caleb rolling his chair next to mine.

'We can suggest it, but I'm not including them in the main designs just so she can make us change it again.'

'Yeah, you're right,' he looks as disappointed as me, but the difference is I've already embraced what Haley wants.

'Queen, I know it sucks. I feel you. Not everyone will agree with our ideas, but it doesn't mean we can't still have them, right?' I'm not sure if I say this more to him or to myself.

I'm also in need of reassurance. Every single day of the past week I've been trying to convince myself Secretive is still the right fit for me. Maybe I just need to find a way of implementing my ideas in a smoother approach. Or maybe I should just make that change my guts are telling me to do and ignore my rational thoughts.

'If I ask you a question, promise you'll be honest?' I say, not yet sure if I should. Caleb and I have been working together for a while now, but our relationship is mainly professional. Of course, we talk about our personal lives here and there, but when the topic is work, there's only Secretive.

'You can ask me anything. And when am I not honest with you, Olivia?' he lowers his face, and peeking under the rose frame of his glasses, he rolls his eyes. It makes me chuckle and gives me the opening I need to ask what I want to.

'Have you ever considered leaving Secretive?'

'Was that the question?' he sighs.

'Yep.'

'Of course, silly. Of course,' he says in a way that tells me he has been putting some thought into the possibility.

Caleb and I end up getting into a whole deep conversation about work, and our future plans. Then as he drank his coffee and I my green tea, we imagined how amazing it would be if clothing brands were to invest more on sourcing recyclable and fair-trade materials. It would be costly at first, but then, in the long run, what a big difference it would make in the world. The textile industry is, after all, the second most pollutive in the world, behind oil. I just wish more people thought like we do, and that more companies believed in this and proved how possible it is.

With back-to-back meetings, I barely had time to breathe, let alone eat. By the time I get home my stomach is complaining, and I have already forgotten all about the weird feeling of being watched this morning.

I kick my heels to the side, place my bag and laptop on the kitchen island and realise how much I'm starving. All I want is to eat something, and ok, who am I kidding? I want to see Luc.

Just as I open the fridge to consider my dinner options—realising there aren't many—the cause of my routine disturbance shows up at the door. As I pass by the mirror in the hall, I see myself with an expression I'm not familiar with. It's a mix of joy and excitement, but not like when I receive a gift or when someone makes me laugh or when I'm praised. It's the kind of joy and excitement that's only celebrated between my heart and mind.

'Hi, Olivia.'

Luc's standing in front of me with a bottle of champagne in his hands.

'Does that mean you had a good day in the office?' I ask, my eyes roaming between the champagne bottle and gleam of his eyes.

A grin comes without warning and takes over my face.

'Yes.'

He kisses me when I'm still stupidly beaming at him.

'Wait. Is this granddad's Lamaire champagne?'

His eyes grow excited and intense, implying so much my breath catches in my throat for a moment.

'Come in,' I manage, tugging on his T-shirt, pulling him inside.

I close the door behind us and he says, 'I'm cooking for you tonight. Then, we'll open the champagne …' He's holding me tight, and walking against me, leading me backwards to the kitchen island, where he sets the bottle that's already cold.

'… and then?' I say, slipping my arms around his neck.

'We'll see what happens.' He lifts me up and places me on the island.

He's glaring at me like I'm some kind of prize. I sink my fingers into his hair, leaving it the way I like it. Messy.

'I like you there,' he says, stepping back and away from me, sizing me up. His eyes take a trip over my body and send sparks through me.

'It seems so.' I wrap my legs around Luc's sexy waist, where his jeans hang low, and pull him back closer to me. He responds with a gentle bite on my neck, making me groan.

'If you intend to cook for me, then I believe a short trip to the supermarket is advisable. I'm afraid my fridge is empty,' I say.

Now he's slowly and patiently running his tongue up my throat, his stubbles tingling my skin. I feel a thrill on my spine, from my tailbone all the way up my nape.

'Then we better hurry up …' He speaks against my mouth, our lips barely touching. I'm impatiently expecting him to kiss me, instead, he places me on the floor again.

Despite being frustrated with hunger and need, I decide Luc's worth the wait, especially when he's the one cooking.

We're in the produce section of the supermarket, picking cherry tomatoes and onions and spinach.

'What are you making?' I ask.

'My grandma's secret quiche recipe,' he says as he picks some champignons, seeming to carefully choose the ideal ones.

'Is it still a secret?'

Luc smirks.

'*Our* secret. Mine and hers. It's called Quiche Lamaire,' he says.

I find this incredibly sweet, and my reaction is to wrap my arms around him from behind as he finally selects the best champignons. It's a reaction that I wasn't expecting to have until it happened. I might have a thing for men who cook, or maybe for men who share secrets with their grannies.

'Are you serious?' I'm suppressing a grin.

'That's what my grandma calls it.'

'Seems like you two are close.'

'Yeah, we are. She practically raised me.' The way his face lights up is so sweet and warm I want to bite him. I manage to keep it together.

Once we have everything, we head to the automatic cashier. People are paying on either side of us we wait in line. One of the two guys on our left smiles childishly when he sees us, and whispers something to his partner, who then looks back to check us out. The woman on the right side keeps discreetly peeking at us, she looks as though she recognises us from somewhere. I ignore all this when my attention is called to the hands that are now filling the back pockets of my jeans. The gesture is so unexpected it makes me smile from ear to ear as I feel blushing all over.

'Are you smiling, Olivia?' he whispers in my ear, from behind me. I let my head fall onto his chest and he kisses the tip of my nose. Waiting in line has never been so entertaining.

Since he's already cooking, I insisted on paying—more like pushed him away from the machine and paid at lightspeed before he could recover from the push. As vengeance against my violent act, he's carrying the shopping bags.

To say I'm having fun cooking with Luc is an understatement. I'm having a blast, and I'm feeling like a child who's getting all the attention from the most important person in the room. At the sound of *Je ne sais pas* by Joyce Jonathan—part of Luc's playlist—I cut the cherry tomatoes in half and feed him some. On the kitchen island he's kneading pastry—which he swears is where his grandmother's secret lies—and decides to scrub his dirty hands on my bottom, leaving marks of his greasy palms on my jeans. I take advantage of the fact that his hands are dirty and busy pressing the pastry onto the quiche pan, and tickle him just under his ribcage just to discover that he's immune to tickles. I'm delighted. I try a few more times with different tricks and different places: blowing his ear, sticking a finger under his arm, and slowly and softly running my index finger from his belly button down his pelvis, as low as I can get without having to open his jeans.

'This way you're going to achieve something else, Miss Charlton,' he teases, chuckling and having fun at my expense, and still with his hands on the dough.

'How can someone be immune to tickles?'

He kisses me, shutting me up, his buttery hands holding my face. Now I also have pastry on my face too.

'I'm not feeding you tomatoes anymore,' I say.

Luc presses his mouth against mine again, and I find myself chuckling against his lips. He responds with a low groan before breaking our kiss.

As he goes back to the pastry, I grab the bottle of champagne from the fridge and analyse the label.

Champagne Lamaire
BRUT
Maison Fondée en 1770
Élaboré par Maison de Champagne Lamaire à Reims, France

'What?' he asks, curious why I'm staring at him.

'Must be really cool to grow up tasting champagne,' I say.

'Yeah, it was really cool,' he says, washing his hands in the sink.

'Was it really founded in 1770?'

'It was. It's on its eighth generation already, it's always belonged to the family.'

I'm still analysing the bottle when he comes to stand in front of me.

'Should we open it? I know you might still be hungover from last week, but …' he teases.

'I'm not …' I say, punching his hard-worked stomach. He doesn't even budge.

We open the champagne before we eat, soon after he's put the quiche in the oven. I get the flutes, he pours.

Staring into each other's eyes—we're better not risking the seven-years-without-sex curse—we toast.

'To kitchen teamwork,' he says.

'To men who are immune to tickles,' I say in return.

He laughs, tipping his head back in amusement. We take a sip from our flutes, and it's delicious. I might retire my rosé drinking and upgrade it for champagne.

Luc's eyes don't leave mine, his dark eyebrows are serious, making his gaze even more intense. I'd say he's planning something.

'What?' I ask.

'Give me your phone,' he says.

'Why do you want my phone?'

'Just give me your phone, Olivia,' he commands, the corner of his mouth curving into a mischievous grin. I think I like mischievous Luc.

I obey and give it to him, still sceptical. He takes the phone and rolls his eyes at me because it's locked. He uses my face to unlock it.

He snorts as he types something onto it, then some more. I'm watching, curious to know what he's doing. I wait impatiently until he gives my phone back.

On the screen are my last calls. The first on the list is an outgoing call to someone named *Immune to Tickles*. He waits for my reaction and looks like the most satisfied person when he sees me laughing. He types something on his own phone then tells me to call him. When I do, he shows it to me, and on its screen appears the picture he took from me at Fresh Me Up yesterday, and the caller's name: Olivia followed by a heart.

Oh God.

My stomach flips. It might just be because I'm hungry.

'Just thought that by now you might have thought it was weird we hadn't exchanged phone numbers yet,' he says, tugging on the hem of my T-shirt, pulling me to him and closing the distance.

'I might have thought about it once or twice,' I confess.

We're now as close as we can get to one another, and his big warm hands have found their way onto my waist.

'Oh yeah?'

'Yeah.'

Now it's my turn to fill his back jeans pocket with my hands, then give his ass a proper squeeze.

'Why haven't you said anything?' Luc pulls a strand of my hair behind my ear and leaves his hand there, his long fingers entangled in my hair.

'I know where you're staying.'

He smirks.

'Fair enough.'

Our eyes keep locked for a long while, as he strokes my lips with his thumb.

'I like that,' I say, lifting my hand to his stubbled face.

'What?'

'Your stubble.'

The magnetic field created between our eyes is still intact.

'Oh yeah? I'm thinking about shaving it off tomorrow.' He narrows his eyes as if daring me to say something about it.

'Don't.'

The mischievous grin is back.

'Yes, ma'am.'

Then he kisses me, soft and wet and slowly, our hands tugging on each other's hair. His playlist's still on, and the air smells like baked butter and flour. This feels better than Christmas, than taking a plane to a new place—even better than buying new lingerie. The feeling does weird things to me, I don't know how to explain. All I know is that it's better than anything I felt before.

Beep. The quiche's ready.

Chapter Fourteen

I end up having to beg him for his grandma's secret. Of course, without success.

'This was amazing. I could eat this dough non-stop,' I say, running my tongue over my lips. My stomach has stopped complaining long ago.

'I know, right?' Luc looks happy.

I can see satisfaction all over his face at the sight of my full belly.

'You'll need me if you ever want to eat Quiche Lamaire again,' he says, watching me.

'Or your grannie.' This makes him laugh his delicious, easy laugh.

'If my grandma ever shares her secret with you, I'll have to marry you,' he says, teasing, but it makes me flush. I down the remaining champagne in my flute.

'Why?'

'So the secret stays in the family,' he winks at me and our eyes stay fixed on each other for what feels like minutes.

He pulls my stool closer to his, placing me between his legs. His face's flushed too, his eyes pinkish. He looks tired, but relaxed. He decides that burying his face between my collarbone and neck is a good idea. I agree. He lingers there, breathing in my scent, his strong arms embracing me around my waist. I'm caught by surprise at first, but after a moment I let down my guard. I sniff his hair, hold him back and let my shoulders relax. Though it feels good, it's scary as hell too. Whatever this is, it's too late to stop without leaving marks. We stay like this for a while, until I realise I feel like sharing something he has asked me about before, something I never talk about.

'Josh,' I say. The name I avoid speaking out loud at all costs. Saying it right now even feels wrong, because Luc has nothing to do with Josh. Both names should never be said in the same room, it's almost a crime.

He stays where he is, waiting for me to elaborate.

'My ex.' I open my eyes and stare into nothing, past Luc's amazing hair, and continue, 'One day I told him I wanted to spend my summer doing a design course in Paris. He wouldn't let me, as if he was my owner. The day I told him everything was already arranged was the first day he hit me.'

Luc sits up straight on his stool, but before I miss his warmth, I'm greeted with his warm hand on my knee and eyes watching me. It gives me the courage to continue.

'I was the one who started it when I pushed him against the wall, so I told myself I kind of deserved it. I also thought it was a one-time thing. I was mad because I really did want to go, and he wasn't going to change my mind. He slapped me hard across my face. I fell on the couch. But I stood up and hit him back. He hit me again, harder than the first time. There was no way I was going to win that fight. It was the day I realised that fighting back was never going to end well for me.'

Luc threads his fingers through mine, holding my hand in his. He props his elbow on the island and watches me attentively. His wide eyes are fully awake, studying me.

'After I sobbed for an hour, guilt hit him hard. He fell on his knees and begged me to forgive him, that he was drunk and didn't know what he was doing.' I say this, rolling my eyes at my old self, for wanting to believe him.

'It was the first of many times that he'd beg for forgiveness for hitting me. I stayed the night because I didn't have the courage to let my friends see how my face looked. I also didn't want to answer their questions.'

I feel a lump building in my throat—more disgusted than painful— as I revisit the moment.

'Everyone loved him, my family, my friends. We stayed together for two more years after that day. At some point I got used to having to hide bruises. Each time, I hid at his place until it got better, at least enough to be covered with makeup. And so it became a vicious circle. We would have some kind of fight, mainly about something that he felt defensive about, he would get angry, hit me, feel guilty, beg for forgiveness, care for my bruises, then do it all again after a couple of months.'

I can tell by the way Luc's watching me that he feels sorry, but his face is full of worry.

'When did you manage to break up with him?' he asks me.

'When it became too much. I could already recognise when it was coming, and it was killing me in many ways. I wasn't even eating anymore, it was as if I was constantly on alert, watching my back all the time, afraid of making mistakes, of saying the wrong thing, doing something that would upset him. I was literally getting sick. I knew it was wrong and that I didn't deserve it, but getting out of that situation was much harder than I thought. He kept saying he loved me, but even though I didn't have much experience, I knew that wasn't love. How could he love me and do what he did to me?'

I'm not proud of what I'm telling Luc, I still feel ashamed of my past. But his calm and the lack of judgement on his face, invites me to share more. Another reason might be because I know he's not actually part of my world. His life is somewhere else and he's leaving soon.

'The day I left him was one of the worst times, to the point where I was on the floor and he was kicking my ribs. I managed to get back to my flat, which I shared with my friend, Lexi. That night I told her everything. And it might sound stupid, but it felt so good to know that she believed me and that I was not carrying this heavy weight alone anymore. It was only then I realised I could have done this all along, shared it with my friends. I could have spared myself two years of being in an abusive relationship.'

Luc sighs and buries his face in his hands. He's speechless, trying to process my confession. After a moment, he looks up, frustrated and says, 'I'm sorry this happened to you. I can't imagine what you've been through.'

I nod. I don't cry. I don't even remember the last time I cried, if I don't count when Gatsby, my Golden Retriever, died two years ago.

He holds me tight, and it feels like the hug is more for him than for me. It's as if by having me in his arms he can protect me from the world and somehow from my past.

'Thank you for sharing this with me,' his voice is low and soft as he speaks into my hair.

'Thank you for listening,' I say.

He watches me with a stern look, and says, 'You're incredible and brave. So brave, Olivia. And yes, you deserve better. Don't let anyone ever make you feel otherwise.' Then he kisses me. There's warmth and need in his kiss. I give him what he needs, because it's just what I need too.

Slowly, his hand finds its way under my T-shirt and cups my breast. He stops immediately and stares at me, raising an eyebrow.

'What are you wearing?' The way his gaze becomes dark and intense makes my heart sparkle inside my chest.

It's a black lacy bra with holes for the nipples.

'You'll find out soon enough,' I say, giving Luc my best wicked grin.

He scoops me up from the stool and takes me to my bedroom.

He sits on the bed with me on his lap straddling him. His mouth fiercely kissing mine. I'm making a mess of his soft hair with my fingers as I feel him harden underneath me. He moves to kiss my collarbone, an insanely arousing combination of his warm soft tongue and his stubbles scratching my skin. He pulls my T-shirt up and watches me for a second with his naughty gaze focused on my exposed nipples.

'Do you have any idea how arousing this is?' he asks with a serious expression, his eyes in flames meeting mine. He gently circles both my nipples with his thumbs, his hands cupping my breasts. I give him a moan as a reply. He has these magical hands, I don't know if it's the rough skin or his long fingers or the warmth of his palms, but when they touch me I feel like I'm under some kind of spell and only he has the power to put me to rest.

I pull his T-shirt over his head and push him onto the bed so I stay on top of him, my breasts on his face. He takes advantage of my strategic position and covers my nipple with his mouth. The contact makes me tip my head back with pleasure. I hold the headboard with one hand for support and start to roll my hips, causing a delicious friction between my sex and the length of his hard cock, our clothes still on. I move faster and if I do this for a little while longer I'm gonna come, because the face he's making as he sucks on the sensitive skin of my nipple is making me lose my mind.

'Slow down or I'm gonna come in my pants,' he says breathing hard, his gaze holding mine. This almost makes me lose it. Though it feels too good, I slow down because I want to make it last longer. I might have spent the day waiting for this moment.

I prop myself on my elbow and kiss him. Hard and hungry, I suck on his tongue. He nibbles on my lower lip and I return the gesture. I cover his stubbled jaw with wet kisses, and with the tip of my tongue I trace a path down his throat, he groans shakily. Then I drag my tongue on the soft skin of his chest, and the hard muscles on his stomach, which are now clenching in reaction to my touch. I keep going down slowly, making him suck air through his teeth as my mouth reaches his jeans. I open his button and fly underneath me, I do it slowly on purpose and as I do so I watch him watching me. He places one arm under his head, flexing his biceps, the other gently tugs on my hair. I pull his Calvin Kleins down just the enough amount to free his erection and take it in my hands. It's hard and hot. It's so arousing to know that I'm doing this to him. It feels so good to be in power, to know that I'm also capable of driving Luc as crazy as he makes me.

I lick his salty precum and he inhales sharply, holding his breath as if containing himself. I cover his cock with my mouth and he stiffens, hardening even more. I circle the crown with the under surface of my tongue. He's pulsing inside my mouth, the muscles of his stomach clenching with the building pleasure, his tongue running along his lower lip, his gaze fixed on my mouth. When he's close, I stop, and he swallows hard.

He pulls me up so we are face to face, my legs on each side of him. He strokes my mouth with his thumb and lifts his eyes to meet mine. In one move he places me underneath him, one knee on each side of me, reversing our positions. He pulls my jeans down. He studies my panties and realises there is a very strategic hole there too. He smirks and shakes his head.

'You're evil, Olivia.' He raises an eyebrow and bites his lower lip as his hooded eyes lock with mine.

Then he slides his middle finger inside of me through the hole in my panties, making me gasp. He does it a few more times, then fills me in with his hard, thick cock. He does it slowly, every inch of his skin sliding inside of me, filling me in. All the while he watches, having fun with the fact that he doesn't need to take my panties off.

He rolls his hips and glides inside of me, in and out, in and out. I'm so close, and he knows it. In and out. He pinches my nipple hard and keeps doing it as he slides in and out. My sex's tightening and pulsing faster around him. Just as I begin to tremble and moan, he retreats from me and releases himself on my belly. It is so insanely erotic it makes me lose any rational thought. It prolongs my own orgasm.

'Fuck,' Luc moans and quivers, holding his length in one hand, propping himself on the other so he doesn't fall on top of me.

I watch him collapse beside me, trying to even his breathing. Once we recover from the intensity of the moment, he faces me and says, 'I've made a mess.'

'Yeah, you did,' I say grinning, not even close to being mad about it.

He smirks and says, 'Sorry, let me help you.'

We clean ourselves up and snuggle on the bed, wearing only our underwear.

'What is it with you and lingerie, woman? You're gonna make me crazy,' he says, playing with the lace of my bra.

'What is it with *you* and lingerie?' I ask back.

'I blame it on the designer and model,' he speaks against my mouth.

He traces a path with his finger between my breasts and down my belly. I immediately start to laugh and he begins to tickle-attack me. He's on top, holding me between his legs as he tickles me everywhere, I'm almost crying with laughter.

'Stop. What is it with you and tickles?' I say with effort, laughing so much I can feel tears rolling down the corner of my eye to my ear.

Then he stops. He's watching me with a serious, almost painful expression. I stop smiling immediately.

'What's wrong?' I ask. Luc can be so expressive and intense sometimes.

'Nothing. I just …' he sighs and continues, 'I wish I'd never make you cry. Unless it's of joy,' he says it in such a deep way I feel my heart squeezing inside my chest.

I raise a hand to his jawline, running my thumb over his scruff.

'Good news is, I haven't cried in almost two years, so the chances are very slim,' I say, giving him a reassuring smile, but his smile isn't so convincing.

I pull him toward me and he rests his head on my chest, his ear against my heart. I realise he enjoys doing this, listening to my heart. I bury my nose in his head and wish we could stay like this for days, in this bubble, on this bed, alone, the smell of sex lingering in the air.

Chapter Fifteen

We wake up to the sound of our alarms. It seems as though my routine isn't as messed up as I thought it was. At least I can't blame him for making me sleep longer, considering we have a similar wake up routine.

'Up for a run?' he asks, his sleepy face is something I could see every day and never tire of. The messier his hair, the better.

'Catch me if you can,' I say, daring him because I know he still needs to go to his place and get ready.

'Deal!'

He takes the dare seriously and gets up as fast as he can and searches for his clothes. Meanwhile, I'm already brushing my teeth and watching him from the bathroom mirror, laughing at him. His T-shirt is missing. From where I'm standing I see it under the bed, but I don't say anything. I just bought myself at least five minutes.

Eventually he gives up and leaves. Not before planting a kiss on my cheek. The way he looks right now makes me rethink this dare, wanting to make him stay a little longer. And it almost makes me feel bad that he's going to lose the dare because of me.

I'm already finishing stretching by the time he arrives downstairs. He's wearing his black cap, strands of his hair are escaping on the sides, I can still spot lines on his sleepy face. I can't stop thinking about last night. I've never felt this way before. Just thinking about it makes my chest warm up and my stomach flutter.

'I win,' I say, teasing him.

'What do you want as your prize?'

He's stretching, pressing his hands against the wall and extending each of his lower legs.

'Surprise me.'

He likes my answer, I can tell by his amused grin.

We run for an hour and a half. I almost forget the amount of work I have waiting for me at home. It was just too entertaining to watch him strip off his sweaty T-shirt and run alongside me with his bare chest, his muscles flexing each time he moved his hands back and forth. Lines of sweat run down along his skin, disappearing into the fabric of his shorts. I think now I know what he means by losing focus. He's doing the same to me, not only while running. He's making me do things I never do, and consider doing things I never did before. I wonder what the girls would say if they knew I've been this involved with him. I bet they'd tease me, and they'd make me tell every detail of what I've been doing to him and him to me. But I brush the thought away, because I'm not ready to share Luc with anyone.

We stop for our smoothies on the way back. Andi's in. He glances at me with a smirk on his face, which makes me blush. Right now, he knows more about me and Luc than my own friends. I kind of feel bad about it, maybe I should call today and tell them everything. Or maybe not, where would I start? Besides, I like how Luc and I aren't under pressure to define what's happening between us.

'Just so you know, this is not your prize,' says Luc after paying for my smoothie and handing it to me.

'I didn't think so,' I say, teasing.

On the way back home, though distracted, I feel kind of uneasy. Something like what I felt yesterday on the way to work, the feeling of being watched. Then it hits me. Hard. Like when you are walking into a glass door and don't see it, crashing against it, startling you in an extremely unexpected way. *Josh*. How could I ever forget? I guess that day was so intense, I forgot about how it started. My brain had found a way to keep it hidden as deep as it could, just so I don't have to live with it.

Now, it all comes back to me. Three years later, I feel it all over again, stronger than the nightmares I have at night. Right here as I'm crossing the street with Luc, I feel like I'm being dragged back to that day. I wonder if those memories will ever stop haunting me.

It had been three weeks after I'd left Josh and told my friends about what kind of relationship we had. All this time, he kept calling and texting me, and even trying his usual shit—sending me flowers and gift cards and notes with promises he would never keep. I didn't answer or reply to any of it, partly because I didn't want to, but mostly because Naomi and Lexi didn't let me. It felt as though I was an addict and they were trying to help me get clean. The drug was Josh. I knew he was bad for me, but still I kept him in my life. I didn't know how to get rid of him, it'd gotten this far. I was in the stage of possible relapse, which I could never do alone. I'll be forever indebted to the girls.

Of course he tried reaching out to them too. My silence, I knew, was driving him crazy. Unlike all the other times, I ignored him and everything related to him during those three weeks.

He also attempted contacting me on social media, but I tried to be as far from social networks as possible, because of him and especially because I didn't feel like checking other's people lives when mine was hell. It got to the point that Josh even called Mum and Nate, making them worry and call me back sick with worry as if I had disappeared. I hadn't told them about the kind of relationship we had. I had decided they didn't have to know about it. It was already over anyways. It wouldn't have made any difference. It was all in the past, I thought. Besides, I didn't know how to start a conversation like that. They would question me and I wasn't ready to talk about it with them. I even avoided seeing them at all costs because of the bruises Josh left me with in our last encounter.

What had happened so far with Josh was already enough to leave scars for the rest of my life, but on that Monday morning everything changed. Everything escalated from very bad to extremely awful. It was a Monday just like yesterday. I got out of the tube and felt like someone was watching me. When I was in front of Secretive, Josh was at the front door, waiting for me.

I pretended to not see him. I went for the door handle to open it as fast as I could, as if I was running for my life.

I was. Oh, I was.

The next thing he did was something he always did, something that always worked pretty well on me.

'Love bug, please. Listen to me. I just want to talk.'

How dare he call me that.

I ignored him. I tried again pushing the door open. He didn't let me. I looked around and considered running away.

'You can't leave me. Let's just talk about it. Please.'

He held my arm. I started shaking, because I didn't know what to do. I didn't know what to say. I was already in a fragile state, it was too early in the detox phase to find yourself having to be strong enough to ignore your addiction.

'I swear I'll kill myself, Livvy. You're everything to me.'

When I think about his words now it makes me so sick I want to throw up. But back then, I really believed he was capable of doing it.

'Leave me alone, Josh. I need to get to work,' I said, unable to look him in the eye.

He tightened his grip around my arm.

'Give me five minutes. My car is right here. Just listen to me and I'll let you go.'

I'll let you go. I wanted to hear those words so badly, I allowed myself to believe them.

How could I think that listening to him was ever going to be a good decision? I did, always. I gave him the chance to say what he needed to, even though deep inside I knew there was nothing else left to say. But I thought this would be my chance for closure. I was wrong. What happened afterwards changed everything.

'Olivia?'

Only one person calls me by my name and makes me feel this good about it. Luc.

'Are you okay?' he stares at me, worry all over his face. 'You look scared. What happened?'

'I …' I trail off. He takes the smoothie from me and holds my hand. He presses his thumb into the middle of my palm, and begins rubbing soothing circles. The touch makes me come back to the present, it grounds me.

'I just wanna go home,' I say.

I don't need to ask Luc to accompany me to me front door and wait for me to get into my flat. He goes in with me and pours me water. He watches me, patiently and understandably. He doesn't demand any explanation nor ask me any questions. He's worried, but he gives me space to breathe. I don't think I'd handle this as well as he does. I'm not as calm and patient as he is.

'Thank you,' I say. My voice comes out shakily and frail.

He stays with me until I assure him I'm fine. He holds me tight and his embrace tells me he's there for me, that I can count on him, no matter the circumstances.

After I take a good long shower filled with heavy memories I wish were erased, I come back to the kitchen and there are eggs and bread and orange juice on the kitchen island.

'EAT ME!' says the post it attached to the plate. I feel much better already. I even force myself to eat, and realise I actually needed it. It gives me the energy I need for the rest of the day.

I bury myself deep into work. In the afternoon, Luc texts me for the first time since we exchanged phone numbers. He's asking how I'm doing, and I catch myself smiling at the name he chose for himself on my contact list.

Today at 3:44 pm

Immune to tickles: I'm glad you're better. I was worried about you.
Me: Thank you for being patient with me, and thank you for breakfast. It was the best I've had in weeks.
Immune to tickles: where have you been eating your breakfast?
Me: laughing-with-tears emoji.
Immune to tickles: I'll knock at yours later.
Me: Sounds like a plan.
Immune to tickles: emoji surrounded by tiny hearts.
Me: little monkey with hands on its eyes.

Luc's profile photo is him with his boyish grin, tanned skin, white cap backwards and white Nike T-shirt in a sunny place. The sight of it is so amusing I let out a snort. I find myself craving to see him again, and anticipation taking over me.

Instead of letting the heavy feeling of today's early morning haunt me for the rest of the day, I cheer myself up. I put on some music, sing and dance while I cook dinner. This might slightly have something to do with knowing that Luc might knock at the door any minute now.

I'm in the mood for some comfy food, so I bake meatballs in homemade tomato sauce, Grana Padano cheese and spaghetti. I'm pretty sure he will like it too, considering pasta is his favourite food.

But this time, he doesn't knock. My phone rings and I see the picture he chose for his contact information, a selfie of him here last night, with my favourite grin on his face. My insides light up with warmth. I answer it and I'm pretty sure he can tell I'm smiling when I do.

'Hey,' I say.

'You should check your front door,' he says.

Curious, I immediately stop what I'm doing and go to the door. When I open it, Luc's there.

'Hi,' he says, still with his phone pressed on his ear and the most mischievous smile on his face.

'Hi,' I say, also still with my phone in my ear.

We both put our phones away and he sweeps me up from the floor and carries me around the house, crashing his mouth against mine as if he hasn't seen me in ages. I'm starting to get used to the way he enters my flat.

'Hmm, what's that smell?' he speaks hovering over my mouth.

'Dinner,' I smile innocently, happy to have him here with me now.

'Can you hit pause? I wanna do something to you first,' he says.

'Hmm, I like that idea.'

He begins kissing my collarbone, the softness and warmth of his mouth makes me suck in air.

'The dish is in the oven. We have twenty minutes until it's ready,' I say, my mouth dry.

'That's plenty of time,' he whispers against my skin.

Oh God.

He places me on the edge of the kitchen island and for a very brief moment I wonder what he's planning on doing to me that will last twenty minutes. As soon as he steps between my legs, I know what his intentions are. They're as crazy and naughty as I feel right now. And they might involve the rock-hard erection I'm staring at.

'How are you feeling now?' he asks.

'Right now? Like you,' I say, darting my gaze at the bulge on his jeans.

He lets out an erotic groan, there's so much lust in it.

'I've missed you today,' he says, his intense gaze holding mine.

Shit. When did we go from *see you around* to *I've missed you today*? I guess today. Between leaving breakfast on the kitchen island for me in the morning and now.

I can see the waistband of his Calvin Klein boxer briefs peeking out of his black skinny jeans. His length is begging to be freed from both. I don't waste another second, both because I want to make the most of the nineteen minutes we now have, and because I'm avoiding saying *I missed you too* to him.

He steps out of his jeans and boxer briefs. Then he pulls my shorts down. I like how Luc never pulls my panties down straight away, he always enjoys taking a peek at them first. This time is no different.

His hands are holding me in place, on each side of my waist, while mine have found his hot erection. My touch induces lustful sounds from deep inside him. I stroke his throbbing shaft a few times. I shiver when I see the way he's watching my hand working around him, blue flames in his eyes. He presses his mouth to mine, sucking the air out of me, making me groan wildly. The kiss burns me from inside out, enticing me to bite and suck on his soft lips. I barely recognise the sounds I'm making. I guess once he leaves and we go our separate ways, my mind will enjoy revisiting all these intimate moments we've been having the past few days. I push these thoughts away because I still get to enjoy him now, and possibly for a few more days.

I have no idea how long we still have before the oven beeps. I have completely lost track of time. I don't care.

He's playing with his swollen cock in my entrance, my panties pushed to the side giving free passage to his length. Once he feels how wet I am, he rolls his eyes up to the back of his head and lets out a soft and slow moan, the sound vibrates through me and makes me ache for him. Then he fills me, slow and firm. He watches me as I welcome him inside of me, gasping and sinking my fingers through his ever-so-soft hair. Then Luc pushes my top up and my bra strategically a bit lower so that he can suck on my nipples.

Ok, I definitely don't need more than a few seconds like this.

He knows it, because he keeps gliding slowly and firmly inside of me, while sucking my nipples, one after the other. I come with my mouth and nose buried in his hair, muffling the sounds I make when I feel the tiny explosions of pleasure throughout my body. Intoxicated by his permanent smell of sex, I grab his hair tighter and pull him even closer to me. I clench around him, taking him with me, making him tremble and fill me with his release.

'I like you, Olivia. I like you a lot,' he says in my ear. His voice is as vulnerable as his body right now. My heart hammers against my chest echoing through my ears. It riots trying to make sense of what Luc just said.

Did he just say what I heard? I'm trying to wrap my mind around it, but it doesn't feel real. Actually, I'm not sure I want it to be real or just something I imagined. Either way, it doesn't change how I feel right now: freaking afraid of ruining everything, especially my heart.

We stare into each other's eyes for way too long, and I'm glad when the oven beeps.

Chapter Sixteen

He loves the meatballs. His eyes light up with pleasure in each bite. Also, he's so hungry he helps himself with two other servings. I'm so pleased to watch him enjoy what I cooked that even I eat more than I normally do.

'Olivia, I—' Luc begins after swallowing his pasta.

'Sorry about this morning,' I cut him off.

'Why are you sorry?' he asks.

'I know it seemed weird,' I say.

'I just noticed something was off. Didn't want to make you talk about it. I figured if you wanted to tell me, you would,' he says. And I like him even more because of it.

'I know. You did everything right. It was exactly what I needed,' I say.

He stops for a moment, and leans his head on his fist, propped on his elbow and watches me. An invitation for me to talk. If I want to.

'Yesterday on the way to work I felt like I was being followed. It felt like *déjà vu*, but I didn't know where the weird feeling in my chest was coming from. Then today in the morning as we were walking back home from the café I felt it again, and the memories started flowing in my head.'

Then I tell him about one of the worst days of my life—sparing him from details that make me cringe—and my mind once again revisits my darkest moment.

'As soon as I got into Josh's car that day, my phone rang. I didn't even get to see who it was, because he took my phone from my hand as fast as he could,' I begin.

Luc stops chewing and turns to face me, giving me his full attention, because he knows where this is going.

'For the first time that day, I looked him in the eyes. All I could see were the million reasons why I shouldn't have him in my life, and how sick he was making me. I felt disgusted. The fury in his eyes, the rough way he moved his arms and hands, the tone of his voice, already changing from overly sweet to aggressive, possessive. I already knew that pretty well,' I say.

'I tried to get my phone back. He didn't give it to me. I tried to open the door. It was too late, he had locked them. I shouted at him, asking him to open the door. He said, "SHUT UP and listen to me, Olivia." The way he said my name shouldn't be allowed. How could I have gotten myself into such a sick relationship? Why did it take me so long to realise it? In that moment I could finally see it clearly. It was a co-dependency, he manipulated me into depending on him and into believing that nothing out there could be better for me than him.'

Luc takes my hand and his thumb finds the centre of my palm.

'I was shaking and doing my best not to cry. He hated when I cried. He used to hit me harder when I cried. I didn't want to aggravate things so I swallowed hard, as if by doing so I was making the tears go back to where they belonged.'

I close my eyes and can hear so clear Josh's voice that day.

'I love you. I cannot live without you. Do you understand what I'm saying?' Josh said.

I kept my mouth shut.

'Tell me that you love me, Olivia,' he said through gritted teeth.

I heard it so many times, him begging me to tell him those words. I never did.

'TALK TO ME.' Though his scream was so loud, I kept my hands under my thighs, I didn't dare look vulnerable in front of him—not anymore—by lifting them to my ears to muffle the terrifying sounds he was making.

I looked away, at the passers-by on the sidewalk leading their normal lives while I was trapped with the worst thing that ever happened to me, in a car.

'LOOK AT ME.'

More shouting. I flinched with every shout, my heart racing, protesting inside my chest. I kept waiting for him to hit me, but he didn't.

I continued staring outside, as if by doing so someone would eventually notice how much I needed help in that moment. No help came. Londoners were too busy trying to get to work, to run their errands, to fully wake up, to accept that the weekend was over and it was time to begin a new week. How would they ever think that some girl inside an Aston Martin with a handsome bachelor wearing a suit would be begging for help in plain daylight on a busy street?'

'Olivia?' says Luc, after I don't say anything for a long while—taking a moment to deal with the memories.

'He turned the engine on and started driving. I dug my nails deep onto the leather seat, the same seat where he bruised me so many times, where we had so many discussions, where only he could ever win an argument. I felt as if I were trapped in a terrifying rollercoaster against my will,' I continue.

Please, God, let me out of here, I remember thinking.

'He drove us to a quiet street. There was no one around, so it was only him and I,' I say.

Luc squeezes my hand, letting me know he's right there with me.

'He had this way of changing his voice from one second to the other. Using his soft tone he said, "Look at me, love bug." I didn't obey. If I did, I wasn't going to be able to hold the tears trying to escape. I was beyond terrified of him. "Why are you ignoring me? Why haven't you been answering my calls?" he continued to press. That's when I said it was over. But instead of just accepting it, he asked if I had met someone else. I said I hadn't, and he called me a liar,' I say, then take a deep breath before continuing. Luc's eyes meet mine for a brief moment, then I go back to talking and staring at his hand on mine.

'Then I felt brave enough to say that there was nothing he could ever do to make me go back to him again. I said he was sick, and before I said anything else there was blood coming out of my nose. He hit me with his elbow. Hard. My eyes wouldn't stop watering because of the pain, and I hated myself because of it. *Suck it up, Olivia*, I told myself.'

Right now Luc winces, and his reaction is the same one Nate had when he learned the truth. Like he could kill someone.

'I remember the tiny drops of blood on my white blouse, but that was the least of my problems. I tried to open the door again, probably on instinct, because I knew it wouldn't work. He laughed his sarcastic laugh I hated so much. My stomach twisted into a million painful knots. I kept my eyes shut and tried to take my mind to a place where I could be free, where this man wouldn't be a part of my life anymore.

'Then he asked me if I thought someone was ever going to love me the way he did. Again, I felt brave enough to say what I really thought. I said it wouldn't be the hardest thing. That was the last thing I told him. The next memory I have is of waking up in a hospital bed. My Mum crying by my side. My family only managed to find me the next day. My phone had disappeared. Someone anonymously brought me to the hospital and I had no ID with me. The hospital staff said the guy who brought me in left before identifying himself.'

'Fuck, what a bastard,' says Luc, raking a hand through his hair in frustration.

'We never told Dad. Nate went after Josh when he found out, but he was nowhere to be found, the coward. That's when I moved. It worked out perfectly that Lexi was already planning on moving in with Thomas. I got a new phone, new address. That's when Nate banned him from their group of friends. That's when I said goodbye to social media; even fake profiles. I wanted to give him as little chance as possible to find me again. Lucky for me, I also got promoted at Secretive and my office was in a new location too.'

'And you never pressed charges against him?' asks Luc.

'No, despite the insistence of my friends and family. I just wanted to put it all behind me as fast as I could. Pressing charges would prolong my torture,' I say.

'Do you ever regret not doing it?'

'Sometimes. But then, I remember how painful it was at the time. I couldn't see anything beyond what I was going through, you know? I couldn't think clearly,' I say.

He exhales sharply, taking in what I just told him. Then he holds me, tightly, and supportive, burying his face in my neck.

'I'm really sorry you had to go through this. I wish I could do something to make it go away,' he says.

'It's ok. It was a long time ago,' I say, both reassuring him and myself, but glad for the words he just said.

'Is that the reason for your nightmares?' he asks as his warm hand takes the side of my face as his eyes lock on mine.

What?

I'm stunned, my eyes focused on his. I didn't know someone could tell I had those dreadful nightmares. No one has ever told me that. It might be because I almost never sleep with anyone, other than the girls.

'Yes. I didn't know you could tell. Is it bad?'

'I wouldn't say it would stop me from sleeping with you again,' he says grinning, immediately brightening up my face with a smile once again. My shoulders relax a little, and I feel like I can breathe again.

'You have tomato sauce right here,' I wipe the corner of his mouth with my thumb.

'All this time you were watching me with tomato sauce on the corner of my mouth and didn't say anything?' He holds back a smirk arching up one eyebrow. 'You're evil, Olivia,' he says, then crashes his mouth against mine.

'So you keep saying,' I tease.

'I like your kind of evil,' he says into my mouth, then kisses me again. He tastes of tomato sauce and Luc, and he feels warm and soft in my mouth.

He helps me clean up the kitchen and once we're done he holds me from behind, his hands firm and warm around my waist. His mouth brushes my neck and stops in my ear, sending tickles through my bloodstream.

'I've gotta go. I have a very important day at work tomorrow,' he whispers.

Though that sounds a bit disappointing, it doesn't feel like it when he's touching me like this and speaking with his French accent in my ear.

Chapter Seventeen

It's late afternoon when I'm coming out of the supermarket—hands busy with my grocery bags—when Naomi calls. I see it on my watch, but I need my phone to answer it, otherwise I don't listen to a word she's saying. I lean on a wall so I can hold one of the bags between my waist and the wall and use the free hand to get my phone from the back pocket of my jeans. I don't even have time to say hello.

'Can you tell me why you're on UK Gossip Today's Instagram post?' she blurts out, as if I'm supposed to know what the fuck she's talking about.

'What?' I'm still trying not to drop my groceries.

'Well, you are. You didn't tell me you were seeing someone, let alone a famous guy.'

I think she called the wrong number.

'Naomi, just … slow down. I have no idea what you're talking about. Aren't you supposed to be calling one of your clients?'

A bus drives by and that makes it even harder to hear her and think clearly.

'Honey, do you actually think I talk to my clients like this?'

'I sincerely hope not,' I joke.

'Is this your cute guy? Lucas Lamaire?'

What? How does she know his last name?

'Now you're talking nonsense.'

'It is, isn't it?'

'How do you know his name?'

'Who doesn't know who Lucas Lamaire is, Olivia?'

She never calls me Olivia. Ok, that's not the point. Again, what the hell is she talking about?

'Can you just tell me what's going on? No sarcasm, or jokes, or bossiness. Please, be gentle.' I feel like the floor has disappeared and I'm on a free fall. My head's trying to make sense of what I just heard, but it's doing a very slow and poor job of it.

'There are photos of you and Lucas Lamaire on the biggest gossip Instagram account of the UK,' she says.

My breath catches, and the air seeps out of my lungs. My head does a 360-degree spin and the floor under my feet are shaking like an earthquake.

'Livvy, are you there?'

One of my bags full of groceries falls on the sidewalk and tomatoes and carrots are everywhere, and broken eggs too. A guy stops to help. We're both squatting on our knees to save what's left. I don't even know what I'm doing.

'I am, I just … wait a second,' I tell Naomi. 'Thank you, thank you so much,' I say to the guy, who gives me an apologetic smile back.

'Livvy? Livvy, who are you talking to?'

'A guy on the street who helped with my groceries.'

What a mess. People are going to hate those eggs splashed on the floor, I don't know why right now this seems to bother me more than anything else. I keep walking, I need to get home.

'Naomi, can I call you back?' Before she starts protesting, I end the call.

When I'm finally home, I drop the groceries on the island and call her back, my hands shaking. There are a million different thoughts running through my head.

'What's going on, Livvy?' She sounds much calmer now, whereas I'm still trying to wrap my head around what she was saying.

'I don't know Naomi, this is such a mess,' I sit on one of the stools.

'Have you been seeing him?'

'Who?' I'm still in a state of trance.

'Livvy, listen to me. There are photos of you on the Instagram of the most popular gossip blog in the UK, with Lucas Lamaire, famous tennis player, hello?'

I wish I could hit pause on this conversation right there.

'Do you know who he is?' she asks.

Apparently not.

'Do you?' It's all I can manage.

'Yeah, I do … but it seems to me that you don't.' She begins the sentence with an indignant tone, but ends it softly, feeling guilty realising I'm in shock.

'Oh, shit,' she says. 'Ok. First things first. I advise you to get over your shock, do what you have to, but do it fast. Then go check the photos on Instagram. And then, my friend, you're going to have a lot explaining to do.'

'I don't have an Instagram profile.'

I'm pretty sure right now she rolled her eyes, but she doesn't say anything.

'I will send you my login and password, you can check it from my profile.'

'Ok,' I agree without discussing, I still don't know what I'm doing.

'Call me back when you can.'

'Yeah, bye.'

I go to the kitchen sink and splash cold water on my face, take a few slow deep breaths, but when I finally manage to open Naomi's Instagram and find UK Gossip Today's profile, I'm still in shock. Even more after I see the most recent post.

It's there. I'm there. The first photo is the two of us holding hands in front of Sketch. I swipe to the left, and there's more. It's me running alongside Luc by the Thames, me at Fresh Me Up having breakfast with Luc on Sunday, the two of us entering the building as Luc holds the front door open for me. Luc, Luc, Luc. Lucas Lamaire.

It gets worse when I read the caption.

UK Gossip Today's Instagram

Has Lucas Lamaire found a new match for his heart? The current number two tennis player in the world was seen in London on different occasions with the same brunette. The four-time Grand Slam champion hasn't been seen with a woman in public since he and his last girlfriend, the Spanish tennis player Malia Ferdinand, broke up two years ago. Lamaire is currently in London pursuing the most renowned championship in the tennis world: Wimbledon. Today he's playing for a spot in the semi-finals on Friday. If he wins, he'll play against Andrej Dordevic. Who's the hottie who's been getting Lamaire's attention? Is it a match before the match?

What in the fuck? Why do I feel like the world's stupidest person alive? Why do I feel like the whole world has just seen me naked on social media? Why can't I breathe?

There are so many things wrong about this Instagram post, about today, about this very moment. Over 30,000 people have liked the post, and almost the same amount have left a comment. There are people trying to guess who I am, others are saying how they wish they were me, 'lucky girl,' and others are mean comments I'd rather not mention.

Fuckfuckfuck.

I don't know what's worse—the betrayal or the violation of privacy.

I lean forward and press my forehead on the hard stone of the kitchen island. I close my eyes and stay there, because I don't know what else to do apart from giving myself time to let it all sink in. But the world has other plans for me today. My phone starts vibrating non-stop. There are messages from Mum asking what's going on. Nate has sent me links and screenshots of different news sources, including ESPN.

Today at 6:05 pm

Nate: Keeping secrets aren't you?

It's everywhere! There are calls from Dad and Lexi, and even from some of my co-workers, including Caleb and Haley.

The only person I want to talk to is unreachable, because I just found out he happens to be playing a tennis match at Wimbledon right now. The realisation that that's what he has been doing this whole time since he arrived hits me hard.

How did I get here?

A wave of moments come flushing in my mind all at once. Him giving his phone number to Lesley must have been an autograph and how Andi looked at the two of us together. The way he's always hiding his face under his cap, his athletic body and the calluses on his hand, the way he's always amused when we talk about tennis, or the way he acted when I asked his name. The private dinner at Sketch, how he's often wearing sports clothes. His temporary stay. The whole team behind him.

How could I have been so blind?

I don't feel like talking to anyone, instead, I make things worse by checking the news. Things escalate when I decide to google his name. Photos of the two of us come up first, then news about the matches he played in the past week, and then photos of his ex. His *gorgeous* ex, Malia Ferdinand.

I settle for checking his Wikipedia profile. Another bad idea.

Lucas Dominique Lamaire

French tennis player

Lucas Dominique Lamaire is a French tennis player. He is currently ranked No. 2 in the world by the Association of Tennis Professionals, after winning the most recent French Open.

Born: November 6, 1993 (age 27 years), Reims, France
Residence: Monte Carlo, Monaco
Height: 6' 1"/ 1.85m
Country (sports): France
Grand Slam titles (singles): 4
Plays: right-handed (one-handed backhand)
Coaches: Florian Provost (2002–2018), Maurice Bellegarde (2018–)
Prize money: USD $85,657,178
Official website: lucaslamaire.com

Early life and background

Lucas was born in Reims, France on November 6th, 1993, to Annette and Dominique Lamaire—who was also a professional tennis player and became tennis coach and founder of the Lamaire Academy after his retirement. Lucas has a younger brother, Jules Dominique Lamaire, who is also a professional tennis player in the boy's category. Lucas grew up between Paris and Reims, where his family owns the Champagne House Lamaire. He started playing tennis when he was only six years old.

Personal life

Lucas Lamaire dated tennis player Malia Ferdinand for almost two years. The pair decided to part ways because of distance and busy schedules. Lamaire hasn't had a public relationship since.

Lamaire is an avid advocate for raising awareness for ocean pollution and is passionate about nature and wildlife.

There's more. Way more than I can handle right now, or ever. I'm afraid of looking out the window and finding out that there are reporters crowding the front of the building. I can't look at my phone because I don't know what to do with all the messages and people calling.

Today at 6:25 pm

Caleb: Damn girl, why am I finding out about this on the news?
Haley: Why didn't you mention the simple fact that you're dating one of the hottest men in the world? You go Olivia!
Lexi: Livvy, are you ok?

I toss my phone at the couch.

I turn on ESPN and there he is, playing. I can't even believe what my eyes are seeing. It's as though I still hoped that everyone around me was wrong and that it was only a misunderstanding, despite what Wikipedia said.

It's really him, dressed in white sports clothes with his cap backwards. I'd recognise that ass and those magnetic eyes anywhere in the world. His last name's on the corner of the TV, LAMAIRE, indicating his score, probably. I have no idea. And I don't care. I can't focus on anything right now. I turn it off, get dressed and go out for a run, because that's the only thing that can help me clear my head.

Yes, I already ran this morning, and yes it's pouring outside, but I go anyways. The least of my problems is getting wet running in the rain. And so I run. Faster than I normally do. Angrier than I ever have. Hurt and betrayed. The only person in the world most unaware of my own life. I want to run until I burn all my thoughts away, because organising them won't do.

By the time I get back home it's late. 10:00 pm kinda late. At some point during my run I stopped and screamed at a tree. As if she were the one to be blamed. I cursed and yelled all my reasons for being mad and angry. I talked to her as if she were myself. I did not cry. Tears didn't even try to form. I guess they were afraid of me, of what I would do if they dared come out. I stopped when my voice became hoarse and I started coughing.

I left a trail of water behind me. It started at the hall of the building, then the lift until my front door, where I'm taking off my soaking wet running shoes and socks.

'Who's there?'

Oh for fuck's sake, is Mrs. Thompson still awake?

This time she opens the door before I open mine. I consider ignoring her and try to get in my flat as fast as I can, but I don't make it in time.

'Olivia, is that you?' she says, peeking out her half-opened door, as if she could see clearly. She's holding on to her walker, which is now trapped between the door and the door frame. I feel bad and go help her.

'Yes, Mrs. Thompson, it's me. Do you need help?'

'No, no, no help.' She raises her hand at me.

Despite her age and the fact that she spends most of her time at home, Mrs. Thompson always looks impeccable. Her grey hair is neatly combed and tied in a perfect bun, and her strong perfume penetrates my nostrils as soon as she opens the door. She doesn't smell like old people, she smells heavenly.

'There was a young man knocking on your door. He was waiting for you until half an hour ago,' she says.

I don't know what to say to that, I'm not in the mood for small talk. I'm not in the mood to talk at all. My voice is still hoarse from screaming at the tree.

'We talked for a while. He sounds like a gentleman, and way too French.'

I'm glad she can't see me rolling my eyes.

'He said he had a long day. He sounded exhausted. Did you know he's a tennis player?'

Great, even Mrs. Thompson who can only see shadows knows who Luc is. Ok, that was mean.

'Did he tell you that?'

And why am I interested to know that again?

'He just told me his name. I recognised it from the TV,' she says with a happy grin on her face.

I sigh.

'I even asked for an autograph. If my Paul were still alive he'd have loved to have an autograph of a famous tennis player,' she says beaming. 'Anyways, he seemed worried, and I'd say even a bit sad.'

I bet.

'Right,' I say.

'Didn't know you had a famous boyfriend, love,' she says, fishing for some gossip.

'I don't. He's not—' I begin but don't finish. I don't have the energy. I'm just not up for explaining something I don't even understand myself.

'Well, that's too bad. He seems like the kind of man every woman would want,' she says and winks at where she believes my face is.

Exactly.

'I'm tired Mrs. Thompson. I should get going. Can I help you with your walker?'

'No, I'm fine, thank you, love.'

I hold the door for her anyway.

'Have a good night,' I say.

'You too,' she says, slowly closing the door behind her.

I go straight to the bathroom, and after leaving my wet clothes on the sink, I shower silently, listening to the drops of water falling on the bathroom floor.

I put on my favourite grey pyjama set of tank top and shorts and hide myself under the duvet. Luc's scent has adhered to the side of the bed he has been sleeping on. *Great.* The T-shirts he left behind are neatly folded on one corner of the bed. I kick them to the floor as an act of vengeance. I'm glad I don't think much more until I black out.

Chapter Eighteen

The muffled sound of my alarm is coming from somewhere. It feels like a dream. It keeps ringing and ringing. I open my eyes and look at my watch, which isn't on my wrist. I fumble around the bed trying to find my phone, but remember I left it on the couch last night. This forces me to get up.

I find my phone under one of the cushions, and I can't believe what my eyes are seeing. There are over sixty missed calls from different people, even more messages. From Mum, Dad, Nate, Lexi, Naomi, and … Luc. I close my eyes, take a deep breath and think that eventually I'll have to face the world, but not now, because my phone's battery just died and someone's knocking at the door.

I don't bother checking myself in the mirror on the way to the door, as soon as I open it my heart stops pumping for an excruciating minute.

'I'm sorry.'

It's Luc, lines on one of his cheeks, sleepy face, hair sticking up, and narrowed eyes staring apologetically down at me.

Why God? Why does he have to be so goddamn hot?

He can probably see flames in my eyes as I stare back at him. I don't say a word, and I consider closing the door in his face but I need to get this over with. I can't go the rest of the day without having some kind of explanation. I leave the door open, and go to charge my phone. He lets himself in.

I'm in my room placing my phone on the charger on the nightstand, and he has followed me. I glare at him from across the room, and even though I have so much to say and ask, I can't find the words. I'm too mad. Fuming.

'Olivia, talk to me.' He swallows hard. His face is covered in guilt and sprinkled with remorse.

I walk towards the kitchen, but he's blocking the door. He folds his arms over his chest and blocks the way even more, giving me no option but to stop in front of him.

I sigh in frustration.

'Why?' I ask him calmly. My eyes meet his, my voice finally shows up.

'I wanted to tell you, but—'

I don't let him finish.

'That's not what I asked.'

He closes his eyes as he inhales deeply and opens them as he exhales sharply.

'I don't know,' he says, to my disappointment.

'You don't know?'

I press against him, making him move out of the way so I can pass. His touch sends me to hell and back.

'You didn't recognise me, and it's not like I brag about who I am. It felt good to be treated as a normal person, no pressure or expectations or secondary intentions,' he says to my back.

I close my eyes and try to calm my heart, which is rioting inside my chest.

'It's not like you had to brag about yourself, just be honest about who you are when you realised I didn't know,' I point out.

I go over the kitchen counter and grab my vitamins, somehow, right at this moment it feels important I don't forget to take them. It gives me something to do apart from looking at Luc as he tries to explain himself.

'Olivia.'

'What?'

He's still talking to my back.

'Will you look at me?'

I hesitate. I'm burning with fury. I swallow the vitamins with one big gulp of water and turn to face him. I catch him checking me out in my pyjamas. He could have pretended otherwise, but he didn't. His stare almost puts me off balance. Almost.

When his eyes stop to meet mine, he says, 'I am very sorry you found out this way. I really don't know why I let it go this far. It wasn't meant to be like this,' his eyes are begging. 'But I felt like myself, being with you not knowing what I do for a living,' he says, and I don't know how to deal with this truth.

'You mean, I don't know *who* you are,' I say.

'No, that's not what I'm trying to say.' He runs a hand through the waves of his messy hair. I haven't seen him nervous until now.

Silence. Way too much silence hanging heavy in the air.

'After one week you know more about me than many people I've seen every day for years,' he says.

'Don't. Don't try to make it better like this, it's not gonna work.'

'I'm just saying.'

He holds my gaze and my fury is stronger than my weakness for him.

'How could you do this knowing about Josh?'

I'm barely keeping it together, rage is crawling all over my skin.

'I …' I see hurt in his eyes. I just hope he doesn't see any in mine. It's not a good moment to show my weaknesses and be vulnerable.

'I told you my deepest secret. I trusted you with the worst thing that ever happened to me,' I say, raising my voice.

He sighs.

'I know. I wanted to tell you on Tuesday night, but then after hearing your story about Josh, I just couldn't bring myself to do it.'

I give him a stern look. Adrenaline moved by anger is taking over me. My skin's prickling.

'You're so freaking selfish, Lucas,' I hiss.

His eyes grow wide, he almost winces at my harsh tone.

'Tell me how I can make it better,' he says, more like pleading.

'That's the thing, you can't.'

I walk to the bathroom and go brush my teeth, leaving him ignored in the kitchen. I turn on my electric brush and when I look up, our eyes meet in the mirror. He's standing behind me, leaning his shoulder against the door frame. He patiently waits, watching me. I can tell this is driving him crazy, so I take my time.

'I'm sorry, Olivia. There were many times I thought you had figured it out. I know there aren't any convincing explanations for keeping this from you. I was unfair to you.'

'Damn right you were,' I say with my mouth full of toothpaste.

His eyes dart through the reflexion of mine.

I wash my mouth and face. I pass him by the door, bumping my shoulder on his arm, and take angry steps towards my closet. I push open the mirrored sliding door to my lingerie collection. My eyes browse through the hangers and open a few drawers. I end up choosing a black bodysuit I designed for myself, a mix of lace, tule and leather. It's the most erotic I ever designed, of course my pick is intentional. I lay it on the bed and move to the other part of the closet to pick something to wear for the office. I'm fully aware that he's watching me, but I pretend I'm alone in the room.

As I pull my pyjama top over my head in front of the mirrored closet—my breasts are fully exposed, I'm not wearing a bra—I see him watching from behind. It looks like I'm slowly killing him.

Good.

'Olivia. Stop it,' he begs.

I ignore him. I push my shorts down and hear him sigh—I'm not wearing panties either. I grab the bodysuit from the bed and start to put it on, stepping in with one foot at a time. When I'm done with the second, he's in front of me.

'What are you trying to do?' he asks.

To drive you crazy.

'To get ready for work.' I'm fully aware it's not even 6:00 am yet, and that normally I'd be getting ready for a run. But I guess yesterday I ran enough for the rest of the week, and besides, I'd rather arrive early and avoid walking the hallways feeling as if I were walking the runway with all the stares following me.

He presses his fingers to his eyelids, pushing the skin to the bridge of his nose. He's doing his best to be patient. I know I'm pushing him to the edge and for some wicked vengeful reason, that's exactly what I want.

'What do you want, Luc?' I say, staring at myself in the mirror, checking how the bodysuit hugs my body.

'I want you to talk to me, like an adult.'

'I don't know what to say to you,' I say, picking up the dress I chose. He stops me, holding my hands and dress. His touch makes me gasp for air.

'Say what you want. Scream, hit me, kick me, hurt me. I know I deserve it, but don't ignore me,' he pleads.

I might have just found his weakness. Lucas Lamaire hates to be ignored.

'How did you think I'd react when I found out? Because you know, eventually I would.'

My face is so hot I think it's audible, my skin feels like it's cracking with fire.

'So what if I don't know who's famous and who's not? So what if I didn't recognise you? I still had the right to know, and you had plenty of time to tell me.'

'I'm not saying you should have recognised me,' he says in a low tone.

'You took advantage of the situation. You omitted a huge part of your life, a part that is now hurting my privacy.'

'What would you have done if I'd told you from the start?' he asks.

I make him let go of my hands and start putting my dress on.

'Probably wouldn't have had invited you for breakfast in the first place.'

'Really?' he raises an eyebrow.

'Yes, *really*,' I say, sounding more aggressive than I meant.

I thought talking to him would calm my nerves, but it's doing the opposite. I honestly don't think now is a good time for this conversation.

'Well then, it's good that I didn't tell you the truth so soon.'

Now I'm in flames. Our eyes are speaking their own language, studying each other, trying to find out what the other's going to do next.

'Do you hear yourself? You're so damn selfish you still don't regret lying to me,' I say through gritted teeth.

I manage to break the magnetic field between us and go put makeup on before I make his hair messier. Because despite my rage, there's something about the way my body craves his.

'Are you telling me you didn't enjoy the past week?' he asks, dodging the question as if he senses what's going through me.

Low blow.

'I hate that I feel so betrayed, Luc,' I confess, applying concealer under my eyes.

'I know. I'm sorry and I'm sorry that your privacy was invaded too.'

'How can you be sorry when you don't regret it?'

'I'm sorry I hurt you, that was never my intention. But now that I know you wouldn't have given me a chance if I had told you the truth from the start, I don't regret it.'

'God, you are …' I'm staring at him in the mirror.

'Are you telling me you regret us?' he asks. 'I don't know how you feel when we are together, but I can tell you I feel damn good.'

I feel my legs shaking, and the heat building between my thighs, but I don't dare give in to what he just said. At the same time I also can't deny the things it's doing to my heart.

'Do you have any idea how much it means to me to open up to someone? To have that much intimacy with someone?' I say.

'I'm aware.'

'Are you really?'

'Yes.'

His guilty face is everything, and at the same time nothing I want to see now. I'm still insanely mad at him.

I stop what I'm doing and close my eyes for a second. I hope that when I open them none of this will have happened.

'You were supposed to leave. I'd miss you for a day or two, then I'd go back to my life. Maybe we'd talk again, maybe not. I'd never have to tell my friends I let you occupy such a big chunk of my time in the past week. They'd never have to find out on the news that I lied to them. And above all, I wouldn't be all over the news.'

'Oh. That's it?' His face is clouded with disappointment and hurt.

'Yes, that's it.' I'm evil and I know it.

'Is that what you're worried about? Lying to your friends? Well, I won't take the blame for that. You judge me when you also lied,' his tone has changed, his face flushed with the heat of the sudden mood shift.

I think I finally managed to drive him crazy. And mad.

'Just go, Luc.'

My heart protests against my mind and mouth. He's looking at me like he hasn't understood me right, but the way I stare back tells him he has.

'Just so you know, the way I pictured things between us … it's nothing like the way you did,' he says.

I want to ask how he pictured it, but I don't. I'm not sure I want to know.

'Anyways, I'm sorry again. I'll leave you to it. You know where to find me if you change your mind and decide to talk.'

What does he mean by change my mind? Is he for real?

'By the way, I'm leaving on Monday,' he turns around and walks away, leaving me trapped with my own misery and anger.

Chapter Nineteen

As soon as he closes the door behind him I do the least expected thing. I ask Google if he won the match yesterday. He did. I should have known, considering he said he's staying until Monday.

Was I too hard on him? What did he expect anyway? That I wouldn't be angry? That I'd be happy to discover who he is through the tabloids of all things?

After our conversation I feel worse than yesterday. My shoulders are heavy with the number of thoughts in my head. I make myself a cup of strong green tea—no smoothie for me today—and start dealing with the aftermath of my life's mess.

I begin by replying to my family's messages, letting them know I'm ok, that I'm not dating Lucas Lamaire and that, funny enough, I didn't know he was famous. No one believes me, of course, especially Dad.

Yesterday at 8:26 pm

Mum: You were with him when you disappeared on Sunday, weren't you? Those T-shirts on your bed ... were his? And the condoms in the trash can too?
Oh my God. Help me.

Today at 6:30 am

Me: Mum! I can't believe you checked my trash can.

Wait! I just realised she has been checking my flat when I'm not home, because on Sunday Luc and I hadn't had sex yet, which means she came over some time during this week. Probably on Monday when I was in the office.

Me: Mum, have you been snooping around my place when I'm not here? Since when?
Mum: That's not the point!
Me: fire and red angry emoji
That's what I mean when I say she's a control freak. I guess the apple doesn't fall far from the tree.

Yesterday at 8:38 pm

Nate: Thea's saying we gotta do a double date soon.

Today at 6:35 am

Me: Sorry to disappoint her, it won't happen. We're not together, Nate.
Nate: Thea's asking why not …
Me: Thea or you?
Nate: Are you going to answer or not?
Me: We're not together.

We're not. Whatever it was that we had going on in the past week, was just some kind of messing around. Nothing more than that. Now anything between us is completely over.
It is.

Yesterday at 8:48 pm

Dad: Hey love, just checking in on you. Never knew you liked tennis so much. Winking emoji.
Dad: Do you think you can get me an autograph? Or maybe a ticket to watch the finals? Maybe in the player box?

Today at 6:40 am

Me: I don't think so, Dad.

I can't even believe all this. I try not to be rude to Dad, after all it's not his fault, it's my own for never watching tennis with him.

Someone's knocking at the door. Again. It's not even 8:00 am in the morning and it's as though I'm throwing a party. I'm fuming when I open the door already saying, 'I just need …' but it's not who I think it is, or who, I just realised, I wanted it to be. It's Naomi and Lexi.

Shit.

In normal times, seeing my friends on a weekday would be a highlight; right now, I just want to hide from the world. And I'm honestly not prepared to talk about Luc or admit to them how I'm such a bad friend and good liar.

'You know, if I didn't love you as much as I do, I'd call you a bitch, but right now I'd be happy if you just give us an explanation about this mess,' says Naomi, storming into my flat.

Lexi gives me a tight hug, and it lasts longer than normal. She knows I need it. She has always been the most sensitive and emotive one. Naomi, is the firm, bossy and reassuring one.

'First, I can't believe you lied to us about seeing him. Why would you do something like that?' Naomi says as she jumps to sit on the kitchen island.

Lexi goes make coffee. I sit on one of the stools and take a deep breath before I begin.

'I don't know.' Now I'm talking like Luc. Great.

Naomi stares me down and raises one of her thick black eyebrows, she knows how intimidating she can be when she does that. So I try again.

'I never get this involved, you know that. On one side I was embarrassed to admit that being with him was different, is, I don't know anymore. On the other side I didn't want anyone to have expectations of me being in a relationship again, you know? Especially because this was going nowhere anyways. I just … I wanted to figure things out by myself.'

There's silence as they both stare at me curiously, as if surprised with my answer. Probably because for once, I'm being honest about this.

'Just how involved are we talking?' asks Lexi from the counter, as she waits for the coffee machine to do its job—though I don't drink coffee, I keep one for them.

'Huh. From having a private dinner date at Sketch, to having sex on the kitchen island to him sleeping over. More than once.' I flush with the admission.

'More than once what, sex on the kitchen island or sleeping over?' asks Lexi.

'Sleeping over. More than once, yes,' I say, burying my face in my hands.

'Wait. *This* kitchen island?' asks Naomi.

Lifting my head from my palms, I nod.

She jumps off the island and says, 'Damn you, Olivia Charlton, you fucked Lucas Lamaire on your damn kitchen island.'

I give her my best eye roll.

'I can't believe you let him stay over,' says Lexi, with two coffee mugs in her hand, the steam dissipating in the air just under her nose.

'Worse. *I* asked him to stay, and when I did, we hadn't even had sex yet,' I speak burying my face in my hands once again.

'Who are you?' Naomi bumps her shoulder against mine.

'Good for you,' says Lexi, innocently, as if forgetting one tiny detail.

'Is it?' I ask, lamely, lifting my gaze at them.

They exchange glances.

'How in hell didn't you know who he was and for what plausible reason didn't he tell you when he realised you didn't know?' asks Naomi the question of the week.

I let out a long and slow exhale.

'I don't watch tennis, I don't follow tabloids or social media. The famous people I know are the ones on TV Series, in movies and fashion. Maybe if he had been on a scene playing tennis with Daniel Craig in the last James Bond movie I'd have recognised him. But …'

They watch me attentively, sipping from their coffee at the same time, waiting for me to continue.

'As for the reason he didn't tell me, according to him, it felt good to get involved with someone who doesn't know who he is,' I say, rolling my eyes.

'That makes sense,' says Lexi, getting a stern look from me.

'What?' she asks as I give her my laser eyes.

'Are you on his side? He lied to me. He's a selfish bastard.'

'Technically it wasn't a lie,' points out Naomi, of all people.

'Oh my God, you're defending him. Both of you.'

'We are not defending anyone, but the guy must be good to be able to mess up your perfectly controlled world. He deserves the credit, besides, he's fucking hot,' says Naomi, her terrifying eyebrow raised again.

'Naomi!' I scold her.

'Just stating the real facts here,' she says.

'Is that how you two describe my life when you talk among yourselves? A "perfectly controlled world"?'

'That's not the point,' says Lexi setting her coffee mug on the kitchen island and pulling her golden hair into a ponytail.

'Exactly. The point is, he's the only guy you've opened up to since Josh. This is a huge thing. So what if he omitted what he does for a living? It's not like he's a gangster or something,' says Naomi matter-of-factly.

Now it's my turn to raise an eyebrow at her, but I get the feeling it's not as intimidating as when she does it because she ignores it completely and says, 'Besides, he's sorry, he came to apologise.'

'As if an apology would make any difference right now,' I say.

When I tell them he said he didn't regret not telling the truth from the start because otherwise I wouldn't have given him a chance, they almost melt like butter. I lost the battle, clearly.

'Okay, we definitely want to know more about your sex life with the tennis star, but right now, my friend, we need to talk about your face being all over the news,' says Naomi.

'Livvy, everyone is wondering who you are. It won't take long until they find out,' points out Lexi.

To be honest, as soon as I saw my face on those photos I already felt so exposed I hadn't thought that people still don't actually know my name and who I am.

'I guess putting a name to the face might make things more complicated,' I say, scratching my forehead.

'It could, yes,' says Naomi.

The three of us look at each other, because there's a name hovering above our heads.

'But, you know, it will be fine. Do you think that after such a long time he'd still come after you?' says Lexi.

'I don't know,' I say.

Eventually I make it to work. I leave with the girls, and we share an Uber to our respective destinations. The driver, a red haired woman with freckles dusted on her nose and cheeks, keeps watching me from the rear-view mirror.

'I think I might know you from somewhere,' she says, her eyes narrow as she tries hard to remember from where. I might have an idea, but I don't say anything, and sink a bit deeper on the seat.

'Hey, you never told me how things have been with Lewis after Saturday's date,' I say to Naomi.

'You were too busy having sex on the kitchen island,' she teases me, and for the first time since I discovered that the person I had sex with on the kitchen island is famous, I smile. Then the three of us laugh. The driver's still watching us, me, from the rear-view mirror.

'It has been ... interesting,' says Naomi. I can almost see her blushing.

When I'm about to get out of the car, the driver says—more like shouts—'Oh, I know, I know!' She sounds so excited, her voice so childish. 'You're dating Lamaire, the tennis player aren't you?'

Oh God.

I basically try to camouflage myself all the way from the Uber to the front door to my desk. I'm glad the few people in the office are too busy to come and talk, but I still notice some look up at me, wink and smile or gesture some *talk to you laters* on my way.

I have a busy schedule today, with back-to-back meetings. On one hand I'm glad, it will keep my mind occupied. On the other hand, this means I'll see a lot of people today, and for those who are more into tennis than I am, I'll be something close to a tourist attraction.

I'm preparing for my 11:00 am meeting with the other designers, making sure presentations are saved on the cloud and confirming in which meeting room it's going to happen when I receive the Google alert I was hoping I'd never receive. Now the media knows my name, and if they do, the world does too.

UK Gossip Today's Blog
Lamaire's next match is against Dordevic, but his heart match is Olivia Charlton.

I click on it to see what it says.

Everyone has been wondering who the hot brunette Lamaire has been seen with all over London is in the past days. Wonder no more, you gossipers, we have her name figured out for you: Olivia Charlton, a twenty-six-year-old Londoner and nothing less than a lingerie designer working for one of the most luxurious brands in the world, Secretive.

How the two met is still a mystery, one we'll certainly try to find out for you. According to sources the pair is staying in the same building, not far from Wimbledon, in the quiet neighbourhood of Richmond. The question is, is she staying with him or is he staying with her?

Tomorrow Lamaire is playing Wimbledon's semi-finals against Andrej Dordevic. Is Miss Charlton going to be there to support her beau? We can't wait to find out. Who's going to watch the match and be wondering who is going to be at Lamaire's player box cheering for him? We know we will.

Wimbledon News
Lamaire's affair: lingerie designer Olivia Charlton.

Tennis World
Miss Charlton's keeping Lamaire busy out of the court.

Daily Mail
Who's Lamaire's new girlfriend?

They all have photos. Some I've seen before, of me and Luc. Others were taken of myself, alone. I freeze when I see one of myself coming to work on Monday, when I thought I was being watched. I don't know if I feel relieved or furious when I see it.

I don't bother scrolling down, there are way more than that. I also do my best not to click on each one of these headlines and read what's being said—I'm almost late for my meeting. It takes all the self-control I have in me not to have a meltdown and to maintain my focus on the next couple of hours, in which I'll be discussing details about the changes we need to make so that all the designs will be approved by Haley on Monday.

I'm the last one to arrive in the meeting room, which is already occupied by my team of five. I'm used to getting the *wow, you look gorgeous today* and the *love your outfit* looks. But I'm not used to get the kind of look that means they know something about what I've been doing in my private life. Because as friendly as I am, I'm not an open book, I'm no public figure, I'm no selfie taker, let alone someone who makes the headlines.

'Good morning, everyone,' I say, pulling out a chair, ignoring their gazes. As soon as I sit down and place my tablet and notebook on the glassed table, I decide it's best to face the devil now than later.

'Ok, spit it out, you have five minutes, then we'll focus on what really matters,' I say, looking around with a big sarcastic smile on my face.

'Is it true?' asks Steph, unable to hide her curiosity despite her insecurity.

Everyone else is waiting for my reply.

'Partially,' I say.

They don't look happy with my answer, so I do my best to elaborate. 'We're not in a relationship, if that's what you want to know. He's a friend.'

A friend? God, even I can't believe this lie. Of course I also omit the fact that I didn't know he was famous, that would be the end of me.

They are all grinning, and Caleb chuckles.

'Friends who hold hands and kiss?' he teases. He winks at me, he knows there's more to the story.

When no one's looking but Caleb, I let out a flushed smile.

'Are you going to the game tomorrow?' asks Taylor.

'I don't know about you, but I have a lot of work to do for Monday, so no,' I say. 'Any more questions?'

No one else feels like speaking out, but I know they're still curious about the whole thing. I attend three other meetings and have no time for lunch whatsoever. People keep looking, grinning, winking and asking a question here and there wanting to know more.

I handle the meetings as professionally as I always do, focused even though there's a little tiny red light blinking inside my brain telling me I'm in trouble. I ignore it for most of the day.

Chapter Twenty

I kept my phone turned off the entire day. It was the right decision, because right now, as I'm headed back home, I turn it on and find an atrocious number of Google alerts, text messages, and calls. The only one I decide to give my attention to is from Luc.

Today at 11:15 am

Immune to tickles: I'm sorry your name's out. I know you don't want to, but we need to talk.
Immune to tickles: It's important, especially for you.

Do I have a choice? Maybe he has some kind of magical plan to undo it all. I just want my normal life back. I just want to go back in time; rewind the tape to when I had control over my life. First he messes up my routine—okay, I let him. Then, the media takes control of the rest.

I've been fighting so hard to avoid changes and getting out of my comfort zone, and for what? I didn't even need to look for it. It found its way to me, through Luc.

Today at 6:33 pm

Me: I'll be home in an hour.
Immune to tickles: I'll meet you there.

Note to self: consider changing his name on the contact list. Maybe deleting it?

I get home a little bit over an hour later. He's sitting on the steps next to my door, the same ones where he saved me from a possible disastrous fall just a few days ago.

'Hey,' he says, immediately standing up.

It looks like he doesn't know where to put his hands, but only for a brief moment. He puts them in his pockets when he realises I'm not greeting him physically.

'Hey,' I say, avoiding his gaze. Better safe than sorry, I don't want to succumb to his magnetic blue eyes ever again.

I unlock my door and leave it open for him, but he stands outside.

'Do you mind if we go to my apartment?' he says as I place my purse and keys on the kitchen island.

I look at him, puzzled. I just realised I've never been to his apartment before, not only during his stay, but ever. Not even when Mr. Sorensen used to live there.

Noticing my confusion, he says, 'I was hoping we could talk to my media advisor, Margot.'

Of course he has a media advisor. Wait, Margot? The same one he was on the phone with on Saturday night?

I raise an eyebrow at him, not sure what this conversation will involve, but since I'm in need of advice on what to do with the media, I don't protest.

'It's her job to advise what we should communicate to the press. She might be able to help you. You know, with keeping your privacy,' he says.

'Or what's left of it.' I don't mean to sound so snappy, but I do.

Our eyes meet, and I'm in dangerous territory. His usual messy hair looks even more perfect, his smell of sex is already lingering in the air and finding its way through my airways. Only now I realise I miss him. In my bed and cooking in my kitchen, and ... *keep it together, Olivia.*

'So?' he says, his eyes hopeful.

'Fine. Let's do this,' I say, not in an excited way. I sound like I'm being taken to be tortured.

I follow him up the stairs and on the last steps he says, 'I forgot to mention, my parents are here.'

Fuck me.

'Are you kidding me?' I say, freezing where I am, considering going back to where I came from.

'They don't bite,' he says with a shy innocent grin, the same one from our first encounter in the lift. My heart considers rioting.

I close my eyes and hesitate for a moment, then I decide to keep following him.

I was so not prepared for this.

He opens the door and it feels like my heart's beating at the speed of light.

I see Maurice talking to a blond woman by the window, she must be Margot, because she looks too young to be Luc's mum. On the couch must be his parents, and talking to them, standing, is Jules. Everyone stops their conversation when they notice our presence in the room.

'Hey, Olivia,' says Jules, already walking toward me with a happy smile washing over his face.

He gives me a kiss on the cheek. He's so cheerful I wonder if he realises how badly I'm taking this whole situation.

Their parents get up from the couch and walk in my direction. The smile on their faces tells me they might be excited to meet me. I have no idea why that would be, but I take it. Luc's got his mum's dark hair, but his stature, dimple, perfect nose and eyes, from his father.

'Olivia, it's a pleasure to meet you,' says his mum first, giving me a hug. She smells so good and bold, I'm pretty sure her scent will stick to my hair where she touched, until I shower again.

'Nice to meet you, Mrs. Lamaire,' I say, politely.

I notice Luc's flushed face in my peripheral.

'Oh, no. Please, call me Annette, dear,' she lifts her hand to my cheek and gives it a light pinch, as if she wants to make sure I actually exist. I smile back.

Then his father pulls me into a hug.

'You look even prettier in person,' he says.

I feel my whole face burn.

'*Papa,*' says Luc, clearing his throat.

I see Jules smirking from behind his dad.

'I'm Dominique,' says his father, now looking me in the eyes. 'But call me Dom, *chérie*,' he winks at me.

I don't know where to put my hands. This is so awkward and unexpected I feel a bit overwhelmed.

I'm used to being introduced to a lot of people in a room. I'm good at remembering names and faces, and most of the time I know exactly what to say. I also can tell when someone likes me or not. Maurice doesn't, I can tell by the sceptical look he's giving me, and the lack of interest in offering me a friendly smile. I guess he sees me as the worst distraction Luc could have right now. As for Margot, I can't tell because she seems neutral, like nude colours and Switzerland. She chooses to shake hands, no hugs, no kisses on the cheeks like the French normally do. Once we're done with the introductions, Luc's mum grabs her purse and plants a kiss on his cheek.

'We'll leave you to it then. Jules's taking us to explore London a bit,' says Annette, in her strong accent, pronouncing *beat*, not *bit*. She then kisses my cheek too.

Luc's eyes meet mine and he gives me a half-smile. I'm not sure what to do now. If I smile back would it mean I'm telling him I'm ok with all the mess going on? Or just that I find his mum the sweetest? I smile, but only after I leave his gaze.

'I hope to see you sometime soon, *chérie*,' says Dom.

Once his parents and brother are gone, Maurice and Luc exchange glances and he too leaves us alone with Margot, who goes straight to the point.

'Olivia, I'm Luc's media advisor, I guess you know what that is,' she says.

I nod.

'Good, I'm here to provide support and suggest a few options on how to deal with the media, and what can be said and done, at least for the time being.' She glances at Luc, some words unspoken between the two of them.

She suggests we sit. I pick one of the big chairs facing the couch, where Luc and Margot are. Luc holds my gaze for a moment, he looks serious, focused, but worried. I fidget with my fingers, my index running along the thumb.

'Luc tells me you want to preserve your privacy,' says Margot.

Obviously.

I nod.

Luc moves forward and props his elbows on his legs and interlace his fingers as he watches me attentively.

'Of course, now it's too late to undo the damage already done. There's no way we can make the media delete all the images and make people forget your name. Well, they might eventually, but not now.' She clears her throat before continuing. 'Before deciding which approach we're going to take to deal with the media, it's important you two define the level of your relationship.'

I'm sorry, what?

She looks at Luc, then at me, and continues, 'As I said to Luc a few days ago, when the paparazzi contacted me about seeing you together last week—'

'What? Did you know about this?' I interrupt Margot and stare at Luc.

'Olivia—' he seems to reconsider, guiltily, and says, 'Yes, I knew, I'm sorry.'

Margot's looking between me and Luc, then rushes to intervene before we get into a different kind of discussion.

'As I was saying, if this is just a fling and you'll lead your separate ways, or if you're still not sure to which level you're taking your relationship, you can't be seen together in public anymore, unless that's what you want. But unless we communicate that you two are officially a couple, they'll keep speculating and they won't leave you alone, Olivia.'

Margot is incredibly professional, not because she's wearing a suit and looks busy with an iPad and two different phones on top of each other on her lap, but because of the way she talks about our affair as if it were a business deal. To me, she seems more like a lawyer than a media advisor.

'If you decide to commit to each other and pursue this relationship, you still need to find a common ground and choose whether you want to make it public or not,' she says this so calmly and impartial it makes me want to crawl out of my skin. 'And that's where our plan comes in.'

The idea of pursuing a relationship hasn't crossed my mind, so when I hear her saying that, my eyes involuntarily search for Luc's, and they have a gleam of … hope? I believe he's had a debrief with Margot before I got here, it's as if he already knows what she's going to say.

I don't say anything, I let her finish her speech and avoid meeting Luc's eyes.

'If you decide to make a relationship public, the media will harass you for a few months, but eventually they will tire. You'll then be able to have a public relationship, but at the same time, private, giving them what info when you want to.'

Silence. I stare at anything but him. I know my face is flushed just at the thought of being his girlfriend. So much for enjoying not having to label what was going on between us.

'If you decide to keep a relationship fully private, it will be a hell of a job to contain leaks and paparazzi. Not saying I can't help you, but it will depend more on you than me. It's gonna be a lot of work from your side to watch your backs all the time. In this case you won't be able to have a normal couple life walking hand in hand on the streets. It also goes without saying that you, Olivia, won't be able to attend Luc's matches.'

God, as if a relationship with someone famous like he is would ever work. The way Margot says this all feels like she's laying all the options I have in my life and I need to pick the one that's less worse. I inhale deeply and hold the air inside for longer than normal. I can't even think past today, let alone think about a possible relationship with a famous tennis player and worrying whether I'll be able to attend his matches or not.

Fuck me.

They're both watching me, expecting me to say something. So far, all I did was listen, fidget, cross and uncross my legs, sigh and try to breathe.

'I don't know what you expect me to say,' I sigh.

Margot watches us both in neutral silence. Luc closes his eyes briefly and runs his fingers over his forehead.

'Then, there's also the option which involves you deciding not to pursue a relationship. In this case it's pretty simple, I'll prepare an official press release declaring you're both only friends. But then, you can't be seen together again, or it will mess up things even more,' she says.

I wonder if that's how it works with all the stars when there are rumours about their love life. This is unbelievable. Right now my head is unable to process all this.

'I'll give you two some privacy. We can talk about it tomorrow, or whenever you're ready. But I'd suggest you do it soon. If Luc wins tomorrow, the media will be all over him, which means you too, Olivia.' She stands up, making us both stand up too.

I guess one of her job descriptions might include dropping a bomb and leaving before it goes off.

'It was a pleasure to meet you, Olivia,' she shakes my hand again.

I almost beg her to stay, because I don't want to be alone with him right now. I might not be as strong as I was this morning or have the same will power.

'Luc, give me a call. We also need to prepare for tomorrow's press conference,' she also shakes his hand.

As soon as she closes the door, it's only the two of us in this enormous penthouse and an even bigger elephant in the room. Only now I notice the sports equipment in the opposite corner of the living room, which is as big as my flat. I never realised that this penthouse occupied the entire floor.

'I know it's too much to take in,' he says.

'It is,' I sigh.

'I'm sorry it has to be this way. I know it's complicated,' he says.

'Very, especially when you haven't been honest about any of this.'

'I'm sorry,' his eyebrows furrow.

'So the phone call, on Saturday—'

'Yes. She called to ask me who you were because some reporter she knows asked her directly. I told her to try and keep the photos from leaking,' he says. I can tell by his pained expression and his low voice that this was hard for him to admit.

I sigh in frustration. I don't even know if I still have the energy to discuss this any further.

'I like you, Olivia.' *Bang*, my heart. 'I like you a lot. Enough to give you space and respect that you might not want to see me again.' The way he says it squeezes out every drop of blood in my heart. He sounds as hurt as I feel.

He steps closer. It becomes hard to breathe through this tension.

'This is a mess, Luc. I don't want to have to discuss the level of our "relationship" with other people, especially when *we* don't even know what it is,' I let out.

'I know. I don't either,' he pulls me into a hug. I'm so weak and tired and needy I don't fight it. Instead, I listen to his heart beating against my ear and take in his smell. His nose gets lost in my hair and one big hand finds its way on the small of my back, the other in the nape of my neck. The touch reminds me of how much I crave him, even though I shouldn't.

'I need time to think. I can't do this right now,' I say.

He breaks our hug and holds my face, his eyes meeting mine. Time stops for a moment, and everything else is nothing compared to the intensity of his gaze. It's taking a lot of effort not slip my hands in his hair and smash my mouth against his.

'Good luck tomorrow,' I say instead, and take a step back. I don't want things to get even more complicated than they already are.

I turn to leave, and I hear him sigh.

'Thank you,' he says.

Why do I get the feeling that my heart breaks a little more with every encounter we have now?

Just as I close the door behind me, Maurice is coming out of the lift.

'Hey,' I say, politely.

He studies me and his bright blue eyes tell me he's pondering whether he should say hello back or just ignore me.

'Miss Charlton,' he says, too formal. It's kind of weird to hear him call me that. Should I call him by his last name too? I don't even remember it anyways.

We cross in the hall, each one of us going our separate directions. Then he stops on the way and says, 'You know, he doesn't need drama right now.'

I turn my back to face him, 'Excuse me?'

'This championship is his dream, you're not helping.' He shoves his hands in his shorts pockets. His face is so judgemental I want to slap it. You know, I'm not good at pretending but I'm very good with answers at unrequested comments at the wrong time.

'Did you know I didn't know who he is?' I say.

'Yes.'

'Then you too should be blamed for not helping him achieve his dream.'

'Oh, I told him from the start this was a bad idea.'

'Apparently your opinion wasn't enough.'

His smirk is sarcastic. I narrow my eyes at him, daring him to say more. He doesn't.

'Good night, Maurice,' I say, cutting the conversation short because I just don't have the energy to continue it.

I hear him shutting the door when I begin walking down the steps to my flat. I feel my blood boiling through my veins.

When I get home I pour myself a very chilled rosé in the hopes it will chill me too. I drink it straight down as I look at the dried up flowers Luc gave me, still in the vase on the kitchen island. I'm so tired and mentally drained I can barely stand. I look at my phone and it's still full of messages and unanswered calls. Everyone that matters already knows I'm alive, all the rest can get an answer another time.

After a long shower I literally throw myself onto my bed. I can feel my brain pulsing, trying to organise thoughts and memories and emotions. It feels like it's an overworked computer about to shut down. I just want tomorrow to be better.

Chapter Twenty-One

I wake up when my alarm goes off at its usual time. Slowly I open my eyes and instead of getting up, I linger a little longer in bed. My brain feels a bit less worked up right now and I take advantage of this to try to assimilate the last twenty-four hours. But I quickly realise it's still all too much and roll to my side.

Why couldn't Luc be just a normal guy with a normal life? Like all the others of the past couple of years? But then, if he were like them would I have gone this far?

I get my phone, and staring at the screen I decide to check his Instagram profile. It hasn't occurred to me yet. I use Naomi's account and type in his name on the search box. I shouldn't be surprised that she already follows him, Lexi and Nate too. This all makes me think that if I'd ever told them his full name, they'd have recognised it immediately and I probably wouldn't be in this mess. I feel stupid all over again. And mother of God, he has over seven million followers. SEVEN FREAKING MILLION.

luclamaire

900 Posts 7,3 M Followers 370 Following
Lucas Lamaire
Athlete
French tennis player

There are so many photos of him I feel overwhelmed. There's him playing on the grass just two days ago in Wimbledon when he won. There's a video of him training with his brother and Maurice. There's him thanking the public, and another of him punching the air cheering a win, wearing his white cap backwards and that daredevil stare of his aimed at something on his side. I keep scrolling.

There's him wearing a suit, receiving some kind of trophy, him giving press interviews, hitting his racket against another tennis player's outside of court, both smiling. There's also photos of him on holidays by the beach, having dinner out with his brother, in a private jet, with a Golden Retriever, giving press conferences, running, sweaty, shirtless, smiling, raising a trophy in the air, many more of him shaking his fist flexing his arm mouthing something close to *yes*, shouting, and so many of him in action playing on blue, green and brown courts.

God.

All this time all of this was here, out for everyone—but me—to see. All his life in squares, accessible to millions of people to like and comment on his photos. It's almost unbelievable. It's unthinkable that this man held my hair while I was throwing up, cooked for me, slept on my bed and asked whether I wanted to make love or fuck.

I realise I've been checking his posts for over an hour. How did that happen? I set my phone on the bed and close my eyes. Thoughts are racing in my head. I want to make them go away. I let out a long and slow exhale. Reopen my eyes and make myself get up and get ready for a run.

I see him nowhere, and I'm relieved.

'Are you telling me the media lady basically pushed both of you against the wall to make a decision about your relationship?' asks Naomi on the screen as she sips her coffee while she's walking the streets on her way to work.

'Something like that, at least that's how it felt,' I say, opening my laptop on my desk as I hold my phone.

'How are you feeling?' asks Lexi, always worried about my feelings.

'A mess. I mean, it seems like the whole world has been watching me in some kind of reality show and I wasn't aware of it.'

'I'm sorry, Livvy,' says Lexi. I'm glad she doesn't say *if you had told us…*

'Including you two, who I realised already followed him on Instagram,' I say, a bit bitter, even though I know it's not their fault. I keep trying to find people to blame for what's happening, but in the end it's all on me. And, well, Luc.

'Well, you can't blame us for knowing who he is, and finding him hot,' says Naomi, and there's so much honesty in what she says it hurts.

'Oh God. I know. Sorry. I just, I feel so stupid. I'm so sorry I kept things from you.'

'Livvy, you would have found out eventually, through us, the media or him,' says Lexi.

'I know, but I wish it was from him. He had so many chances to tell me, yet he didn't.'

'What are you going to do?' asks Naomi.

'I have no idea.'

'You like him,' says Lexi.

'That's not the point,' I say.

'You like him a lot, otherwise you would know exactly what to do,' says Lexi.

'Lexi's right. Things are simpler when there are no feelings involved. I don't remember you having any trouble telling Mike, Conor or all the others to go live their lives,' says Naomi.

I say nothing, because it's true. None of those guys were Luc.

'Honey, there's nothing wrong with liking someone. Did you really believe it would never happen again?' asks Lexi.

Maybe. And maybe I hoped it wouldn't hurt ever again.

'Guys, I have a meeting now. Talk to you later?' I say. It's true, but right now I'm glad I have a lot going on at work so I don't have to carry on with this conversation. I feel like being alone today.

'Sure, we're here if you need us,' says Naomi.

'I know, thank you. Bye.'

His match is at 1:00 pm. I have never in my life watched a tennis match until the end. I don't know the rules, I never understood why people enjoy seeing two players screaming *Oh's* and *Ah's* as they hit the yellow balls from one side to the other for hours. If it weren't for Dad who occasionally watches the games, I'd never know who Roger Federer, Rafael Nadal and Novak Djokovic are. If he ever mentioned the name Lamaire before, I wasn't paying attention.

Today I actually check my watch more times than normal, to make sure I turn on the TV to watch him play. Even though I don't know how a player scores or understand the point count, I trust I will recognise when and if he wins the match.

My heart feels heavy in my chest when I see him on TV. The camera is showing him in a corridor waiting to be called out to the court. He's all dressed in white, as is his opponent, Dordevic. That I know about Wimbledon—it's mandatory that all players wear white. He has his white cap backwards, his eyes serious and focused, really focused, like he's in his own parallel world.

Dordevic is the first to go out to the court, then it's his turn. He salutes the public looking up, raising his arm to wave his hand, the other holding the straps of his racket bag hanging over his shoulder. He spins slowly in a circle, making sure he has greeted everyone. My heart beats faster.

Then he walks toward one of the benches and sets his bag on it. He opens it and chooses a racket. He discards the plastic that covers it, and tests it by touching his fingers on its strings and hits it against his hand. Then the two players head to the centre of the court, each on one side of the net, to hear some kind of explanation from the jury—or chair umpire, as they're apparently called. The chair umpire tosses a coin to decide who's serving first, whatever that means. Luc wins. Then he and Dordevic officially greet each other and stand side by side for some official photo.

Each player goes back to their bench. Luc takes off the white Adidas jacket covering his T-shirt and goes to warm up on the court.

The narrator talks about previous games in which they played each other, Luc has won more matches, but the previous two Dordevic has won. He also talks about the numbers and achievements of the two players during the championship and who of the two would have a better chance against Moretti in the final on Sunday.

Once they finish the warmup, the game begins. I suspect then that the server gets to hit the ball first, because it's Luc who starts. His face is so composed, his eyes so focused on the ball and on his own movement. I don't know how he can look so calm. Right there I meet a different Luc. An athlete, a public figure, someone who people cheer for at each point won. A determined and competitive man who's already won some of the most important tennis championships in the world.

I can't keep my eyes off the TV even though I'm struggling to understand what's going on. I notice that the numbers change from 0 to 15 when he scores one point, then from 15 to 30 then from 30 to 40 when he scores again and again. The narrator says he has won the first game. *How many games are there?* Then after a little over one hour into the match, he wins the set. *How long is this going to take?* I decide to take my laptop and get some work done while I watch the match.

After three hours I find myself on my couch still watching the match, my laptop now on the side. I learned that watching a tennis match and trying to focus on getting some work done on my computer doesn't really happen. It's either one or the other.

Luc is doing good, but Dordevic is fighting strong against him now, winning one point after the other. Luc has won two sets. As far as I understood, if he wins this set he wins the match, but both are point against point. It's like a never-ending story.

By now I know that Luc has a thing before he serves, he always tugs his T-shirt on the shoulder, touches his nose and pulls strands of his hair behind his ear. Only then he takes position, throws the ball in the air then hits it. He does this every. Single. Time. Also, whenever there is some kind of a break he gets something to drink and uses a towel to dry himself. While he sits on the bench, he eats a banana or a fruit bar here and there, takes his cap off to dry his hair too, combing it with his fingers, then puts it back on. To my complete despair, he also changes T-shirts, as well as his racket—twice—and now even though he still looks incredibly focused, he seems tired. The camera zooms on his face and there's sweat and grass on his forehead.

The third set is taking ages, they have been on something called *deuce* and *advantage* for what seems like one hundred times. *Deuce*, I realise, is when they are tied on a game 40 - 40, and *advantage* is when one of them scores and the next point favours him on winning the game. The crowd gets crazy each time a *deuce* is announced. I can't even tell for which player they are cheering for, because it doesn't matter who scores, people go wild, so much that at different occasions the jury needs to ask them for silence.

I'm no longer sitting, I'm pacing my living room from one side to the other. I just heard the narrator saying that if Dordevic wins this set, there will be a fourth one. God, I can't handle watching another one of these.

Today at 4:36 pm

Dad: Your boy's doing good.

Oh God. My boy, as if.

Mum: Your dad is going bonkers. He's already thinking he's an in-law.

Oh God.

I toss my phone on the couch.

The TV is showing the box of each player, where their families are. I see Luc's brother and parents, Maurice and Daniel—who I discovered is his physiotherapist—and some people I haven't seen before going nuts cheering for him. Each point he makes, he does that thing with his clenched hand, shaking his fist and flexing his elbow against his body mouthing a *yes*. Sometimes, when the point is very hard to win, some of them taking over twenty-five strokes, he shouts hard and throws his daredevil look at the crowd as if saying *see what I can do?* God, that makes my heart go wild.

His white T-shirt is completely glued to his abdomen. His white shorts are now green from the grass. I bite my nails. I catch myself cheering, screaming, jumping, then back to biting my nails again. They've been playing for almost four hours. It makes me remember how tired he often looked when he was here. After playing such a long match he must feel exhausted. I wonder how he managed to keep this other life from me for over a week.

Then is a *deuce* again. If Luc wins this point he will win the game and the match. But he doesn't. The match goes on. Luc begins to lose one point after the other, now he doesn't look as focused, he looks furious, something I've never seen. He begins to hit the net more than he should. He lets out screams of frustration at the sky. Dordevic wins the third set. God, I can't believe there will be another one of those.

The TV goes for a break, I open a bottle of rosé and make popcorn. Something, anything that can help me with my nerves will do. I can't even believe I've been watching him play the whole afternoon. Even this makes me mad at him. How could I have let someone else wreck my plans and routine like this? Why am I watching him play? Why do I care if he wins or loses?

Slow motion replays of the match's best moments are being shown on the screen. Both players are already exhausted. Luc sits on the bench staring absentminded at the court and drinking some kind of pink liquid, possibly an isotonic, while Dordevic changes his racket one more time.

Suddenly everyone goes silent and they resume the match. Luc seems determined once again, his body expression says he's giving his all to win this match, but Dordevic is number one in the world for a reason, comments the narrator.

Whether he's number one in the world or not, Dordevic gets smashed by Luc on the fourth set. Luc is on a winning streak, now Dordevic is hitting his racket on the grass with rage. He's making too many mistakes, while Luc is now celebrating each point in silence, more focused than when the match began. It's more than clear that Luc will win now, even Dordevic has already accepted his fate, he lets out an honest smile when Luc scores the last point and uses his racket and hand to applaud him. The crowd laughs in unison at the scene.

I only let my shoulders relax when I see Luc celebrating his win, going on his knees and looking up at the sky, as if thanking God, then lying on his back on the grass. The narrator says it's his first time advancing to a final in Wimbledon, so I can only imagine how important this match was for him. It even makes me feel a bit childish for worrying about my problems, while he's about to accomplish a dream.

I still watch the two players greet each other with a friendly side hug and a strong pat on each other's back. Dordevic tells Luc something, probably congratulating him. Luc lets out a smile and I can read a thank you on his mouth. He then grabs his stuff, takes off his T-shirt only to make the women in the crowd go crazy. He lets out that boyish grin of his to the camera that has now zoomed in on his face. He puts on another T-shirt, only to make the females go crazy again with his defined muscles on display. The ones I have been taking advantage of these past days.

On the way out of the court he talks to some of the fans, signing tennis balls and some big versions of it and taking selfies with the people on the green chairs. That moment a realization hits me hard— being with him means I'll need to share him. With a lot of people.

I finally sit again and lean back on the couch, sighing.

Today at 5:36 pm

Dad: Tell him congratulations from me, love.

I roll my eyes, but smile, at Dad, and at the fact that Luc won.

After the match, there's a press conference. I was never one to watch sports press conferences, until now. Luc answers a few questions about the match, using many technical words I don't understand. The press likes him, it might have something to do with his kindness, how he replies to every question patiently and almost always with a smile on his face despite his visible tiredness. When he's about to stand up and leave, one more reporter throws him a question.

'Is Olivia Charlton your girlfriend? Is she going to attend the match on Sunday?'

Luc puts on an impartial face, like he gets asked this question all the time.

'I'm not discussing my private life. Does anyone else have another question about tennis? If not, I guess we're done here,' he says in such a calm tone it makes you think he just said something nice and not something that if said in another tone would sound rude.

I still manage to work for one more hour. I'll probably need to work over the weekend to finish what I need. It is extremely important that everything goes as planned for Monday. But right now I'm exhausted, and looking forward to an evening read and early bedtime. The universe, however, is still conspiring against me, and before I make my way to the balcony, someone's at the door. It's probably Amazon for a neighbour who's not home. Working from home also involves receiving packages for the neighbours.

But when I open the door, it's no Amazon, or any neighbour, or Luc or any friendly face. In fact, it's my worst nightmare.

Chapter Twenty-Two

It's Josh. The same Josh that hurt me from the inside out, not in that order. It's the cause of my nightmares, of my control freakiness, of the walls built around me and my heart, the one who hit me until I blacked out, the one I've been running from for three years.

Right now, as I hold the door and my eyes quickly take in the tall male dressed in a million-dollar suit, my first reaction after the brief shock, is to close the door on his face. But it's too late—he's faster than me and his foot is already blocking the door.

'Livvy,' he says with the voice that has been haunting me all these years. The voice that puts me down when I'm cheerful, that wakes me up at night when I think he's sleeping beside me. I flinch at the sound of it.

What do you do when you have to face your worst fear, alone?

I don't run. I knew this encounter was a possibility, and trust me, I've been preparing for this moment for way too long. I'm not running, but I'm not stupid.

'How did you find me, Josh?' It's the first question that comes to my mind. Because the most obvious one would be *what are you doing here*, but I already know the answer to that one.

I take a few steps back.

He lets out a sarcastic smirk, the one he used to give me that said *do you think I'm stupid?*

I turn around slowly and walk toward the kitchen. I grab my phone from my jeans pocket as imperceptibly as I can. I go behind my kitchen island, as if this was enough to make him stay away from me. It's enough for me to gain time and send the letter *H* to Naomi and Lexi, on our group chat. I hope they remember the code. It was Lexi's idea after what happened the last time I saw Josh. *H* is for help, and it's an easy letter to find and press on the keyboard, being right in the centre.

'You're all over the press, love bug.'

Hearing him call me by the nickname he gave me years ago makes my blood heat up through my veins and burn my insides. The smug smile on his face makes it even worse.

'How you've been? I haven't heard from you in a long while,' he says, making himself comfortable on one of the stools.

My body is trying to find a way to cope with his presence, but I'm panicking—I can feel my heartbeats in my throat, my voice trying to find its way out. My legs are trembling, trying hard to keep me standing.

'I've missed you,' he says.

I close my eyes and wish very very hard that this isn't real. I still don't run. I also don't cry.

Breathe, don't forget to breathe.

'What do you want?' I say, finally.

'Just wanted to stop by and say hello, see how you're doing. It seems as though everyone that knows you disappeared or don't know anything about you all of a sudden.'

All of a sudden? It's been three fucking years.

'Well, you've seen me now. You can leave,' I say, my voice trembling.

'So you've got a new boyfriend,' he says, completely ignoring what I just said. Typical Josh.

'Please, leave,' I beg.

I've played different scenarios in my head over and over again of what I'd say if I ever saw him again, but now everything seems to have disappeared from my mind.

'Do you have a beer, or something?'

I sigh. How long is it going to take until he leaves?

'I don't,' I say, crossing my arms over my chest, as if creating a shield against him. But today, there is no right lingerie or strong enough armour to wear against him.

Josh is manipulative, he knows what to say and how, he knows how to make something complex turn into water and sugar. Everyone who meets him falls for it. I did, my family and friends too. Not anymore.

Now he sits across from me, his red hair darker than I remember. His blue eyes trying to meet mine, but I avoid the contact as much as possible.

'Do you think your tennis player will love you like I do?'

I don't answer him. I know where this is going. He wants me to answer, but no matter what I say, it will be the wrong answer. He will use it against me.

'He won't, love bug. No one will ever love you like I do.'

Now I let out my sarcastic laugh. He used to hate it, too.

'I'm also pretty sure he won't fuck you like I did,' he says, now standing up.

I clench my hands, digging my nails deep into the skin of my palms.

'That, I'm pretty sure too. No one will ever fuck up my life like you did,' I say, anger taking over me. Courage is showing up.

He laughs hard. His sarcasm drives me crazy.

'I'm not that girl anymore.'

'Oh, I know. You're a woman now, successful, and apparently famous too,' he mocks.

'Does it bother you?'

He smirks.

'Looking at you now, looking like a loser, unable to get over me after three years, I don't know why I didn't press charges against you,' I say, now with clenched teeth.

'Maybe you should have, but I always knew you didn't have the courage to do it. It was never something I worried about,' he says, his eyes darkening like a thunderstorm about to begin as he walks toward me.

'Get the fuck out, Josh,' I shout at him as he gets closer to me. I try to walk away, but he grabs my arm, his grip strong and tight. He shakes me hard. My instinct is to close my eyes and wait for the punch.

'Shut up, Olivia,' he raises his voice, squeezing my arm even harder. Veins are popping across his forehead, his face has reddened with rage.

'Why is it so hard for you to accept defeat? You lost me, get over it and leave me alone.'

'Get out.'

When I hear the familiar voice coming from behind me, I know everything will be fine, no matter what.

'You must be the boyfriend,' says Josh, letting go of my arm, yanking it in a way I almost fall backwards.

'And you must be the jerk ex,' says Luc firmly. The door must have been open, and I'm so glad.

Luc's wearing an expression I've never seen before. It's as if he transformed himself, now prepared for a cold war. He gets to me and wraps an arm around my waist, holding me in place. Then he takes my hand and uses his thumb to apply pressure to my palm, just like he did when I had my *déjà vu* on the street.

Josh's sarcastic smile doesn't work with Luc.

'Get the hell out,' Luc's voice is calm, but firm. His eyes are focused on Josh's every movement, as if he's ready to act if it comes to it. Josh doesn't feel intimidated, he takes one more step towards the two of us.

Luc's reaction is to shift me behind him as he acts as a shield against my ex. His hands still clasped through mine.

'GET OUT,' this time Luc shouts and I flinch in surprise. I'm shaking all over and my heart rate is through the roof.

'Do you think she will want anything to do with someone who exposes her life like you do?' Josh is furious, his face all shades of red. It brings back even more memories. He takes a few steps towards us and for a moment I fear he will attack Luc.

'You'll die waiting for her to tell you she loves you,' says Josh.

'I'm not going to say it again. Get out or I'm calling the police,' Luc's voice lowers again, but the way he speaks has much more weight than when he shouts. He chooses to ignore Josh's comment, but I know he will eventually wonder what he meant by that.

'Fine,' says Josh, holding his arms up in the air in defeat, but still with his smug smile.

He starts to walk toward the door, around the kitchen island, opposite to where I'm standing with Luc, who's still keeping me behind him, protecting me from the threat across the room.

'Nice match, by the way,' says Josh to Luc. It sounds more mocking than praising.

'Get out,' says Luc once again.

'You know, love bug, relationships with stars never last too long. Soon enough I'll be reading the news about your breakup.'

I feel every strong and fast beat of my heart in my extremities. My entire body is alert and aware from the fear of having to face Josh again. Luc and I watch him leave the flat in silence.

Chapter Twenty-Three

It's only after Luc pulls me into him and hugs me that I let my guard down, realisation of what just happened hitting hard. I let the tears stinging behind my eyes roll out. They come thick and fast, I can't control them or what I'm feeling. I sob onto his chest, shaking. He tightens his arms around me. In silence, he feels and watches me fall apart. I can't believe I'm having this breakdown now. My body is betraying me by letting my emotions show so easily when I fought so hard to keep them inside for the past years.

Luc holds me until I feel like letting go of him, which only happens several minutes later. His white T-shirt is wet, but he doesn't seem to care.

'Can I get you anything?' he asks, his eyes searching for mine, but I'm feeling so ashamed of him seeing me this way I avoid his gaze.

He takes my chin and lifts it so I have no choice but to look at him. He wipes a tear from my cheek with his thumb and pulls me back onto his chest again, 'Come here.'

I'm pretty sure he can feel my heart hammering inside of me.

Once the wave of emotions that took over me eases down, he lets go of me and hands me a tissue, then pours a glass of water for me. I must look like a mess, but right now I don't care anymore. I realise, finally, that I'm just glad Josh isn't here anymore, and that Luc is.

With his ass pressed against the kitchen island and arms crossed over his chest, he watches me as I blow my nose, then take a sip of water. His expression's still of worry, forehead creased, his shoulders tense.

'Congratulations on your win,' I manage to say, my nose and eyes swollen from the unexpected crying. I must look like a mess, as I always do when I cry.

He looks at me surprised, his face now softening.

'Oh Olivia. Of all the things you could say,' he half-smiles. 'Thanks,' he says as if it weren't that big of a deal, even though now I know how big of a deal it is.

'I watched it,' I say after taking a sip of the water once again. My hands finally stopped shaking, but there is still the electrifying current running through my veins.

'You did?'

'I did. All of it.'

'Did you understand anything?' he smiles shyly. How I missed his smile. It brings some normality back after the intense moment I just had with Josh.

'Only that you beat him after four hours and twenty-two minutes,' I say.

Luc laughs and stares down at me, amused, probably because despite the fact that I have no idea how a tennis match is played, I'm perfectly capable of memorising how long his lasted.

'I might have also learned a thing or two about what a serve is. And surely by now I know what *deuce* and *advantage* are,' I say, half crying, half smiling, my nose still full.

He reaches for my hand, pulling me and placing me between his legs. We can't keep our eyes apart and I'm finding it hard not to kiss him right now. But then I remember the reasons why I shouldn't. He and I can only end in heartbreak, and it's most probably going to be mine first.

'You should be celebrating with your family, I don't want to keep you,' I say, pretending I'm not enjoying the fact that he's here standing in front of me after winning a Wimbledon's semi-final. Pretending I'm a cold-hearted woman, just because I still haven't fully forgiven him for omitting that he happens to be the current number two tennis player in the world.

He smiles and exhales sharply.

'I don't want your family to resent me without even knowing me,' I say.

'They'd never resent you,' he slides his hand through my hair, so that his fingers are touching the nape of my neck and his thumb's stroking my cheek.

'Maurice already does,' I say.

'That's not true. Maurice is just a coach who wants his player to focus on winning the most important tennis championship in the world.'

'When you put it like that, I feel like I'm the villain of your story,' I tease, but it has some truth to it. That's what he meant when he said I made him lose focus.

'Never,' he says, pulling me closer to him and into a gentle hug. My ear is against his strong beating heart, his hands tight around me. It feels good, safe and just what I need right now. His nose is on the crown of my head, breathing in my hair. For a moment I even forget why I'm so mad at him.

After enjoying a long moment of silence, he takes my face in his hand, lifting my chin so my eyes are fully connected to his and says, 'I'm sorry. I really am.'

He could be saying this because he's sorry for what just happened, but as I stare into his eyes, taking him in, reading him, breathing him, I know the reason he's saying it's because of his betrayal.

'I know you are. It's just, I need to think, right now it's all too much,' I say.

'I know,' he says, and touches his lips to my forehead. 'I'm not used to getting involved with women who don't know who I am. I enjoyed being myself with you. I was selfish and unfair to you, and for that I will always ask for your forgiveness. But ...' He doesn't finish his sentence, because another storm seems to have invaded my home, Naomi and Lexi are breathless and desperate walking through the front door that was still open. I'm surprised Mrs. Thompson doesn't follow after them. I'm pretty sure she isn't enjoying all the commotion.

'Oh. Is that why you needed help?' says Naomi, panting.

Luc and I immediately break apart, more me than him. He stays where he is and I go hug the girls.

'Josh was here.' As I say it, it all comes back to me, the realisation, the fear, the tears.

'You're ok now,' says Lexi in our triple hug.

'How did that happen?' asks Naomi, shaking her head in disbelief.

'He saw the news, he must have found out where I'm living somehow. Maybe following me from work, I don't know. You know how he is,' I say, fully aware that Luc is listening just behind me.

'But how did he get in?' asks Lexi innocently.

'You know, it's not hard to get in the building, just wait for someone to open the front door,' I say.

'Shit,' says Naomi. She lifts her gaze to find Luc and I feel my face flushing.

'Hi, I'm Luc,' he says with a shy smile on his face, hands in his pockets. Now watching him from where I am he looks so tired.

'Oh we know who you are,' says Lexi with a big smile on her face. She has always been easily charmed, it'd be alarming if she wasn't charmed by Luc.

He walks towards us and greets the girls with a kiss on their cheeks. My heart beats faster seeing them all together in one room. I honestly didn't think this would ever happen.

'I guess I should let you girls talk,' he says looking at me. 'Now I believe you're in good hands,' he says to me.

I walk him to the door, and it's awkward, because I know the girls are watching us.

'Celebrate tonight, you deserve it,' I say.

'That's ok. I need to focus on Sunday, get some rest,' he says, running his fingers through his ever so perfect hair.

'Thank you,' I say.

'For what?'

'For being here when I needed you.'

He pulls me into his arms again. My face presses against his chest and I can't help but breathe him in.

'I hope to see you tomorrow,' he says close to my ear.

I don't say anything, I pull away from him and say good night. Then I close the door behind me and find the girls frozen, staring at me.

'What?' I say.

'I know you don't wanna hear this right now, and it probably doesn't go well with the fact that your stalker ex was just here, but … you are one lucky bitch,' says Naomi.

I tell the girls how it happened, what Josh said, how he came to be in the same room as Luc, and how Luc protected me, intimidating my crazy ex. They listen attentively. We're lying on the couch on the balcony, drinking frozen Margaritas because Lexi insisted on making them for us. It's not only her favourite drink, it's her specialty. I'm in such a state that I accept any kind of alcohol, even very sweet strawberry frozen margaritas with extra shots of tequila. With today's heat, it certainly helps cool things down.

When I'm done talking, they look at each other, speaking their own language.

'Can I ask you something?' says Lexi first.

I roll my eyes, 'Go ahead.'

'What's the worst that can happen if you give him a chance?' asks Lexi with puppy eyes.

I sigh.

'So much can happen.' I feel lightheaded from the alcohol. Margaritas are dangerous when they're this sweet.

'I think the worst has already happened. Josh,' says Naomi.

I process what she has just said, because in a way it's true. I've been hiding from Josh for the past three years, even though he should be the one hiding. I let him haunt me and become my nightmare. I felt like watching my back all the time, I keep having nightmares where I'm still with him, trapped and unable to tell anyone about it.

'Yeah, Naomi's right,' says Lexi.

'What if he comes back? Should I move again? Should I restart my life one more time?'

'Honey, I think it's time for you stop hiding,' says Naomi.

'How? I don't think he's given up yet. I can't believe he came over here and told me he missed me. How sick is that? I should have pressed charges when I had the chance.'

'There's no point in thinking about the should-haves, honey. If he comes back, you kick him out, you call the police, you scream, you do whatever it takes to keep him away, but that's *if* he comes back. What else can he do? You're a strong woman, you're not innocent or unaware like you were back then,' says Naomi.

'Live your life, that's what we've been trying to tell you for a long time,' says Lexi.

Their words keep playing in my mind. I get the feeling I'll need to organise all these thoughts at some point. I say nothing for a while, I only sip my margarita. They are silent too, respecting my silence.

'Now, will you give him a chance or not?' asks Lexi again after a long while, really not giving up on getting her answer.

'We don't even live in the same country, I don't even know what kind of chance we both have,' I take a big, long sip of my margarita. I should stop drinking about now.

'So that's it? You're not even going to try?' says Naomi.

'It's not like that,' I say defensively.

'Yes, Livvy, it is like that. We're kind of tired of seeing you sabotaging yourself, making excuses to pass on opportunities to be happy,' says Naomi.

'First, I'm not unhappy. Second, this is not sabotaging myself, this is protecting myself from what I know has a minimal chance of working and maximum chance of breaking me,' I say.

'You know, it takes two to make a relationship work. It depends on both of you,' says Lexi.

'Sure, that's why I cannot give myself fully to someone I don't know will give their all too.'

'Then you're going to have to trust him. You'll never know if you don't try,' says Naomi, and I know she's got a point. The thing is, I don't know how and if I can trust a man again. Besides, me and Luc haven't started on the right foot when it comes to honesty.

'You guys, you're talking like he has asked me to be his girlfriend, which is not the case.'

'Yeah, but what if you don't even give him a chance to ask?' says

Lexi.

I exhale sharply, emptying my lungs. I wish I could pause this all for a while until I wrap my head around it. There's just so much going on, I don't even know which problem I should solve first. My nightmares, my reality or my dreams.

'Look, until we talked to the media advisor, I hadn't thought about us beyond Monday. I knew from the start it wouldn't go beyond that.'

'But now you are,' says Lexi.

'I am what?'

'Thinking about it.'

'It's complicated, Lexi.'

'I know it is. But he might be just what you need.'

I laugh, because I can't believe she's saying this. She knows me better than I know myself.

'Look, from how I see it, it's up to you. Whether you need time or not to figure out where being with him will take you, it's up to you,' says Naomi.

'And we're just questioning and saying all this to you because we want you to be happy and have a life beyond work and one-night stands.'

I give her a stern look, because when she says it aloud it kind of sounds bad.

'I know.' I give in, because she's right anyways.

I lay on Naomi's lap, she plays with my hair. It feels so reassuring, it feels like my comfort zone.

'Can you imagine yourself dating the number two tennis player in the world?' says Lexi all excited, tickling my belly. I curve my body in reflex and swat her hand away as I laugh. What a crazy day filled with mixed feelings and confusion.

'He's probably number one now,' I say.

'Ohhh, she's keeping track,' teases Lexi as Naomi smirks while still playing with my hair.

I'm glad when the topic moves on from Josh and Luc to their lives, it helps me take my mind off my own. I have the impression I've neglected them these past days. I've always been the one to listen more than talk, because for the past years I had nothing more interesting than work and an occasional flirt to talk about.

'So, does that mean you're in a relationship?' I ask Naomi after she told me Lewis asked her if they could be exclusive. My eyes widen in excitement as I wait for her response.

'Yes!' she says, so excited I can almost see tears in her eyes.

'Oh my God, why didn't you tell me before?' I sit up again and hug her tight.

'It just happened, last night. I wanted to tell you in person,' she says.

'I'm so happy for you, honey. Wow, this is huge,' I say.

If there's someone I know who deserves a good guy who takes her seriously, it's Naomi. We've known each other for over five years, but the only guy to get as close was Ryan, and well, it didn't last longer than three months. It took her way longer than that to get over him.

'I talked to Tommy,' says Lexi.

'And?' I ask.

'He didn't say anything, he just listened. When I asked him why he wouldn't, you know, initiate things in the bedroom, he still didn't answer,' she says.

'He said nothing? Nothing at all?' says Naomi.

'He just said he's sorry and that I caught him by surprise and now he needs to think about it. I mean, what is there to think about?'

I look at Naomi and I know she's probably thinking the same as I am. Our high school sweetheart friends are going through a crisis, and it's strange, because they are this kind of couple that belong together and you can never imagine them apart.

'Well, I like Tommy, but I like you best so I think you should get a vibrator,' I say and we all burst out laughing. I'm glad I thought of saying something silly to wipe the sadness from Lexi's face.

Despite all the craziness in my life, there's nothing that makes me happier than seeing people I love happy. Even if I need to get them a vibrator myself.

We put on our playlist in the surround system and upgrade to sipping from the tequila bottle. We eat popcorn and order pizza. We strip off our clothes and try on lingerie, and we dance, and we sing to The Chainsmokers and Coldplay's *Something just like this* in our underwear in the kitchen, then in my room in front of the mirrored closet pretending we have microphones in our hands, then jumping on the bed almost falling off, bumping into each other. If we're going crazy, we do it properly. I feel like I'm on a high.

This is nice.

Sometimes it's good to forget that we need to be strong all the freaking time, once in a while taking a break from being an adult helps to keep you sane.

After the dancing fit, we lay on my bed and stare at the ceiling. I'm so drunk I see stars spinning.

'I can't believe you coldly changed into your most sexy lingerie in front of Lucas Lamaire, making him watch,' says Lexi sounding just as drunk as myself.

We all laugh hard until our bellies hurt and tears roll down our faces.

'You're such a little devil. Poor guy,' says Naomi.

'I was mad, so freaking mad. I'd have used any power I had to make him suffer,' I say, vengeful.

'Did he get hard?'

'God, Naomi. I don't think so, he left so …' I say, remembering the face he made when he turned to leave. It still makes my heart ache a little.

'So …?' says Lexi.

'Hurt,' I say, finally finding the word.

'I zhink he's crayz 'bout you,' mumbles Lexi.

'From the things you told us and seeing the way he looked at you tonight when we arrived, he really is,' says Naomi, shooting her dark green eyes at me like a laser.

I shake my head.

'What have you done to him?' asks Lexi.

'The question is, what has he done to me?' I say, covering my eyes with my forearm.

'Will you go to the match?' asks Lexi.

'What? Are you crazy?' I say sitting up.

'Sorry, it was just a question! Please don't hurt me,' says Lexi, defensive but holding in a laugh. This makes me laugh.

I lay back on the bed again and we stay silent for a while.

'Are you saying goodbye before he leaves?' asks Naomi.

I let her question hang in the air. There's also that. Sometimes I forget he's leaving. The alcohol has slowed my brain down, and I'm glad for it, because the past three days I felt like it was crashing with so many thoughts. I have to make a life changing decision about work by Monday, then there's the truth Luc failed to tell me, my face and private life all over the news, and Luc's media advisor, and my encounter with Josh, and … Luc leaving. *Luc's leaving.*

How much can someone change you and mess up your life in a matter of two weeks?

Chapter Twenty-Four

I spend the next day dealing with my hangover, which is better than dealing with everything else. The girls leave after brunch, also hungover. Once they're gone I grab my bottle of water and jump back on the bed, which I haven't made since the last time Luc slept here. His T-shirts are still here, I should probably return them to him. I fish them out from under the pillow and sniff them before I do that. There's probably a malfunction with my nose, because how does he smell like sex all the time?

I cover my face with one of his T-shirts. I stay way too long like this, searching for answers, thinking of possibilities, wondering about consequences, pondering my next steps. All the while taking in his scent.

It's like he knows I'm thinking of him, because right then I get a message.

Today at 2:58 pm

Immune to tickles: I thought this might be helpful in case you want to press charges against him.

It's a video from Josh when he's jerking my arm, my body lurching with violent motion. It looks even worse than it felt at the moment. I can't believe Luc got this on camera.

Me: Wow. Thank you for that.
Immune to tickles: No problem, I hope you can use it somehow.

I could. I now definitely have proof against Josh and he didn't even need to leave another mark on my face. It's probably proof enough to at least file for a restraining order to keep him away from me isn't it? The question is, do I have the courage to do it this time?

I stop for a moment and stare at the ceiling, with the phone placed over my heart. Then I remember I've been wanting to know something Luc never got to tell me.

Me: Can I ask you something?
Immune to tickles: Yes
Me: When I told you how I pictured us, you said it wasn't how you did. How did you picture us?
Immune to tickles is typing …

Two minutes later I hear a knock on my door. My heart takes a leap. *Traitor*. I push Luc's T-shirts aside and head for the door. When I open it I find him with his forearm propped on the door frame, his forehead pressed against it. His eyes immediately lock with mine.

'Together,' he says.

For a moment I have no idea what he means by that, I'm too distracted trying to divert my eyes from the indecent Calvin Klein waistband showing. His joggers are hanging too low on his hips, and *… goddamn it, why is he shirtless and barefooted?* Then I quickly realise it's his answer to my question.

'I pictured us together. Cooking, eating popcorn, running, getting to know each other, travelling, sleeping together, making love,' he says it with such calm I envy him, because on my side, I feel everything but stable.

I lean my head on the half open door and watch him for a moment. I have no idea what to say to that, I never imagined he would be so straightforward.

'Come with me tomorrow, to the match,' he says, filling in the silence.

I smirk, because this is so not a possibility for me.

'I'm serious, Olivia. I know it's too much to ask of you right now.'

Too much to ask is an understatement.

'Yes, it is,' I say.

'I also know I fucked up by not telling you who I am. I know now how much it hurt you, and I don't ever want to hurt you again,' he says.

Seeing the hurt and hope in his eyes makes my whole body ache.

'But you will, Luc. There's no such thing as not hurting someone. Eventually we'll hurt each other,' I say.

'I never said it won't happen, I just said I never want to. We're not perfect, we'll make mistakes. As long as we're there for each other and trust each other, we'll make it work.'

'How can I ever trust you?'

'I'll fight for your trust, no matter what.'

I sigh. What is he trying to tell me? What does he want?

'Last night—' he says, then swallows before continuing. 'Last night I was about to tell you something before your friends arrived.'

I almost forgot about that. I wait for him to continue.

'Whether you forgive me or not, whether you want to be with me or not, it doesn't change how I feel. I want to be with you more than anything,' he says.

Here's your chance to give him a chance, Olivia.

I stay silent for too long, hearing my heartbeats echoing in my head. Would it be too crazy to tell him yes? Would it be too stupid to tell him no? I don't know. Why is it so hard for me to open my heart? Why is it so difficult to believe a relationship can work?

Then as I watch him there, standing in front of me, saying things any woman would like to hear and believe in, Josh's words come to my mind like a hurricane, wiping everything out with it. *Relationships with stars never last too long.* Why would ours be different?

He's waiting for me to say something and I can tell it's killing him, because he has narrowed his eyes and creased his forehead as if in pain. I shake my head and just like that I decide my heart should remain protected.

'I have something for you,' I say.

I turn around and go to my room and leave him at the door. When I come back he's still at the same spot, the same way I left him, only he's looking at my hands, where I'm holding his T-shirts. I give them to him, he almost doesn't take them, and when he does, it's as though he's accepted defeat.

'So I guess this is goodbye then?' he says.

It hurts, it hurts way more than I expected it would. The word goodbye is lingering in the air between us, making my aching heart beg me to change my mind. But I'd like to believe that it hurts less now than it would hurt later if I decided to give him my heart. Sometimes, the heart doesn't know what's best for it.

I nod. Because I can't bring myself to say it aloud.

'What are you so afraid of, Olivia?'

'What makes you think I'm afraid?'

'Because I know you are, I can tell by the way your eyes are looking at me right now, and how hard you're fighting not to take one more step closer to me.'

What?

'And right now you're trying to find excuses not to be happy,' he says.

'What are you talking about? I'm not making excuses. You lied to me—'

'And I have apologised. Because yes, I was selfish. I *am* selfish, because of what I do. I always put myself first, I have to. But with you, Olivia, I want to be selfless.'

Why isn't his apology enough?

He's breathing so hard the ridges on his stomach are contracting strong and fast.

'This, us, it can never work, Luc.' I fold my arms across my chest to avoid fidgeting with my fingers in front of him.

'And how do you know that if you don't even want to try?'

'I don't need to, this has been all wrong from the first moment,' I say through gritted teeth. He might have hit a nerve.

'You see how afraid you are?'

Why is he doing this?

'I'm not afraid.'

'Now say that looking me in the eyes and convince me,' he says.

'Damn it Luc, just leave it,' I hiss.

He hesitates for a second, and says, 'You know, I'm not him. I'll never hurt you like he did. Just, remember that.' Now he sounds angry.

I close my eyes, taking in the pain of hearing him say those words. I don't reply. I just watch him hurt like the devil I am. Sometimes I wonder how my heart still manages to beat when it's surrounded by so many layers of iron.

He stands there for one more second, his eyes not wanting to leave mine, maybe still hoping I change my mind.

Once he fully gives up and turns to leave, I say, 'Good luck tomorrow. I know how much this match means to you.'

He doesn't even look back when he says, 'Goodbye, Olivia,' as he begins to climb up the stairs back to his apartment. Is this the last time I'm seeing him do this?

One day this man will belong to one lucky bitch. He will ask her, too, whether she wants to fuck or make love, he will take her to fancy private dinners, she will get to meet his family and see his home, she will get to travel with him and cheer for him during his matches, they will celebrate his wins together, he will cook his grandma's recipe and tell her the same story about its secret, only this girl will get to have that recipe and he will marry her. He will declare his love for her in front of everyone, and I will be reading about it on the news.

Will I be wondering what would it have been like if I said yes to us? Or will I be smiling and thinking how he deserved to find someone that has a place for him in her life?

Chapter Twenty-Five

I almost didn't get any sleep last night. Instead of succumbing to my thoughts, I worked my brains out on my presentation for Monday. My biological clock makes me wake up at 5:00 am today even though my alarm isn't set. Before I begin to think too much, I get up and go for a run. It feels like forever since the last time I went running.

It's so quiet outside. I'm glad. It feels quieter than my mind. London's still sleeping, only the birds seem to be awake with me. As I begin to run, focused on the path, my thoughts begin coming one by one, and I take my time to deal with them. Work. Josh. Luc. Luc. Luc. Then it's all about Luc until I clear my head and decide it's time to get back and have my smoothie. I don't even remember the last time I had one.

Today Lesley's there and, of course, I have to tell her what I'm having. No surprise. I've lost hope in her.

She's watching me with a weird grin on her face, she never grins at me. I might know the reason, so I don't bother asking. She offers an answer anyways.

'Saw you on the news,' she says handing me my smoothie.

I shoot her a fake smile.

'The other day, a guy, a reporter or photographer, not sure, came asking about you.'

I was about to turn and leave when she said it.

'What do you mean?'

'He was asking if I knew who you were, and if I'd seen you … you know, with him,' she winks at me.

Of course he did.

'And what did you tell him?' My curiosity is bigger than my desire to ignore her.

By the look on her face and her expression, I know she was the one who leaked my name to the press.

'I might have told him your name,' she says, wincing.

I sigh. Now who'd have guessed that Lesley, who can't even remember my usual order, would be the one to remember my name at the most inconvenient time?

'Sorry,' she says with a guilty face.

I let out my most sarcastic smirk.

'Whatever,' I say, turning to leave. What's done it's done, right?

Before I reach for the door handle I look back and tell her, 'At least you've got his autograph.'

'Oh, and a selfie too,' she looks proud, innocent, and in that moment I realise Lesley's just naive, not stupid. And I confirm the fact that Luc never gave her his phone number, not that I had any doubt.

Just as the lift doors open, I bump into Jules. As soon as he sees me, a smile tugs at the corner of his mouth. His smile and his eyes are identical to his brother's, but younger.

'Hey, Olivia,' he says.

'Hi, Jules,' I say, a bit shy, something I'm normally not. I wonder how much he knows about me and Luc.

'Funny, I'm headed to the café to get the same thing for Luc.'

I smile at him. My heart feels the pain of hearing his name. Will I ever be able to drink this smoothie again without thinking about him?

The doors almost close, but he holds them open. I'm not sure what else he has to say.

'You know, I told him to tell you as soon as he realised you didn't know,' he says with a guilty expression. This makes me like him even more, this younger version of Luc.

'That's ok, Jules. It was his decision.'

'I know,' he says.

I step onto the lift and press the button. He's still blocking the doors.

'Would it have made any difference if he had told you sooner?' he asks.

So he knows.

'I don't know. It still wouldn't change the fact that he's famous.'

'Right,' he says, studying my face for a second. 'You know, he's still a person despite the fame. There's so much about him you don't know,' he says, his expression changing from hopeful to disappointed.

I feel a pang in my heart. For some reason I'm disappointed in myself for disappointing Jules. Why? I have no idea.

'So it seems,' I say, more to myself than to him.

'He likes you, he really does. Just thought you should know,' he finishes his sentence just as the doors begin to close again, this time he steps out of the way and lets them close without an answer from my side.

After a long shower that has failed to help me organise my thoughts, I dress and get ready for lunch. Nate's supposed to pick me up and will be downstairs at any moment now.

I grab my purse and check my bangs in the mirror on the way out. As soon as I open the door I bump into Mrs. Thompson and her caretaker, a young girl that is helping her walk past her door.

'Morning Mrs. Thompson,' I say and nod politely to her caretaker.

'Good morning, Olivia,' says Mrs. Thompson.

The lift arrives and I hold the door open for the two.

'Going for a walk?' I ask her once we're in the lift.

'Yes. Are you going to watch your boyfriend play?' she asks with an excited grin on her face.

'My boyfriend? Oh no, he's not my boyfriend,' I say, embarrassed, blushing.

'Why not?' she asks curious.

If only it was that easy.

'It's complicated.'

'Love, complicated was having a boyfriend in a war zone not knowing if he'd ever reply to the latest letter. If that letter had arrived at all,' she actually smirks at that, making me smile too.

'Don't let complicated turn into regret,' she says, her hand pat my shoulder.

There is much more to what she just said, but I don't have the chance to hear all about it because the lift has reached the ground floor.

When I open the front door to the street, Luc's standing outside on the pavement. He hasn't seen me, he's looking at the street, his Nike white cap backwards. He's holding his big backpack over his shoulder, one hand holding his phone, the other the straps of his backpack. Just what I didn't need right now.

Maurice and Daniel are standing beside him, focused on their conversation. It looks like they're waiting for someone, probably the car that's going to take them to Wimbledon. I don't want to have to talk to him, so I unconsciously freeze where I am. I even consider going in again and give it a few minutes to come out again, but there's no need, the driver has stopped the car by the kerb and they're walking towards it. Maurice gets in first, then Daniel, when it's Luc's turn, he looks back, as if feeling my eyes on him.

He stops and holds my gaze for what it feels like an eternity. He watches me, his eyes seem hopeful, but his expression is closed and hard. For a moment I wonder if he thinks I'm there for him. I want to make it clear that I'm not, I just want him to leave already, so I make myself stop staring and check my phone.

My heart speaks to me in a way it never did before. There's a painful feeling in my throat, something I hadn't experienced before. It reminds me of the feeling of loss, but in a different way. I've lost before, but they were all losses I hadn't had control over. I couldn't do anything about them, other than accept them. Now it's different. I have a choice. And I'm choosing to lose. Him.

When I lift my gaze up again, he has just closed the door, but I can still feel his eyes on me as the car drives away. I can't breathe or move from where I am. Then I'm startled by Mrs. Thompson making her way out the front door.

I hear Thea's voice coming from somewhere, 'We're here, Livvy.' She's leaning on the Range Rover parked by the kerb. A warm smile takes over her face and I sense her contagious morning energy approaching, I could use some today. As soon as I start to walk toward her, I hear someone else from behind me.

'Olivia?'

It's Luc's mum.

I turn to find her and Dom. She has a big smile on her face. She's so gorgeous and elegant, bright red lipstick on, hat and a beautiful dress to suit Wimbledon's style. In some ways she even reminds me of my own mother.

'Annette, hi!' I'm so surprised I can't hide it, my voice comes out like a squeak.

'Are you coming with us?' she asks.

I wonder what made her think that.

'Me? No, I'm not.'

I can't even believe my own voice when it comes out, it sounds like regret.

'I was hoping you would,' I hear the disappointment in her voice.

Dom looks disappointed too.

'I thought you were supposed to go with him,' I say.

'With Luc? Oh no, he always goes first with Jules. He warms up and practices before the match. We go in separate cars,' she says.

'Olivia,' Dom pulls me into a hug. He holds me there for longer that I expect. I don't know why, but I feel like crying. How confusing am I now? And it's not even PMS.

'Hi Dom,' I say into his chest.

'Come with us, I know someone who'd like that very much.' He breaks our hug and looks me in the eyes. I'm pretty sure I'm blushing all shades of pink and red.

'I'm headed to see my parents, but I wish you all good luck for today.' I can't look at their faces. I feel like I'm betraying them in a way. Myself too. Today's an incredibly important day for them all.

'Oh that's too bad. But we get it. I've already kicked his ass for lying to you. He's still going to be able to play today despite the pain in his ass,' says Dom, laughing at his own joke.

I flush at the thought that his family knows about us and talks about it so casually.

'But you know, in case you change your mind ...' He places a card held by a lanyard in my hand. It takes me a few moments to realise what it is.

'Oh, no. It's ok. It won't be necessary.' I give him the card back, I know what he's trying to do.

Touching my upper arm, he looks me in the eyes and says, 'You know, *chérie*, a heart beats fast—you can change your mind fast too, from one second to the other, or in a heartbeat as people say. Sometimes you just need to listen to it.'

I don't know what to say, because I hadn't seen this one coming.

They're both watching me, Dom still holding the lanyard, a gleam in his eye.

Just then, their car arrives. They both hesitate for a moment, I'm the one to say goodbye first and wish them good luck. Then they're gone.

'Olivia?' says Thea from beside me. She lays a hand on my shoulder and when I look at her, she's as confused as I am, but she still has a big smile on her face.

'You look strange. Are you ok?' asks Nate as soon as I enter the car. I nod.

'Who were they?' he asks.

He's watching me in the rear-view mirror. He has a suspicious look on his face, the one he makes when he's fishing for the truth.

'Luc's family,' I say.

'Oh.'

He turns his face to take a proper look at me sitting in the back of his car.

'Are you sure you're ok?'

'Yeah, let's just go,' I say, avoiding his gaze and staring out the window.

He begins to drive but I see him studying me from the rear-view mirror once again. After a moment of silence—yes, it's apparently possible to have a moment of silence with Thea in the car—he says, 'Why are you so in denial? It's pathetic.'

The thing with having a close relationship with siblings is that they just know you too well. Sometimes, more than yourself. In my case, most of the time. They have, at some point in their lives, seen you at your worst and your best, they know your weaknesses and strengths, they know how to get to your head, they know what drives you crazy and what makes you incredibly happy, they had several different opportunities to experience and test it all out throughout your lives. Of course, they also know when you're lying to them and when you're lying to yourself too. Even if they don't always tell you.

When I was at the hospital, after what Josh did to me, Nate came by to visit. Mum and I had agreed we shouldn't tell him or Dad, because we knew they would want to do something about it, and I didn't. When he asked me what happened and I began making something up about an accident, he knew I was lying. I'm not good at faking and pretending. And well, he's my brother, he knows me well. Playing pretend with him wasn't going to cut it, and I knew it. He knew it.

And now he knows too, of course. And maybe he knows it more than I do, he just used the right word for it. Denial. Something I hadn't thought about until now.

'What are you talking about?' I pretend I don't know.

He, of course, throws me a mocking grin.

'Seriously?' now he raises an eyebrow, making sure the other stays as low as possible.

Then everything changes. Because yes, I'm in denial. Luc is the best and most exciting thing that ever happened to me. And yes, he was right: I'm afraid. I'm afraid of trying, of breaking, of losing, of the unknown, of giving my all to someone I don't know will give his all in return. But then, how will I ever know if I never give it a chance?

'I wanna do something crazy,' my mouth speaks before I can even think clearly.

Nate stops the car at a red light and turns his to face me.

'Just how crazy are we talking?' The way the corner of his mouth kicks up in a smile that reaches his eyes just confirms how well he knows me, because right now he knows the crazy I'm referring to.

'How much do you want to make it on time for lunch today?' I ask.

'Hell, I'm in for skipping it,' says Thea looking back at me too. I don't know if she's more excited about my proposition or not having to see Mum today.

Nate laughs, and my mouth trembles as I smile back at them.

'Good, because we need to make it to Wimbledon,' I say.

Cars are honking behind us as the lights have turned green.

'We need to try to find Luc's parents' car. I don't have their number and I don't have a way of getting into Wimbledon,' I say.

'Then we better hurry up,' says Nate stepping his foot on the gas pedal and spinning us in the opposite direction.

Thea searches for Wimbledon's address on the Navi.

'Traffic doesn't look good, guys,' she says.

'I figured,' I say, my heart racing inside my chest.

Nate speeds through lights in every colour and doesn't seem to mind getting a ticket or crashing. He also ignores all the honks. On a normal day I'd curse at him for driving like this, but right now I'm grateful.

With my arms propped on both front seats, I keep my eyes peeled to find the black BMW. I can barely breathe with the adrenaline. I'm doing all this and I don't even know if he'll listen to me, if it will make a difference. The way he looked at me before getting in the car didn't seem promising. My stomach stirs with the thought of our conversation yesterday.

We turn on a few streets until we make it to the main road that leads to Wimbledon. It isn't far from my flat, but traffic on a finals day makes up for the short distance. Nate changes lines a few times and that's when I see them, far ahead, doing just the same. Hope makes its appearance.

'There! They're on the right side,' I say, pointing.

'Shit. They're gonna make it there before we do, Livvy. The traffic's too slow,' says Nate.

And that's exactly what happens. The line has been divided, cars on the left are being let inside, past the barrier to a restricted area, others stay on the right line moving only inches forward. That's when we lose them, as the car has turned into the reserved area.

Fuck.

Thea and Nate look back at me and I know what their stares are telling me.

I have to run. Literally. I don't even think twice before opening the door and stepping out of the car.

'Good luck Livvy,' shouts Thea.

'Good luck sis,' says Nate.

I think I'm gonna need more than luck, because maybe running in heels and wearing a flowing dress isn't the brightest idea, but it will have to do.

People watch me as I dash through the lines of cars. I don't even make it 50 meters before giving up on my heels and taking them off. I now am running barefooted on the road like a mad woman. How did I get here?

I make it to the restricted entrance where the BMW drove into. There is security, of course. I do my best to be discreet as I try to do the craziest thing I've ever attempted to—duck unnoticed into the VIP area.

'Miss,' says the guard.

I pretend I haven't heard her and keep going, holding my heels in my hands. I just need to make it to the black BMW and talk to Luc's parents, I can see them from here.

'Hey, miss. Where do you think you're going?'

I run. I actually run from the guard. I don't even look back. Before I can celebrate my success, I bump into another guard a few steps ahead.

'Please, I just need to talk to them,' I say, pointing at the car.

The guard gives me a once over and fixes his gaze on my dirty feet.

'I'm sorry miss. If you don't have a badge, I can't let you in,' he says, politely.

Shit.

Still not accepting defeat I try shouting Dom's and Anette's names, but they aren't close enough to hear me, and it's useless anyways, they're inside the car. They keep moving ahead. Then I can't see them anymore.

I have no idea how I'm going to make it inside without a pass.

Chapter Twenty-Six

I find myself surrounded by thousands of people in front of an enormous outdoor screen. Everyone's waiting for the match to start, splayed on the grass or steps of the famous Henman Hill. Here's where Dad used to come to watch the matches he didn't get tickets to. I wonder what he'd say seeing me here right now.

In less than an hour Luc's going to step on the Centre Court and I have no way to make it to the player box. The only chance I have is if he responds to the text I sent him a few minutes ago after being kicked out of the restricted area. But I don't think Luc's worried about his phone right now.

Today at 11:46 am

Me: I need to talk to you. Can you reply as soon as you see this?

Maybe I should just wait until the match is over. Maybe I shouldn't have come after all. I cringe when I think of the guard following me out of the restricted area—my second most shameful moment after the bathroom incident with Luc almost two weeks ago. What was I thinking?

Accepting I can't do anything right now but wait, I have joined the fans sitting cross legged on the grass, feeling sorry for myself and wishing I had done things differently. But I guess I deserve this. He tried, didn't he?

Today at 12:10 pm

Immune to tickles: Olivia, it's Jules. What's going on?

As soon as I get the notification on my phone, adrenaline shoots through me.

Me: I'm at Henman Hill. Is there any way I can join you?

Immune to tickles is typing …

Before I can see Jules' message, my phone dies.

Fucking great.

I look around me and desperation makes me brave to ask around the crowd who might have a power bank. People stare as if I've asked them if they have a ticket into Wimbledon. Until someone actually recognises me.

'Hey, aren't you Olivia Charlton? Lamaire's girlfriend?' asks a woman about my age.

'Uhh …' I don't know what to say to that. I just need a freaking power bank.

'Here, you can take mine,' she offers.

'Thank you so so much,' I say, so relieved I immediately forget what she just called me.

I realise now people are staring and whispering. It's spreading fast. I have a feeling I need to get out of here soon.

When my phone screen finally lights up again, I go check my messages.

Immune to tickles: What? are you here?

Immune to tickles: Give me a sec, I'm calling you.

An unknown number has called me, and I believe it's Jules'. I call back.

'Hey, Olivia,' says Jules cheerful.

'Hey, Jules. Sorry, my phone died.'

'Can you meet me at the closest entrance of Henman Hill?'

I have no idea where that is, but I agree.

'Awesome. I'll get you a badge,' he says and relief shoots through me for the first time in this weird day of my life.

Before I go, I give the girl back her power bank. She waves me off and says I can keep it, as long as I give her an autograph and take a selfie with her. I hesitate, but I'm guessing it's the least crazy thing I'll do today. I make sure to ask her where the next entrance to Centre Court is, or whatever that means. She finds it amusing that I don't know this and points me in the right direction after describing the way there.

I put my heels back on and make my way to the meeting point, Jules is not there and I wonder if I have come to the right place. But before I give up, Luc's little brother shows up with a wide grin on his face to greet me by the entrance.

'Jules, I'm so sorry for this,' I say, guilty for causing him so much trouble.

'It's no problem really. But, here, you're going to have to use Mum's badge,' he says discreetly into my ear into our embrace. He places his mum's lanyard around my neck and takes my hand before I can even think.

The security gives me a doubtful glance but decides to turn a blind eye after he checks Jules' badge. Then I'm in. Finally.

'Thank you so much for doing this, Jules.'

He looks back at me, amused as we walk through the crowd heading to the Centre Court in a hurry to catch the beginning of the match.

'What?' I say.

'Nothing.'

I don't know if it's because he's happy I'm here, or because his brother will be happy to see me here. Maybe both.

I find myself once again in front of a screen, this time in a private area inside the Centre Court building. I told Jules I'd rather not make an appearance at the player box right now. I have no idea how Luc will react when he sees me, it can be either bad or good, and I don't want to be a distraction. I might have also taken the advantage of the private bathroom to freshen up. I'm sure I've made the right decision when I rinse my feet under the shower.

The match is about to start. Luc looks focused, but not nervous. I realise that when he enters the court he turns a part of him on and another off. His expression changes, his body language too. My heart is hammering against my chest, my skin is prickling.

He's wearing the same white outfit from his previous matches. The cap backwards. He has ear buds in. I wonder what he's listening to. He waves to the crowd and throws them a wide smile. Someone's taking his and his adversary's—Moretti—backpacks and places each on their respective benches. He picks a racket. He takes his jacket off. A coin is tossed. Moretti wins and is going to serve first. They begin the warmup. The crowd is loud, screaming both their names. Fans are holding signs with messages to their favourite player. A heart shaped one reads *Marry me Lamaire.* I shouldn't be surprised. Still, I am.

The match begins, and I hold my breath. He loses the first and second games easily. Then he also loses the first set after 45 minutes. His expression hasn't changed. He's still focused and determined, but now sweaty. He's doing that thing of his, tugging on his T-shirt on the shoulder, touching his nose then pulling a strand of his hair behind his ear before throwing the ball in the air and hitting it with his racket bouncing it to the other side of the net.

He loses the second set too, after forty minutes. My heart sinks. It seems as though the crowd favourites Moretti. Both players seem to be immune to the cheers and screams and whistles around them, theirs heads are somewhere else. On the game. On the title.

I've been sitting on a chair all this time, but when the third set begins I stand up. If he loses this set, he loses the match and the title. If he wins, he needs to win the next set too so they can go to the fifth set. Don't even ask how I know this, the narrator just said it.

I bite my nails, I curse, I throw punches in the air, I scream *yes.* Moretti is winning 2-3, then it's 3-3, then Luc is winning 4-3, then 5-3, then Moretti comes back for a 5-4 and 5-5. I don't think I can watch this anymore. Luc wins another game, and now it's 6-5, then he wins the next game, and the set too. I feel a rush of adrenaline take over me. He did it. He won the freaking set after almost an hour and a half.

While I'm going out of my mind, despite looking visibly tired and drenched in sweat, Luc seems focused, which seems to me is the most important thing in a game like this. He's drinking water sitting on the bench, waiting for the match to continue, staring pensively at an invisible point somewhere in the middle of the court. I can't imagine what's going through his head now, knowing that he needs to win the next set for a chance to win on the fifth set. I don't know how he can be so calm. But I guess that's part of his job.

During the fourth set, he begins to let out his emotions a little. He mutters something to himself when he hits the ball against the net, or when he doesn't manage to get to the short balls coming from Moretti. He cheers more when he wins a point, making a fist and flexing his elbow closer to his body. He looks at somewhere in the middle of the crowd, which I guess must be his family, Maurice and Daniel in the player box.

He rearranges the cap on his wet hair, which he tugs behind his ears. And now as he wins one more game against Moretti, he lets out a scream. *Yes.* It is as if it's been trapped all this time, there's so much emotion in that scream, I can see the veins on his face.

Luc's winning 5-4 on this set. Now the crowd seems to be entirely in his favour. How insane is that? I guess people just enjoy a good fight, in this case, match. As it stands, if Luc wins the next game, they're on for the fifth set.

Today at 5:31 pm
Me: I'm coming.
Jules: About time!

It's time. As I walk away from the TV, my heart is upset with me. It hammers, it kicks, it rushes, it's loud in my ears and has found its way up my throat. There's no turning back now, I'm here for this, I have to do this, because *I want* to do this.

After walking through long hallways, turning a few times and asking people along the way for directions, I open a door and it feels impossible to control my heart and the goosebumps taking over my body at what I see. I find myself in the middle of the crowd in the famous green seats, the grass court and Luc just before my eyes. It's a feeling I'm not able to describe. It's nothing compared to watching on TV. It's real, it's huge. It's Wimbledon. I stand there frozen, overwhelmed by the cheers. Everyone's standing up from their seats to celebrate one more point, I can't tell from which player, but considering how the crowd seem crazy about Luc's comeback, I'm guessing it was his.

'Olivia, here.' I hear Jules almost shouting a few steps down to the left. He has a big smile on his face. He sits back on his seat next to his parents. I join them and sit between Jules and Annette.

I can't believe I'm here. This is so insane my mind feels foggy.

'Just in time,' says Dom winking at me. Annette seems nervous, just as I am. She looks at me with a smile on her face and gives my hand a little squeeze, then looks back at court, fidgeting with her fingers on her lap.

'Thank you,' I say to Jules, who nods and winks at me.

I try to find myself in the game again, and Jules points out a big green sign in the back of the court where I can follow the game. It has an oversized Rolex watch with the players' names and respective points under it, and for how long they've been playing. Just as I'm finding myself on the game again, I hear Luc letting out a scream and assume he just scored.

'One more for Luc and the fifth set is on,' says Jules.

Oh God.

Luc hasn't seen me yet, he's too focused on moving fast from side to side, sliding his already dirty white shoes on the grass. Both players determined to score this point. The ball keeps bouncing from left to right, right to left. The crowd's holding its breath. I feel like I can't breathe for a long time. Then after twenty-six strokes, Moretti scores. It's 40-30 for Luc now.

C'mon, one more.

Luc goes for his serve. Just as he takes position he decides to look up, and when he does, his eyes are aimed straight at me. Though we are way too far from one another, I feel the magnetic field between our eyes build up despite the distance and everything else in between. He has seen me. He's trying to understand what's going on, probably realising its not a vision, it's really me. He gives me a boyish grin in disbelief, the sight makes my lungs stop working for a few moments. This is good, right? He's smiling.

People must have noticed our exchange, because now everyone's staring my way. Moretti shoots a smile at the box too. Even the royal family, for Christ's sake. When would I ever in this world imagine myself being watched by William and Kate? Then I see my face on the big screen on the court.

Bloody hell.

The crowd is laughing and whistling and cheering and applauding. It's the kind of cheer people do when they're hoping for a couple to kiss.

The screen is now split into two, half is my face, the other half is Luc's. Luc's smiling, his face flushing. I've never seen him flush like this. I don't know if I just keep smiling with my very much blushed face, or if I should hide myself in my hands. I do the latter because I can't help it. This is too much attention for someone, even for Luc, it seems.

Mother of God.

The chair umpire reminds Luc that he only has a couple more seconds to hit the ball or he loses the point. I guess I still ended up being a distraction, almost making him miss a point. Somehow he finds a way to focus again. He does his ritual before the serve, only faster this time because his time's almost up. The chair umpire keeps asking the crowd for silence after the commotion. He still manages to serve.

God, I wasn't expecting this.

My stomach's flipping, my heart's begging for some normality again so it can go back to its normal rate.

Luc scores and wins the set. Jules high fives me, Annette gives me a hug, Dom too. Maurice and Daniel are in the first row of the box, in front of us, they too high five us. It feels weird to high five Maurice, even more to see him smile at me. I guess we might have something in common after all.

Luc and Moretti go inside. They get a little time before the match continues. People still keep staring at our box. I don't know what to do with my heart. I wish I could just hug him already.

I didn't need convincing to be here. I didn't need my conversation with the girls, or to hear what Jules said to me earlier. *He's still a person despite the fame.* I also didn't need Nate telling me I was in denial, or Dom trying to make me accept his access card to Luc's player box, or Mrs. Thompson telling me not to *let complicated turn into regret.* But I needed them all to remind me what I've felt and known all along: I've been trying to convince myself that I don't and can't be with him, even though my heart knows it's completely the opposite. Yes, I've been in denial since our first dinner together. I need him, like I've never needed anyone before.

As soon as I stepped into Nate's car I knew I couldn't go about like today was a normal Sunday with lunch at my parents'.

'I'm glad you stopped to listen,' said Dom, winking.

All this time my heart and mind have been playing against each other. My mind was always ahead in the game, until my heart made a comeback and won the match.

The fifth and last set is about to start, the court goes completely still. They've been playing for over four hours and it feels like an entire day. Luc has gotten a new racket, Moretti, new shoes.

Jules explains me that Wimbledon's fifth set can go on forever. *Forever? Four hours is already torture enough.* Luc scores the first point, then Moretti, then Luc, then Moretti. Each time Moretti scores I think I'm going to die. How can a match last this long?

Five hours of match. I don't even have fingernails to bite anymore. I'm unable to behave myself on the seat, shifting all the time. I scream and jump, despite knowing that there are many eyes staring. A hurricane of emotions is taking over me, of both watching this dreadful match and of wanting to talk to him.

Then Moretti misses one point, which now are counted in a different way 1, 2, 3 and so on. I really hope someday I'll understand this game's rules. I mean, first is 15, 30 and 40—why just 10 for the third point? Then there is 1, 2, 3 … on the fifth set, and Jules just told me this is only for Wimbledon, for other championships it's different.

'This is madness,' I say.

Jules laughs nervously at me and says, 'If he scores now, he wins. That's all you need to know.'

Oh God.

Now there's so much silence you can hear the drops of the heavy rain that just started falling. Everything else is still. The smell of wet grass is dissipating fast in the air, the anticipation of who's going to score next is almost tangible.

Luc serves, and he fucking scores with an ace. I hear him shouting *yes* and going on his knees, his head touching the ground trying to take in what just happened. Then he lays on his back while we all hug each other, screaming. His family in disbelief that he has won Wimbledon for the first time, me in complete disbelief I'm here experiencing this in the first place.

Once Luc gets up, he goes greet Moretti over the net and both players exchange words, a hug and slaps on their backs.

'Vittorio's his best friend,' says Jules.

'Oh, really? I can't imagine what it would feel like to play such an important match against a best friend,' I say.

Things are about to get better. Luc is walking toward us. He has this determined look on his face, this wide grin. It's a combination of happiness, excitement, naughtiness and a hint of tiredness—just a little bit. He's now running and jumping over fences and the crowd is going wild, my heart too at the thought of finally being face to face with him. He climbs all the way up to the box and I stand watching him as he gets engulfed by his family, coach and physiotherapist. His eyes don't leave mine.

He eventually finds his way out of the hugs and taps on the back and freezes for a brief moment as he stands in front of me, only a few inches away. His eyes are curiously searching for an explanation in mine and I hope my face is conveying the answer. I just smile, then I'm in his arms, and his mouth is on mine. Despite the rain, it feels like fire, it feels like home, and belonging, and my heart feels safe. In his embrace he feels whole and I complete.

His delicious warm lips are pressed hard against mine, and his tongue is finding its way into my mouth in a hurry, with need and longing. It's as though the world around us has stopped spinning and moving. For a second I can't even hear the crowd around us. It feels like it's only us, and that's enough. More than enough.

I need him more than I thought I did. I've been lying to myself, an actress around my real feelings. How couldn't I have seen it before as clearly as I see it now? How did I survive days without kissing these soft and wet lips? Away from this embrace and his warmth?

I don't want to ever stop kissing him. This is good, this is a kind of good I've never felt before. But then I hear the world screaming and cheering and clapping around us and we break our kiss, rain still falling.

'What made you change your mind?' he asks, his eyes locked on mine.

'Everything.'

He pulls me harder into him and his face finds its way around my neck. This makes me deeply inhale his smell—sweat and grass and sex lingering on him. I gasp for air, for words. I try to feel my legs but all I feel is the banging of my heart against him. He's soaking wet from the rain, and my dress now also wet from our embrace.

He looks at me, half-smiling, and says, 'I feel like today I've won two titles.' He pulls my bangs to the side and plants a soft kiss on my nose.

Chapter Twenty-Seven

'Ladies and gentlemen, Wimbledon's champion—Mr. Lucas Dominique Lamaire,' says the presenter.

After a long wait for the beginning of the trophy ceremony—due to the heavy rain, the roof needed to be closed—Moretti received his trophy first, now it's Luc's turn. No one less than the Duchess of Cambridge herself hands him the golden trophy. He looks so emotional his eyes might be a bit teary. I like the emotional version of Luc. He raises the trophy in the air, then plants a long kiss on it. The cheer of the crowd gives me goosebumps.

'Lucas. Wow. What a comeback, what a match,' says the presenter. Luc's smile is wide, I'd say his mouth's trembling.

'How does it feel to win Wimbledon for the first time?'

He takes a moment to gather his thoughts, to breathe and find his voice.

'Surreal,' he manages, smiling and sounding a bit breathless.

The crowd cheers with his answer. When there's silence again, the presenter resumes the interview.

'What went through your mind when you lost the second set?'

'Puh. I reminded myself of something my father always tells me, "Giving up is not an option, there's always a chance to turn things around." *Merci, papa.*' There is so much applause I feel the floor shaking under my feet. I look at Dom's reaction and he has tears in his eyes.

227

'Are you aware that tomorrow it's going to be official that you're now number one in the world?' The crowd doesn't just applaud, they shout. Luc's laughing, readjusting his cap with one hand and holding the trophy with another.

'Today's win still hasn't sunk in, let alone that I've moved up to number one in the ranking,' says Luc. The crowd laughs.

After saying kind words to his best friend, he thanks his team and family, the event's organiser and the public.

'I could never be where I am without you,' he says, eyes filled with tears.

'Now, the question of the week, of the hour if you might,' says the presenter. 'Lucas, everyone wants to know …'

I know what's coming, so I feel my heart climbing its way up my throat. He knows what's coming too, because he's flushing in anticipation.

'Can we say the reason for you almost missing your serve today is your girlfriend?'

Laughter takes over the court. Luc's shyly smiling at the presenter, as if he were a little boy asked about his first kiss in front of his parents.

Everyone's now impatiently waiting for a reply, even Moretti seems excited, smiling again after his loss. This past week, Luc and I were on the news spotlight. It's all people could talk about. The fact that he always declined to answer questions regarding our relationship made people speculate even more. Did I mention we even became memes?

'She's a very private person. I don't want to answer for her, so you might want to ask her yourself.'

I can't believe he said that. I immediately find shelter for my face in my hands. Of course, my face is now on the screen, probably on TV too for the entire world to see.

'Miss Charlton. The world wants to know, even the royal family's curious.' A little pause for more laughter. 'Is this man standing right here next to me, holding this humble golden trophy, your boyfriend?'

More laughter, then complete silence as everyone waits for my reaction.

Of all the ways I could have told him I wanted to give him a chance, I definitely hadn't considered this one. Not in a million lifetimes.

I don't say a yes, or at least I don't speak, because first, I don't think I can find my voice right now. Second, I don't think people will be able to listen. So I nod. My face is completely flushed and hot. I firmly nod multiple times, to make sure Luc got it. He did, because as the crowd applauds and shouts, he's as flushed as I am, clearly using the trophy as shield. Seeing him this shy in public makes up for one of our favourite moments so far. I can't wait to hang myself around that neck and make love to him until it's morning. That is, if he's fit enough for such a wild night after playing tennis for five hours.

After the trophy presentation and interview, Luc and Moretti take official photographs side by side, each with their respective trophy. Then they go for a round around the court, showing their trophies, only to finally make their way inside the building. By the door, Luc stops to autograph papers, caps, T-shirts and tennis balls of every size. Then he's gone.

The crowd begins to leave and so do we. Luc's family already knows their way in the building, so I just follow them through doors and corridors and way too many people. I'm still numb from all the past hours, but the only thing I can think about now is finding him.

My eyes keep searching for him, each turn we take inside the busy building I feel a pang of anticipation.

Then I see him, he's talking to some people when he sees me. He excuses himself and begins walking towards me, cameras following him. We meet halfway. He pulls me into his arms. The hug is needy and almost desperate.

'Did you mean it?' he asks into my neck.

'Considering what you got to learn about me in the past days, do you think I'd joke about something like this?'

He looks at me, holds my gaze and takes my face in his hands, and says, 'Hi, girlfriend.'

I blush all over again.

'Hi, boyfriend.'

Then he kisses me, hard. I hear the camera flashes going off, but most importantly, I feel him. I feel all the intensity of this moment, a combination of the roller coaster thrill of the past weeks. Above all, the realisation that sometimes, losing control means you gain something else.

I can't believe I was just introduced to Kate and William. How insane is that? Even though he was clearly exhausted, Luc still had to mingle for photos, hand shakings, and an awfully long press interview, before we finally managed to leave Wimbledon.

We drove home alone in the black BMW, the same one that took us to our private dinner at Sketch, the same driver too. His family and the others left first, in another car.

Luc is tired, he lays on my lap as the car drives us from Wimbledon to my building. As I play with his hair, my fingers entangled in its wavy strands, he asks, 'Do you happen to have a gala dress?'

'Why?'

'You're going to need it for tonight.'

Oh God.

I text the girls and say we need an emergency meeting, they don't even discuss or ask why.

When Naomi and Lexi arrive, they're both carrying dresses and carry-ons.

'Oh my God, you do realise I have clothes and makeup, right?' I say, but they both ignore me and storm into my flat with a mission.

In between deciding on the lingerie, dress, shoes and accessories and getting my hair and makeup done, I tell them about how I made it to Wimbledon today. And how I became Lucas Lamaire's girlfriend in front of everyone.

'I never thought you were one for grand gestures, honey,' says Naomi.

'Huh, that makes two of us,' I say.

'I knew you were a romantic, you just had to find the right person to be romantic with,' says Lexi.

'Tequila shots?' says Naomi.

'Are you kidding?' I ask.

'You need to relax, Lucas Lamaire's your boyfriend,' says Naomi.

I don't know if I laugh or curse first.

'That's exactly the reason why I'm not relaxed. You do realise the media will be all over us tonight, right?'

'So what? He's gonna be there to hold your hand,' says Naomi.

'Let's do it. Tequila shots I mean,' says Lexi.

They manage to rescue me by helping me picking an outfit, doing my hair and makeup in a matter of two hours. Luc went back to his place to get some rest while my adrenaline kept running high, my stomach deciding whether to focus on the butterflies or the stirs caused by my anxiety.

We clink our tiny glasses filled with tequila and slam it down. It burns everything on the way, but it's doing wonders for my nerves.

'You know, I was thinking. If you decide to open your own Instagram account I can be your social media manager,' says Naomi as she sprays hair spray over my braid.

'I wouldn't want it any other way,' I say, smiling.

'We're so proud of you, Livvy,' says Lexi.

There's so much behind this sentence I cannot even begin to tackle.

'You have a fucking boyfriend,' shouts Naomi.

I have Lucas Lamaire as my fucking boyfriend.

We arrive at the famous Champions' Dinner—an event which athletes, their families and the media gather to celebrate one more Wimbledon tournament together—holding hands. Photographers and reporters stop us along the way for photos and questions. Luc confirmed we're in a relationship, but hasn't provided any details, which I'm glad for. I guess we'll need to sit down and have a conversation with Margot about how to deal with the media.

On the way to our table, I just smile and nod at people. Being in the spotlight like this is simply surreal. I feel numb until I finally find my place at our table and have the first sip of champagne.

Right now Luc is giving a speech and I'm at the table with his family, Maurice and Daniel. Jules is making sure I know who is who.

He keeps pointing at people and basically giving me their complete profile. Tennis players, their wives and husbands, coaches, and so on.

'That one's Malia,' he says.

I know who she is.

'Luc's ex,' he says it as if it weren't a big deal.

She's staring at Luc, paying attention to what he's saying. She's so beautiful it hurts. Her shiny dark hair, her tanned skin, her perfect profile, her wide smile with big white teeth, and her eyes, which are now brightly staring right into mine.

Shit.

I look away discreetly, hopefully discreetly enough for her not to notice it.

'Should I be worried about her?' I ask Jules. Somehow, I feel like he's the kind of guy who girls like to confide in, like his brother.

He looks at me immediately, eyes wide, worry all over his innocent face, and says, 'Definitely not.'

He sounds so sure, my heart calms down a bit.

I turn to watch Luc at the stage, where he's being interviewed. He looks incredibly fuckable in that black tuxedo, his shiny hair combed back and his perfectly trimmed stubble on that jaw I want to scrape with my teeth so bad. All I can think about is the moment we'll be alone again. Apart from the moment we had in the car on the way home from Wimbledon, we hadn't had a chance to be alone yet.

'I'm glad you're here, darling,' says Annette, giving my hand a gentle squeeze.

'Me too.'

She looks so proud of her son.

We hear laughter across the room, and I focus on *my boy* again—as Dad would say—and my stomach flips and turns and reminds me I now am officially his girlfriend, and he's going home with me tonight.

When he comes back to the table, he whispers in my ear, 'You have that look on your face again.' He sits by my side, and we have one more drink. It's the longest drink ever. He tortures me, sliding his hand between my thighs, over the light fabric of my black dress.

'Should we have our first dance ever, tonight?' he whispers in my ear, making all my hair stand on end.

'Now?'

'Yes.' Another whisper, and I don't even give it a second thought. When I look at him, his face is lit up with anticipation and excitement. *My boy. My boyfriend. My Luc.*

I'm surprised by how well he can dance, and by how he makes me feel comfortable despite all the stares and cameras. A slow song is playing in the background, but all I hear is his heart beating against my ear. I'm so overwhelmed and inebriated by the moment, I close my eyes and try to relax and let go of what's around. It must be one of the scariest, yet most rewarding moments of my life.

Then he finally says, 'Let's get out of here.'

We're back in the place where we met, the lift, and finally alone again. Luc presses the button to my floor amidst demanding kisses. I'm between him, his erection and the lift's mirror. I have the feeling the mirror will need to be cleaned after our ride up. He moves his mouth down to my collarbone and begins to suck on my skin. The contact of his warm tongue to my sensitive skin is so arousing I bite my lower lip to avoid letting out a moan.

'Are you giving me a hickey?' I ask, smiling.

'Yes,' he whispers against my skin, then resumes his work.

'It's my first,' I say.

He looks up under heated eyes.

'Good,' he rasps, then continues.

When the lift doors open he picks me up and I wrap my legs around his waist, my arms tight around his neck. In front of my door, we fumble for my keys in my tiny clutch when we hear, 'Who's there?'

We can't help but laugh.

'Just me again, Mrs. Thompson,' I say as Luc manages to fish my keys out of my clutch. I'm still straddling him, but now pressed against my flat's door.

'Easier than the first time,' he says, grinning, taking me briefly down memory lane to the night we met.

'The bag's smaller too,' I smirk.

I drop my pink heels on the way to the bedroom. He places me sitting on the bed and makes me watch him slowly strip off his black tux, then bow tie. Then, with one hand, his skilled fingers open his white shirt button after button. Taking his time. When he's done, he leaves it on, but now I can follow his happy trail down to the Calvin Klein's I've grown so familiar with.

He steps closer to stand between my legs. I already made a mess of his hair in the lift, the combination of it and his hard chest with his open shirt does things to my body I can't even explain.

He slowly begins to move my dress up my thighs. The anticipation of what's about to come makes me hold my breath.

'All this time, you weren't wearing anything underneath this dress?' he grins wickedly and shakes his head in disbelief.

'I thought you needed some help after such a long and hard day,' I say, mostly teasing.

He pulls the dress up and over my head then watches me as he unzips his pants. My nipples harden and everything within me contracts and flutters with need for him. I hadn't realised how badly I missed him— as if he was part of me.

Once he steps out of his clothes, he watches me for a second and reaches for my face, our eyes connected with no intention of parting ways whatsoever.

I give him my I-want-to-fuck-you stare as he rasps, 'Make love to me, Olivia.'

'Yes,' I whisper.

Underneath him I feel my body come alive. As he pushes into me, I catch my breath. When the softness of his tongue greets my skin, sounds I don't recognise escape me. The warmth he radiates tells me I'm safe, safe to be myself, with him. When my body reaches its extreme, my heart knows, it simply knows, that he would never have been a one-night stand.

'I guess Margot will have a lot of work to do tomorrow,' I say.

I'm sitting with my back against the headboard and Luc's between my legs. I'm rubbing his sore shoulders and occasionally planting kisses on his neck and treating myself with the smell of his hair.

He smirks and says, 'She will.'

He tips his head back onto my chest and turns to face me, his eyes staring hard at my mouth. I kiss him.

'So, I've heard you've become friends with Mrs. Thompson,' I say.

He laughs.

'She's quite a remarkable lady. You should hear her advice, it tends to work,' he says with a smirk.

'Oh really? And what kind of advice did she give you?' I ask, curious.

'When a man fucks up, he needs to give his lady space. But not enough that she forgets about him. Of course, don't forget to apologise, and always, always tell her the reason why you're apologising,' he says, imitating Mrs. Thompson's hoarse and tired old lady voice.

My belly hurts from the laughter coming out of me.

'She told me early today I shouldn't let "complicated turn into regret",' I say, and tell him about our encounter in the lift.

'And?'

'I guess we're still complicated, but at least now I don't feel regret,' I say.

'Is that so?' he asks, his voice raspy.

'Yeah,' I say and kiss the top of his head.

He falls asleep first. Understandably. I still linger and think and wonder and worry, staring at the ceiling, hearing him breathing peacefully next to me. My mind tries to assimilate and absorb all that happened today, hell, in the past few weeks. Eventually I give in and decide I can worry later and at least for today embrace the happiness that has taken over me and that's much deserved.

Chapter Twenty-Eight

'Hmm ... are you leaving me already?' mumbles Luc still half sleeping, holding my body tightly against his. I consider staying just a bit longer like this. His skin is warm against mine, providing me with the feeling of belonging.

'I don't want to be late,' I say.

I try to get off the bed one more time. He pulls me back to him and tickles my neck and collarbone with his stubbled face.

'Just when I finally can stay in bed longer,' he complains as I fight my way out of his arms, even though all I want right now is to be exactly where I am.

He finally accepts it and lets me go, but not before kissing me sweetly and needy, with a morning erection that was hard to ignore.

Yesterday feels like a dream, but I very much believe it happened. There is enough proof of it: all the messages waiting to be read on my phone, as well as the missed calls. There is also the news articles, which are all over the internet and on the covers of today's newspapers I see on my way to work. I'm glad when I see one featuring a photo of only Luc and his trophy, all the rest have my face stamped on them beside him. The favourite angle and scene seems to be of Luc giving me a kiss in the player box. I think I'll need time to wrap my head around all this.

UK Gossip Today's Blog

What a match! Lamaire wins Wimbledon and gets the boyfriend title.

Yesterday, Lamaire and Moretti played a match that is hard to forget. After over five hours with a memorable tiebreak under the stormy London weather, Lucas, the French Golden Boy, took the most dreamt-of trophy in the tennis world. Lamaire wins Wimbledon for the first time in his career, becoming the current world's number one tennis player. But for us, the highlight of the match was the presence of the most talked about woman of the week, designer Olivia Charlton. Proving the rumours to be true, after surprising Lucas during the match—mind you, almost making him miss a point—Miss Charlton was asked live if he was her boyfriend. The answer, dear gossipers is YES. We told you it was a match, didn't we? Also, can anyone explain how Miss Charlton could be at Henman Hill and the player box almost at the same time?

Tennis World

Wimbledon and love: Lamaire wins dramatic final and celebrates with new girlfriend Olivia Charlton.

Daily Mail

This year's Wimbledon's final goes straight to a romcom movie scene …

Le Figaro

Notre Golden Boy a gagné Wimbledon pour la première fois et a trouvé un match pour son cœur …

I don't remember the girls being so excited about something that happened in my life as much as they are with me dating Luc. It's as if they started to see me in a different way, I could tell by their grins and excited tone as they helped me dress up last night.

Mum bombarded my phone before and during the match, I didn't have time to explain it to her before making my way to Wimbledon.

Yesterday at 11:30 am

Mum: Why are you and Nate taking so long? Your dad's starving.

Mum: For goodness' sake, where are you?

Mum: Nate told us about your plan. We think it's wonderful my love. Your dad says next year he wants to be in the player box too.

Mum: Olivia, I feel like I just watched my favourite movie. I think your dad is going to have a heart attack. I told him he better not or I'll sell his cars.

Yesterday at 6:38 pm

Nate: You owe me one. Just kidding, I'm happy for you. Love you sis. Now we want to meet the boyfriend, you know, we need to approve him…

Right now I'm standing in front of my desk at work. The office is still a bit quiet, it's early Monday morning after all. I enjoy the time and the quiet, taking one more look at the presentation and going over my speech.

When Caleb arrives he comes straight to me, and he looks just as I imagined he would: a pile of nerves, but immaculately dressed for the occasion. He has a black floral suit on, with big red flowers embodied on the shiny fabric. Only he can pull off wearing something like this and still look gorgeously chic.

'Good morning, Queen,' I say, raising my eyes at him, contemplating his nervous smile.

'Good morning, Celeb,' he teases.

He gets an eye roll from me.

'Are you ready for this?' I ask, grabbing my stuff from the desk and standing up.

'Oh, what do we have here?' he stares at me over the frame of his glass and motions his finger in a circle pointing to my collarbone.

I almost forgot about the hickey.

'Shit,' I say, quickly trying to cover it with my blouse.

'Shit? Didn't seem you thought it was shit while you were getting it,' he laughs at my expense.

'Funny Queen,' I tease him sarcastically.

'Let's go, let's do this,' he says, turning on his heel, waiting for me to follow.

Caleb and I are the perfect match at work. When he freaks out, I pull him back to his senses, when I need someone to make things happen under pressure, I have him. When it comes to work, we think alike; when it comes to designs, we complement each other; when it comes to loyalty, it's us before the rest. And so now, as we finish presenting the final changes for the new exclusive private collection of Secretive to our boss, Haley, we have no doubt it will be a success. Honestly? I have never designed a collection like this, and I might as well never do it again, not with these materials anyways.

Haley is looking at us, speechless. I have never seen her speechless, it could mean something really good or really bad. But Caleb and I know for sure that it's good, more than good.

Everyone's holding their breath. The only two people in the room who seem to be self- confident and carefree about this moment are Caleb and me. We have our reasons.

'Wow,' she says, finally. 'This is amazing.' Her mouth's hanging open. She stands up and shakes our hands, congratulating us on our work. She only ever does this when someone manages to impress her.

We gave her what she wanted, what she thought she didn't want and what she'll need until she finds a replacement for the two of us, because right now we are going to tell her that we quit.

Caleb and I look at each other. I see signs of pride for the work we've done all over his face. I can feel my shoulders already happily dismissing the heaviness they carried in the past few months.

'You're joking, right?' says Haley, the blood on her face immediately disappearing. Her big blue eyes almost popping off her face. Desperation taking over her.

Unfortunately for her, she has just lost two of her best designers, and though we still offer her to help with our replacements, we know it will never be enough to help her stop her shaking hands or ease the confused look on her face at this very moment. I almost feel sorry, but then I think about how amazing it will be to have the freedom to design whatever and however I want to. A world of possibilities lays ahead.

Quitting had been on my mind for a while, I'd be lying if I said otherwise. When the opportunity to talk to Caleb about my ideas for the future appeared, without expecting it, I gained an ally. The most important one, because there's no one else I'd rather work with on founding my own brand than him.

And so after presenting my best work so far to the company that used to be my dream, I announced I'm quitting to work on a personal project, my biggest dream. Even though speculations started to appear across the room, I gave them no clue of what is to come. Thanks to that, people forgot that yesterday I was live on TV and all over the press today.

The black BMW is waiting for me just in front of the revolving doors of Secretive's building. The past two weeks are playing like an 8mm movie in my mind, and my heart is jumping with excitement for what's coming next.

I forgot how good it felt to be carefree, at least for a while. Comfort zones feel good, they're safe, you know what to expect from them. But sometimes, stepping out of them can make you question whether it's worth saying no to the new. It's scary, it throws you off balance, and it may make you feel out of control, it's true. But what if this also means you get to feel alive? Wouldn't it have been all worth it?

Steps away from reaching the BMW's door, Luc opens it for me. I join him in the back seat of the car, where he greets me with a Sweet Relief green smoothie in his hand. If this isn't a dream, I don't know what else it could be.

'Thought you needed to celebrate,' he says with a wink.

He showered, but still smells of sex. His hair looks like it dried naturally, and it makes me want to mess it up even more. He didn't shave his stubble, which I'm thankful for. He's all the celebration I need today.

'Stop,' he says, watching me with a wicked smile.

'What?' I pretend I don't know what he's talking about.

'Don't look at me like that, Olivia.'

He can't stop staring at me either.

I take a sip of my smoothie, but my gaze's still holding his.

'Are you bringing that devious design of yours I didn't get to take advantage of?' he asks.

'You mean your punishment?' I tease, thinking of the morning I made him watch me put the black bodysuit on.

'If you say so,' he says with smiling eyes.

'Of course,' I say. 'I'm wearing it right now.'

His mouth envelopes mine, taking me by surprise, spreading heat and longing through every part of my body. Too bad we aren't alone in the car.

'Ready for your prize?' he asks with his lips hovering over mine.

'Yes.'

Outside the tinted windows of the car Londoners are living their usual Monday and the familiar rainy weather, whereas I'm stepping out of my comfort zone and saying yes to a life I never thought I'd have the courage to live just a few days ago.

How much can one person mess up your life within two weeks? A lot, but sometimes, messing up can be a good thing, and I cannot wait to find out how messy my life will be with Luc holding my hand. I cannot wait to find out how I will fit into his life and he into mine. I cannot wait to find out where this summer will take us. But I'm ready. Oh, I'm so ready to find out.

Tennis World

After becoming France's Golden Boy and number 1 tennis player in the world, Lamaire's taking time off this summer to celebrate his 5th Grand Slam title at the Côte-d'Azur with his new girlfriend, Olivia Charlton.

UK Gossip Today's Instagram

Gossipers, Gossipers, what if we told you that the spotlight couple of the moment, Lucas Lamaire and Olivia Charlton, were spotted at Nice's International Airport just yesterday? Oh, we can't wait to see what these two are up to this summer. Should we call the new lovebirds #LOvia or #LOvaire? Share your thoughts in the comments below.

akelly_ *I feel like melted butter right now.*

jonasdddd *Oh yes, #LOvia!*

fansoflamaire *I love you @luclamaire*

***lamairew
eloveu*** *The match of the season. In love with these two already.*

bealoveslamaire *My kind of couple*

marinloveslucas *#LOvaire!*

View all 5.945 comments

Acknowledgements

I know the vast majority of writers had a hard time creating new stories or publishing their work during COVID lockdown. For me, it was when I was most productive in terms of writing. It was when I invited Luc and Olivia into my life, the time I wrote Heart Match, began The Match Series. And here it is, in your hands and out there for the world to read.

I could go on and on about how much work it is to self-publish – to me, the easiest and the best part is the writing – but I rather dedicate this space to use my words to thank all the people involved in the publication of Heart Match, directly and indirectly.

I'm eternally grateful to the first ones who read this story and not judge it or me: my baby sister, Alliane and my dear friends, Ana Lucia and Maria Fernanda. Of course, to all my beta readers: Evi, Ana and Nay for dedicating your time to read the first version of this work.

A warm thank you to the professionals involved on shaping this story, my amazing editor Lucy York and proofreader Elise Hitchings. Took me long enough to publish it, right? But I believe that everything happens at the right time, no matter what we plan or hope.

Fabíola Gonzalez, your talent deserves my respect and admiration. It is not easy to capture ones imagination and put to paper/screen, and yet you did it. You managed to illustrate Lucas and Olivia better than I could have hoped, and with so much love. Another thank you and a chai latte to my patient and talented friend Amelie Henning for designing this perfect cover. To Clara: it means a lot to me that you took the time to format HM, gracias! I'm so lucky to have such a wonderful team of amazing ladies working on this project with me. You ladies rock!

A special thank you to my all the lovely Bookstagrammers who helped me spread the word about HM, and to the hard working lady from Love Notes PR, Ellie for supporting me with the ARCs and PR. I don't think you realise how your time and work are important to indie authors like myself.

To the ones who contributed to my crowdfunding and helped me cover the costs of the professionals involved on getting this book on your hands: YOU made it possible. When I was losing hope to be able to afford this project, YOU gave me hope back. Self-publishing is expensive, and I could never have done it without you. I'm forever grateful to each one of you.

Mom and dad, I hope you never read this book. I just want you to know that I'm a fulfilled person for accomplishing my biggest dream: to write and publish my books. You both taught me two things without even meaning to: always give your best and never give up. I love you.

Madu, you will never remember the amount of hours you saw mommy in front of the laptop writing this novel, editing or marketing it, you were too young for it. I just hope one day you will know how important it is to go after your dreams and that you're aware that sacrifices need to be made to make them happen. I love you more than anything, you give me strength to keep going.

Enzzo, you will always be the brightest star in my sky. I miss you. Always.

Acknowledgements are supposed to be short, but since I'm the boss of this work, I want to use this last paragraph to thank you reader for giving my story a chance. I hope you enjoyed it, and if you did: spread the word!

Allane Milliane wrote on journals throughout her childhood and teenage years. For her, writing and reading has always been the best way to escape reality and live different lives in one. When not writing she is working full time, raising her daughter, running, travelling, watching Tennis matches and Formula 1 races and, of course, reading. She was born and raised in Brazil, has lived in six different countries and today lives in Munich, Germany, but the ocean is her home.

Stay in touch with Allane
Instagram: @allanewrites
TikTok: @allanewrites
Goodreads: Allane Milliane
www.allanemillianewrites.com